STONEWALL INN E[DITIONS]

KEITH KAHLA, GENERA[L EDITOR]

Buddies by Ethan Mordden

Joseph and the Old Man by Christopher Davis

Blackbird by Larry Duplechan

Gay Priest by Malcolm Boyd

One Last Waltz by Ethan Mordden

Gay Spirit by Mark Thompson, ed.

Valley of the Shadow by Christopher Davis

Love Alone by Paul Monette

On Being Gay by Brian McNaught

Everybody Loves You by Ethan Mordden

Untold Decades by Robert Patrick

Gay & Lesbian Poetry in Our Time
by Carl Morse & Joan Larkin, eds.

Tangled Up in Blue by Larry Duplechan

How to Go to the Movies by Quentin Crisp

The Body and Its Dangers and Other Stories
by Allen Barnett

Dancing on Tisha B'Av by Lev Raphael

Arena of Masculinity by Brian Pronger

Boys Like Us by Peter McGehee

Don't Be Afraid Anymore by Reverend Troy
D. Perry with Thomas L. P. Swicegood

The Death of Donna-May Dean
by Joey Manley

Latin Moon in Manhattan by Jaime Manrique

On Ships at Sea by Madelyn Arnold

The Dream of Life by Bo Huston

Show Me the Way to Go Home
by Simmons Jones

Winter Eyes by Lev Raphael

Boys on the Rock by John Fox

End of the Empire by Denise Ohio

Tom of Finland by F. Valentine Hooven III

Reports from the holocaust, revised edition
by Larry Kramer

Created Equal by Michael Nava and
Robert Dawidoff

Spo[rt] by Susan Fox Rogers, ed.

Sacred Lips of the Bronx
by Douglas Sadownick

West of Yesterday, East of Summer
by Paul Monette

I've a Feeling We're Not in Kansas Anymore
by Ethan Mordden

Another Mother by Ruthann Robson

Close Calls by Susan Fox Rogers, ed.

How Long Has This Been Going On?
by Ethan Mordden

My Worst Date by David Leddick

Girljock: The Book by Roxxie, ed.

The Necessary Hunger by Nina Revoyr

Call Me by P. P. Hartnett

My Father's Scar by Michael Cart

Getting Off Clean by Timothy Murphy

Mongrel by Justin Chin

Now That I'm Out, What Do I Do?
by Brian McNaught

Some Men Are Lookers by Ethan Mordden

a/k/a by Ruthann Robson

Execution, Texas: 1987 by D. Travers Scott

Gay Body by Mark Thompson

The Venice Adriana by Ethan Mordden

Women on the Verge by Susan Fox Rogers, ed.

An Arrow's Flight by Mark Merlis

Glove Puppet by Neal Drinnan

The Pleasure Principle by Michael Bronski

And the Band Played On by Randy Shilts

Biological Exuberance by Bruce Bagemihl

The Sex Squad by David Leddick

Bird-Eyes by Madelyn Arnold

Out of the Ordinary by
Noelle Howey and Ellen Samuels, eds.

ALSO BY PAUL RUSSELL

FICTION

Sea of Tranquility
Boys of Life
The Coming Storm

NONFICTION

The Gay 100: A Ranking of the Most Influential
Gay Men and Lesbians, Past and Present

PAUL RUSSELL

THE
SALT
POINT

ST. MARTIN'S PRESS ❧ NEW YORK

Design by Steven N. Stathakis

www.stonewallinn.com

Library of Congress Cataloging-in-Publication Data

Russell, Paul Elliot.
  The salt point / Paul Russell.
    p.   cm.
  ISBN 0-312-26769-X
  I. Title.
  PS3568.U7684S2   1990
  813'.54—dc20   89-34535
                                                              CIP

First published in the United States by E. P. Dutton, a division of Penguin Books USA Inc.

First Stonewall Inn Edition: September 2000

10 9 8 7 6 5 4 3 2 1

For Michael Somoya

It was revealed to me that those things are good which yet are corrupted which neither if they were supremely good nor unless they were good could be corrupted.

—AUGUSTINE

SEPTEMBER

On Poughkeepsie's Main Street, the pedestrian mall, a boy sits. This is how it begins: Lydia and Anatole seeing, out two separate windows, this boy perched on the back of a bench. Lydia leans her forehead against the windowpane of Boutique Elegance, recently opened and soon to go out of business. She's bored. She stares. Across the street at Reflexion Anatole is hectic, darting to the window in between customers. Together they fix the boy in the angle of their gaze.

They don't know his name. They know nothing about him. He eats a frozen chocolate bar—a slight boy, seventeen or eighteen. He crosses his legs like a girl. Behind him, the fountains are dry. The trees have died. The broken concrete underfoot yields up the dust and heat of an afternoon whose temperature tips ninety. This boy has thin arms, dishwater-blond hair that falls in a long lock over one eye. He licks the frozen chocolate bar.

There are five billion people in the world. Nobody matters very much. He wears jeans, a white T-shirt, black loafers without socks. His profile is perfect.

Chris Havilland is drinking scotch in Bertie's when Lydia and Anatole burst in.

"Oh God am I glad you're here," Anatole tells him.

"I'm always here, remember?"

Anatole flings himself exhaustedly down in the booth.

"Every once in a while you just need independent confirmation. You know, a voice from the outside."

"Anatole, what are you talking about? Lydia, what is Anatole talking about?"

"Lydia knows," Anatole exclaims. "Lydia saw. Lydia can tell you I'm not crazy."

"You *are* crazy, Anatole," Lydia reminds him. "It's why we like you, remember?"

"I'm boy crazy," he tells Chris simply.

"Oh please. Not again?" It's a joke among them, how Anatole's always falling in love with teenage boys. He glimpses them in supermarkets, movie theaters, they occupy his whole life for the space of a few hours or days, then he forgets about them. Whenever he and Chris and Lydia are out together, he's always pointing out what boy has just stolen his heart. It alarms Chris, it seems dangerous and ill-advised, and he's always wanting to lead Anatole away to somewhere where it's safe, where he won't be tormented by these visions.

"I *know* what you're thinking," Anatole tells Chris. "But this one was different. The light around him was different."

"Oh?"

"It was *lighter.*"

Chris leans back and draws on his cigarette. He knows it's an affectation, one he suspects his friends used to be impressed by, but now don't notice much anymore.

"Don't tell me you tried to pick him up," he teases, trying to mask a vague unease. "I know you: you leaned out the window and hooted down at him or something embarrassing."

"Don't I wish? You're nothing but a *heretic*," Anatole complains. "This wasn't just *boy*, this was *divine*."

"You saw the vision too?" Chris turns to Lydia. She and Anatole always seem to be noticing exactly the same thing, only from different angles.

"It was one of those moments," she admits.

"You sound almost grim."

"You had to be there."

"Oh God. Why do I feel like groaning?" Chris is conscious of playing the skeptical third. But it's okay—it means he's the one the others defer to, as if they expect him to judge them, to find them wanting.

"You'll see," Anatole tells him.

"Yeah, sure. So when's the shrine going up?"

"You laugh. There'll be healings."

"Shrine of Our Boy of the Mall." Chris tries it out.

"Exactly." Anatole is quiet for a moment, as if considering the implications. "I'll never see him again," he says.

"Think of it as a narrow escape," Chris tells him, but immediately he regrets his tone—it's everything he doesn't like about himself, his aloofness, his shielding wit. He sees how Lydia and Anatole glance at each other—an instant—to say, He doesn't understand these things. We didn't really think he would.

And he hasn't. Or if he has, he wants to keep aloof from it. There's something in the alliances Anatole and Lydia construct that leaves him out—despite his tangled history with both of them. When the three of them are together, he always feels he's the third. Probably it's because he's the newcomer—three years ago he hadn't met either one of them—while Anatole and Lydia both grew up in Poughkeepsie, they've known each other Since When, as they like to say. I'm just visiting this place, Chris will tell himself. I don't live here, but they do—and he doesn't know whether that difference saddens or liberates him. For the three years he's lived in Poughkeepsie, he's lived apart from it—treading water, as it were, never breaking the surface. All he wants is a place to hide, and Immaculate Blue, the record store he manages on Academy Street, allows him exactly that. Poughkeepsie allows him exactly that.

They're best friends, Chris and Anatole and Lydia. Either the first wave of Poughkeepsie's long-awaited gentrification or its last stand, they like to think of themselves as beautiful, chic, to be envied—"the only thing this goddamned city's got going for it," they'll joke among themselves, especially when it's late at night and they're drunk, or stoned, or bored. Together they share complicated pasts, common frustrations. Their friendship is a balancing of forces that would otherwise part them, a constant reorientation of needs, crises, deflections at depths they are reluctant to plumb. For each of them it is different, for none of them does it remain a single, definable thing.

Main Street's deserted, the moon's out, a thin crescent. They walk in a loose contingent, Daniel and Anatole, Lydia and Marion. In a Macy's shopping bag Marion carries bottles of champagne.

Daniel is Anatole's business partner, and he's pretending he's in a Madonna video. He wears an enormous string of pearls, knotted. A tight black skirt, blue turtleneck, a beret with a costume diamond brooch affixed. His long blond hair falls below it. He's singing "Like a Virgin," velvet falsetto. Anatole frisks with him, trying—but failing—to be suave and mysterious as the man wearing the lion mask in the video. With liquid movements Daniel tries to turn Main Street into the canals of Venice. He's in a gondola, he's on an arched bridge, he's in a palace and a twilit Adriatic breeze is blowing the gauze curtains out into the room.

Daniel's the star hairdresser at Reflexion—if it wasn't for him, the salon would go under in a month. But he's also a little crazy. At night he'll do Ecstasy, roam Poughkeepsie's streets in drag, so good he's seldom mistaken for a man. Last month the police picked him up for DWI—he was driving around in his Rabbit with the headlights off. At first the officer thought he was carrying a fake driver's license. " 'Daniel'? Come on, lady, what kind of a name's that?"

Deep in conversation, Lydia and Marion ignore Daniel's and Anatole's antics. Marion's telling Lydia how wonderful the two are to her, how just knowing them has changed her life. Lydia sighs—Marion's simply the latest in a long line of Daniel-and-Anatole groupies, a collection of women who swear miracles by them. In any other city it might be a famous therapist, or a dance teacher. Here it's Daniel and Anatole—who specialize in these lonely women they flatter into expensive dye jobs, elaborate and prolonged programs of hair reconstitution. They made a date with her—come by Saturday, bring champagne, we'll remake you. It'll be fabulous, it'll change your life, doll.

To Lydia—who's just along for the champagne, the company on a Saturday night—it feels sad. This fat woman's really thrilled, she thinks; she's thrilled because they've talked her into thinking this may after all be the thing that *will* change her life. Things'll be different. She'll find love.

Just be careful, Lydia wants to tell Marion. But she doesn't. She walks beside Marion and pretends not to enjoy how Daniel and Anatole cavort. They leap into a dry fountainbed. Daniel pretends to splash, to let the jet of invisible water drench him.

Let Marion learn, Lydia thinks. Anyway, she doesn't like her very much; she's a fat, pathetic intruder. A little overweight herself, or at least convinced she's overweight, Lydia hates without mercy women who are fat.

Marion lopes along in her huge cornflower blue dress, Princess Diana stockings and slippers, and Lydia thinks: Who the hell are you? What Mad Hatter tea party did you stumble out of?

But Marion is drunk, she's talkative. "Aren't they fabulous?" She indicates the two dancing figures. "It's so interesting to me. Women like us."

"What do you mean, 'women like us'?"

Marion seems for a moment to want to backtrack, but then plunges bravely ahead. "Oh, you know. Fag hags."

"I don't consider myself a fag hag," Lydia says politely. She wants to make Marion suffer.

"Oh, I don't mean anything; I mean, I don't want to put you, to put anybody, down or anything. We're all in it together. Am I talking too much? I had a lot to drink before I came here. I was trying to get my nerve up."

Anatole and Daniel are pirouetting in the moonlight. "Like a virgin," they screech at the empty buildings. In the doorway of Schwartz's, two black men lift a sack-wrapped whiskey bottle in a toast, "Yah yah yah," they sing in hoarse chorus. "White girls," they yell. "Come over here, suck my cock, white girls."

Daniel turns to Anatole. "Want to?"

"Sounds fun. I bet they got humongous cocks."

"Foot-long hot dogs."

"Monster dongs."

"Put his foot in yo mouff."

Daniel and Anatole strutting arm in arm, whooping it up. The two black men suddenly seem to be having second thoughts. They shy back into the shadows, brandishing their bottle as if to ward off what it is they've unleashed.

"They're so crazy," Marion observes.

"They're doing it for you." Lydia dry, a bit alienated. "They're trying to work you up to the mood before they get their hands on your hair. So watch out."

"I'm ready for anything."

Then they are clattering up the stairs to Reflexion. "Chez Barbarella, it looks more like," Anatole admits. "Make yourself at home."

Standing on tiptoes, stretching his arms wide, Daniel takes a picture off the wall. It's nearly as big as he is—the Calvin Klein poster of a model naked except for briefs, smooth skin oiled and bronzed, against a backdrop of blindingly white stucco wall. Romantic gaze, off camera, stage right. What sailors does he see entering the harbor? What boys cavorting bare on the beach? Above him the blue sky of Mykonos. Daniel dusts off the glass with a cloth, then proceeds diligently to deposit a pyramid of coke in the center of the picture, where the model's navel is. With his American Express card he cuts it into eight long thin lines, bars across the model's body. "Drugs is a terrible prison," Daniel laughs, inviting Marion and Lydia to partake. "Let's free this boy." Anatole busies himself with opening the champagne bottle. He opens a window, leans far out, lets the cork shoot into the night.

"You should do business like this all the time," Marion tells them, bending low over the picture, closing one nostril with her fingertip.

"Go to it, girl," Daniel advises her, running his hands through his long blond hair, shaking it out luxuriously. "Sniff that crotch."

"Don't make me laugh. It'll be expensive."

"She's got an idea, you know." Anatole pours champagne into plastic cups. "Set up midnight rates. We'll steal Astor Place's clientele. They'll drive up from the City in pink Cadillacs."

"Dream on, darling," Daniel purrs, bending a nostril close to the glass, sniffing up the line. "Ah"—he straightens, breathes deep—"wake up and smell that coffee."

Anatole flicks a tape in the box he's got on the counter: Orchestral Manoeuvres in the Dark. Lydia moves around the room to the beat. The hairdressing equipment looks strange and wonderful in the harsh light. She's bored, but doesn't mind. She likes being here when there're no customers, when it's just them. They know the secret life of the place, and to know the secret life of anything is to lift you out of yourself.

Daniel and Anatole have settled Marion into a chair, draped her with a drop cloth, it's as if a surgery's going to be performed. Daniel is fluent and excited—he only really comes alive when the prospect of hair is before him. He's like a boy about to have sex for the first time. He arranges mirrors around her, contemplates her every way he can. "Doll, you're in for the treat of your life," Anatole assures her. Daniel is snipping shears at thin air; already he's shaping her in the abstract. He runs his hand though her thick dark masses. "Very Irish hair," he tells her. "Very colleen country-girl look."

"I don't want to look like a country girl," Marion tells him.

"Of course you don't. The sophisticated look. Very short, I think. Clipped, sharp. Witty."

"And the color," Anatole adds. "You can't keep that brunette."

"How about giddy blonde?" Daniel keeps looking at her like a painter angling his subject. "I think giddy blonde'd be perfect. Marilyn meets the Marine Corps. It'll accent the Manhattan chop effect, set up a rhythm of tensions, it'll just be fabulous."

"I'm putting my life in your hands," Marion tells them, holding out her cup for more champagne. "I'm just going to lie back and take a nap and when I wake up I'll be a new person. How's that?"

"Doll, you're so trusting. You're like, perfect. Have you considered really dramatic colors?"

"Like?"

"Anatole, get the cellophanes. There. See these? They're really vibrant. Prism cellophanes. They'll wash out in a month. They won't hurt your hair."

Marion considers.

"Go for it," Anatole urges. "In a hundred years, more like ten probably, we'll all be dead. Nobody'll care whether you had a little fun with your life."

"Sure," Marion says. "Why not? Just pour me some more champagne."

"We could do stripes," Daniel says, tapping his chin with his finger, an artist deep in thought. "Eggplant purple in back, fantail effect"—he gestures expressivley at her head, shaping the new look with his hands—"then this lovely wine red and electric blue, alternating, on the sides."

"Does she need to sign a rights waiver? What's our lawyer's current thinking?"

"I'll sign anything," Marion says. She's very drunk. The coke and champagne are an immense wave of light lifting her toward the ceiling, where the view is infinite. In a single motion Daniel flips Marion's reclining chair back—"Whoops!" she cries—so her head rests above the sink. Vigorously he rinses her scalp, applies shampoo. All at once the room smells of fresh coconuts. Another rinse, then conditioner, wheat and honey. "Anybody for tahini?" Marion jokes under Daniel's long, energetic fingers.

It's not turning out to be as fun for Lydia as she expected. Suddenly she's jealous of the attention Daniel and Anatole are giving to Marion. It surprises her, but there's nothing she can do about it. She sits sidesaddle on the window ledge and looks down at Main Street. It's empty, a bleak expanse of concrete and a few straggling trees, none of it made magical by a thin moonlight. Am I like this? she thinks. It's Anatole and Daniel at their worst—Daniel seems to bring it out in Anatole, a kind of desperate camp that's finally heartless, even destructive. If she didn't dislike Marion, fear her as a usurper, a disturbing mirror of her own condition, she'd feel sorry for her. As it is, depressingly enough, what's happening to her at their hands seems a species of sweet revenge.

When she looks back at the trio, Marion is sitting upright, her head covered in a tight rubber cap with holes in it. She could be an experiment in a science fiction movie. Daniel's a demented Marilyn Monroe turned lab assistant as he uses what looks like a crochet needle to pull strands of hair through the holes. "Ow," Marion half cries, half laughs. "That hurts."

"It's art—what do you expect, baby doll?"

"Ow." Marion cringes beneath Daniel's retrieval of her hair from the rubber torture cap.

"All finished." Daniel pats her hand. "You survived. Now we bleach."

"What did one bleached whale say to the other?" Anatole asks.

"I'm so washed up I could dye," Daniel tells him.

"You've heard it?"

"I think I made it up, darling." He twirls a small paintbrush in a bowl, then daubs bleach along the strands of exposed hair. "I think," he notices casually, "the bleached whale is out cold." And she is. She snores, head tilted back, empty champagne cup cradled in her lap like a favorite toy. Beneath Daniel's hands her dark, luxurious brunette dies, whitens like bone. Daniel tips her back once more into the sink and turns on the water. She comes awake spluttering, eyes wild. "Professor, it's alive, we've created life," Daniel shouts. "It's all right," he soothes Marion. "We're ready to paint. Frank Stella would die."

He dips a brush into the bowl, then stands poised, contemplating. "Next stop, Glamourville," he announces.

Anatole watches Marion's face. Her faith in Daniel is touching. Out cold, face gone jelly, she looks like someone who's been expecting the worst but is resigned to it, is convinced it's the best thing. With exaggerated flourishes, Daniel lays the eggplant purple on boldly, thickly.

Anatole hums along with the OMD tape, he mouths the words even though he doesn't know most of them. It exhilarates him, it seems just perfect—this moment, all these people here together. Marion unconscious, Daniel daubing eggplant purple, Lydia sitting on the window ledge sipping champagne. It's the kind of thing he likes more than anything else. At the same time he feels empty, he doesn't want to be here. He wants to be with Chris.

It's the secret he carries around all the time. Whatever he's doing, no matter how much fun he's having, it's empty unless Chris is there. His crush on Chris has dominated his life for two years, ever since he met him one June afternoon on the Metro North between New York and Poughkeepsie. He was coming back from a day spent shopping in the City. At Croton-Harmon, passengers for Poughkeepsie have to change trains. This particular afternoon, the connecting train hadn't pulled in yet, and as the passengers for Poughkeepsie stood waiting on the exposed platform, a thunderstorm sprang up—big drops of water, bolts of lightning that shot into the green hills around the station. The light was eerie the way light in sudden thunderstorms can be, and Anatole was terrified of the lightning. If you hear the thunder, you know it hasn't hit you, he remembered his father telling him when he was a child. Still, the waiting between thunderbursts was unbearable. The sky was alive with crackling bolts. Every instant, not knowing if it would strike you: this instant, or this—was it your last?

He stood shivering under his umbrella, resisting the urge to cower, wondering if it was true that an umbrella acts as a lightning rod. Finally he couldn't stand it any longer. Nervously, he turned to the person next to him to try to make contact with someone else who was in the same predicament.

"I just love risking my life to get to Poughkeepsie."

"I wouldn't stand so close to me," the stranger said. "God's got too many things against me for it to be safe."

Just then there was another flash of light, a blast of thunder, and

Anatole looked at the man he'd spoken to. It was the oddest thing—at the instant of the thunderbolt it seemed as if he were looking at an angel who'd just flashed into being, golden hair slicked down by the rain, soaked through to the skin.

"God's not such a great shot." Anatole laughed nervously.

"You wait." Chris grinned. "He's got a lot of ammunition."

But at that moment the Poughkeepsie train pulled alongside the platform. They scurried inside, sat in seats across the aisle from each other. Wind and rain buffeted the silver Hudson, the gray-green hills. In a few minutes the sun came out. By the time the train got to Poughkeepsie Anatole had volunteered practically everything he could think of about himself, and in the process had managed to learn that this gorgeous stranger's name was Chris Havilland, that he worked in the record store on Academy Street and that the two of them shared the same birthday, July first, the exact middle of the year.

He phoned Lydia later that night.

"So how was New York?" She knew he hadn't looked forward to going down.

"You'll never guess. I'm a wreck. Lydia, sweetheart, I met the man of my dreams."

"Again? Is he over eighteen?"

"Lydia. You'll approve of him. He gave me his phone number, he asked me to call him. He looks like David Bowie."

"David Bowie's old."

"He looks the way David Bowie used to look. He looks like the cover of *Station to Station*."

A few days later he managed to work up the courage to call Chris. At first Chris seemed not to remember him, and Anatole's heart sank, but then something seemed to click and Chris sounded suddenly enthusiastic. "Oh. The train," he said. "Of course. How about dinner? I like the Milanese. Do you ever go there?"

After four glasses of wine, they're both relaxed, talkative. Anatole's content to sit in candlelight and watch the impossibly perfect face before him. I can't believe I'm this lucky, he tells himself. He means—just to be here. Anatole is thankful for small things. It's why people like him, even against their inclination.

"It's nice to meet somebody interesting in this city," Chris tells him. "You were funny in that little rain shower—"

"It was a thunderstorm—"

"—that little rain shower. I liked that. You know, I've been here in Poughkeepsie a year now, and I don't know anybody. I haven't met people I want to know. I didn't grow up here, I didn't grow up in the East at all. I'm from Denver."

"Denver." Anatole's never been west of Buffalo, where he used to visit cousins when he was a child. "So how'd you end up here?"

"I'm here on my father's business, you might say. What I mean is, the record store I manage, Immaculate Blue—it belongs to him. It's some kind of tax dodge or something like that—I don't know exactly, I don't *want* to know. I just look after it. I get to work with records, which is all I really like. Music records." He laughs nervously, lights a cigarette. "My dad's lawyers handle the other records."

"You must be close to your dad," Anatole observes.

"No," Chris laughs abruptly, wryly. "Actually, we don't get along at all. My being here's a kind of deal, I think. My dad's very tough, very air force; he used to be a colonel, then he retired and went into real estate development—made incredible amounts of money. We were always moving to a bigger house, he kept buying boats and Winnebagos. He did it to get me out of his hair, see? I kept dropping out of schools. It was getting too embarrassing for him. He was afraid I'd end up in the East Village as a waiter or something. Dad wants a respectable son. So that's why I'm taking his money. I don't know. Maybe it's a way of getting back at him. Because he likes the wrong things about me. Or maybe it's because I'm afraid to do anything on my own because I know I'll fail, so I have to let him do it for me."

He looks in his wineglass, as if fascinated by some reflection in it. Anatole watches him, afraid to say anything that will sound stupid.

"No," Chris tells him abruptly, "I'll tell you what it is. When I was little—like, the first thing I remember—we were playing follow the leader, Dad and me; we were walking along this little brick wall, the edge of a patio; he was leading, I was following, and then I fell off the wall. I broke my arm. Chipped the elbow. I think that's the source of everything." He pauses, then groans loudly, almost despairingly. "Oh, I don't really care. Anatole, usually I don't talk about these things. I'm not interested in them. I'm just doing this to test you."

"Oh?" It confuses Anatole a bit. "Do I pass?"

Chris looks at him across the tapering candle flame. "We'll see, won't we?"

They look at each other for a minute, neither looking away. Anatole feels dizzy, he feels scared. Then Chris looks down at the table, lights up a cigarette. Anatole's crazy about the way Chris handles his cigarettes. It's enough to make him want to smoke.

"I'm exhausted," Chris says. "I've had a bad day. I'm being too talkative."

"I love it."

"Oh, you'll get bored with it, don't worry."

Later, it's what Anatole holds on to, that phrase "you'll get bored with it." More than anything he wants a chance to get bored with Chris Havilland. He doesn't know if he'll see him again. He doesn't know if the evening has "passed."

But Chris does call. Over the course of that summer they meet once a week for drinks, or for dinner. Chris is never again quite so revealing. He banters, but seldom descends into seriousness. It's Anatole who does most of the talking.

Nevertheless—one humid August night they're standing in the restaurant parking lot beside their respective cars, but neither seems quite to want to go home. "Well," Anatole says. Suddenly he is very nervous. Is this what they've been edging toward over the slow summer? He was quick to admit liking to sleep with men, he has nothing to hide. Chris listened politely, but said nothing. That was two dinners ago; it seems not to have affected their relationship one way or the other. Now tonight Chris says, "We just go on and on like this, don't we?"

"What do you mean?"

"Circling." He laughs. "It's crazy."

Anatole doesn't know what to say. He knows he's supposed to say something, he's conscious of an opportunity and of missing that opportunity, but he can think of nothing that will catch it.

"You could come back to my place for a nightcap," he suggests.

There's a pause, he waits for Chris to say no. The night itself seems to have paused in its business, to be listening to them to see how it will turn out.

"Sure," Chris tells him, smiling. "A nightcap."

In Anatole's apartment—big Victorian rooms, dark wood, lots of furniture he inherited from a grandmother—Chris sits on a sofa while Anatole brings scotch in a cut-glass decanter, glasses and a bowl of ice on a tray.

"Fancy," Chris tells him.

"I just get nervous when I have guests. I overdo it."

They sit together on the sofa and drink in silence. The apartment feels big but intimate. Anatole tries to broach the difficult subject. "It's funny," he says, "when I think back to the beginning of summer. How I didn't know. How I couldn't ever have guessed." He looks at Chris; it's awkward, sitting side by side like this; so he plunges ahead. "It's always hard to talk about, isn't it?" He laughs, but then is grave. "Can I say you've sort of changed my life this summer? That I'm alive now. Is that okay to say?"

He watches Chris for signs of retreat, but there don't seem to be any.

"I guess what I'm saying is," he says, "I think I'm sort of in love with you."

As he says it he puts his hand on Chris's shoulder. His heart is beating so fast, he's afraid he'll have a heart attack.

"Okay." Chris's laugh is halfhearted but gentle. Anatole waits for him to say something more, to touch him, to do something. But nothing happens. Chris lifts Anatole's hand from his shoulder; he pats it. "I like you, Anatole," he says.

"Do you understand what I'm trying to say?" Anatole asks.

"I do understand." Chris is firm but tender. "Remember, you don't want to stand too close to me. Lightning."

"But I want it to strike. I've been waiting my whole life."

Chris smiles fondly, shakes his head. "I was afraid," he says. He takes a sip of his scotch. "I'm going to go now. Call me soon, okay?"

It's the closest they've gotten, that moment—a high-water mark they never reach again. But Anatole remembers it. He'll catch himself thinking of it at moments like this, and then feel far from everything that's happening around him, the chatter and bustle. He thinks about it all the time; even though more than two years have passed since that night and he and Chris have become, as they say, best friends, it makes a lump in his throat to remember. The highest moment of his life. He's slept with lots of other boys, he's slept with Daniel—it's not that. Rather, it's the closest he's ever gotten, he tells himself, to something—he can't name it, he doesn't even know for sure what it is. All he knows is that it matters more to him than anything else in his life.

"Here, doll," Daniel is saying. He pats Marion's cheek, then gives a deft slap to bring her around. She sputters as she hits consciousness again. "Keep your eyes closed, honey. Your heart just stopped for a while. You probably had an out-of-the-body experience, right?"

"Are we finished?" she murmurs groggily. Obedient, she keeps her eyes shut.

Daniel pauses to contemplate her. "They're going to take you right to heaven," he tells her. "You're not even going to have to wait. Patti LaBelle'll *swoon* when she hears about this."

"I'm afraid to look." Marion's trying hard to stay conscious long enough to savor that first glimpse in the mirror, the "You" she's asked for and never thought she'd really get.

It's a losing battle, though.

Daniel addresses the once more inert form in front of him. "Your self-control, darling, is *admirable*." He touches up the sides, then frowns, almost pouts while Anatole puts both hands to his temples, eyes wide, and mouths a silent Yikes.

Lydia watches it all coolly, pensively. She feels far from their antics. They're tiresome, their larks bore her after a while. But they're her friends. Anatole's her best friend in the world. "Fag hag"—Marion's words from earlier in the evening annoy Lydia, but they also haunt her.

It seems impossible that things can have lasted between her and Anatole as long as they have. But then, they've been through everything together: between them there's a special understanding that survives her feelings of entrapment, of futility. I should be dating eligible men, she tells herself, I should find a man to make love to, to marry. But she's paralyzed. She wonders if it's Anatole who paralyzes her. After all, it's safer to tag along on a night like this—watch Anatole and Daniel carry on even though she doesn't entirely approve—than set out alone, stand forlorn on the edge of the action at Let's Dance (somewhere along the way she's lost her old courage) and wait to meet that one man who counts, who'll change everything, who never shows up.

Because it was Anatole who was there when, after taking a leave of absence from Bard her sophomore year and moving to New York for a resounding six-month disaster, she fled back to Poughkeepsie, the waiting arms of her mother, her old friends, the life she was accustomed to. A rat- and roach-infested apartment between Avenues A and B, broken into twice in the same month, her neighbors a sax player with a three-hundred-a-month heroin habit, and a drag queen whose shrieks kept her awake at night.

The defeat is something she seldom thinks about, it's a private failure she nurses much the same way she nurses the memory of a baby she had aborted her freshman year at Bard. Sometimes, even now, she wakes in the morning and feels an unbearable nostalgia for the Lower East Side, its colorful squalor, the shifting life of its streets.

She thinks sometimes of a boy she knew named Demian, a poet always dressed in drab work clothes, scuffed black leather shoes—he wore a Greek sailor's cap perched on the back of his head, his hair black, unwashed—she remembers spending a night with him, stroking his greasy-sweet hair, breathing in the scent of his tense body as he plunged furiously, heartbreakingly into her; later he cried and told her about his lover Marc, the only person he really loved, who was in Bellevue, who'd threatened to kill him. Sometimes (she thinks of Anatole) it's hard not to be bitter. Though of course it's not their fault; nothing's anybody's fault, or it's all God's fault, in which case who cares anyway?

She's always lived with the myth that she'll return one day, that she's only in Poughkeepsie getting her life together—but every year that goes by, it's harder to conceal from herself (and she suspects she's the last it's concealed from) that she's here for the duration, she'll never go back to the Lower East Side, she'll never go back to college; whatever her life is going to be—and she's twenty-nine, this is real life—this is it.

It's been Anatole who's somehow made it bearable, this long exile from whatever her life might otherwise have been. He's amused her, diverted her, he's cried with her and gotten drunk with her. Anatole and Daniel. What else do they signify other than how life might be possible anywhere, how like weeds it can spring up unexpectedly, even where there seems no place for it?

She watches as they pause in their ministrations about Marion to survey the extent of the damage.

"Do you think we should call the fire department?" Anatole asks. "Or at least have a hose ready when she wakes up?"

But Daniel is pleased, triumphant. With a final mad flourish he brings Marion back to life—two deft slaps on her cheeks. Then he is sitting her upright in her seat, now he spins her around to face the mirror. And in the mirror, transformed—her new self.

How exactly, Lydia wonders, would you describe that look on Marion's face when she glimpses her new self for the very first time?

Evening sun inundates the kitchen. Waiting for Anatole and Lydia to show up, Chris chops endives, tosses them into a blue ceramic bowl. He ladles in roasted peppers, six quartered sun-dried tomatoes. Squeezes lemon, crushes garlic, sprinkles dill. This might be one of those perfect moments: every surface, every utensil floats in light.

It may be that Chris is at his best this instant before other people see him. Everything gathers itself into a momentary coherence, the tensions balance as in music. There comes this brief space of calm, a perspective achieved and then forfeited.

Chris watches Anatole and Lydia as they get out of Lydia's Chevy, stroll up the sidewalk. The way they touch each other, gracefully, ironically—Chris imagines that they're married. He's the bachelor friend both are fond of, the one who's had an affair with the wife and the husband doesn't know about it.

He seldom thinks of the night he fucked Lydia. He can't let himself, because it's always there, he doesn't need to think about it to be aware of it: it hangs over perfect moments like a cloud threatening not only rain but storm, havoc, whole cities swept away.

Why did he move to Poughkeepsie in the first place, if not to get away from that other city where he'd hurt too many people? It's something he can't think about, that year in Ithaca with John, that summer with John and Michelle in the big, bare house. If you can bruise a soul, then that's what happened. And now, three and a half years later, Chris is afraid it's started to happen all over again right here, in different circumstances, with different people—but still just the same. After everything he told himself he'd learned painfully, disastrously, how can he have let it begin again here as well?

Anatole was the one who introduced him and Lydia in the first place. They'd have drinks together, the three of them, at Bertie's after work. Occasionally they'd go to a movie, or Anatole would make dinner for them. They'd known each other two or three months when her younger brother Craig drove down from Boston. Chris had always liked Lydia—she struck him from the first as quick, acidic, generous. But to glimpse her reflected in her brother—he was thinner, sharper in definition—well, it made Chris see her in a new light. Her relation to her brother changed her, it enlarged Chris's sense of her. If he could see her in him, he could also make out, just barely, him in her.

He had the two of them over for dinner; Anatole had something else to do; Chris can no longer remember why, fatefully, Anatole wasn't able to come.

It was late, the three of them—Chris and Lydia and her brother—listened to Chris's new CD player and drank scotch.

"I'm so tired," Lydia yawned. "It's pleasant. I feel like just fading away."

"We'll go," Craig told her.

"No. We don't have to go. I'll just stretch out on the bed and take a nap. You two keep on talking. I like listening to you. I'm just going to shut my eyes and listen to you talk from the next room."

They both watched her disappear. For a while they were silent, almost shy with each other. All evening they had talked animatedly, finding a connection in each other's words that led them into an immediate friendliness, even intimacy, that thrilled Chris and at the same time made him wary.

Craig lounged in an armchair, his legs draped over the side, barefoot, his sneakers cast off on the floor beside him. Were they, after all, strangers? Could they go on in Lydia's absence? For a moment they had nothing to say, it was hopeless. But then the next moment there was once again this quiet, electric flurry that sparked between them. He can't reconstruct now, almost two years later, what it might have been that they talked about. But beneath whatever foundation their sentences laid, an underground river roared—you could hear it, sometimes just barely, sometimes rising so near the surface it seemed in the next instant it must break through. But it didn't. Perhaps Craig was too young yet to be attuned to it—he was only a freshman at Boston University. Perhaps Chris was only inventing it all, scotch and the lateness of the hour collaborating to invest innocence with all sorts of nuances that weren't really there. It was three o'clock, then four.

At last Craig stood up to go. "It's so late," he said. He'd driven down for the weekend, he was driving back in a few hours: he had to write a philosophy paper. "It's been really great to talk to you," he told Chris. "I hope we'll see each other again." He seemed to have forgotten Lydia. Perhaps he assumed his sister and Chris were involved. He didn't ask if he should wake her, and Chris forgot about her too, in the intimate moment between them as they shook hands, their touch lingering an instant too long—Chris had learned to read such handshakes as secret, even unconscious gestures. Gestures he was never certain he could accurately interpret, but that he nonetheless thrilled, on occasion, to encounter—as if it gave him purchase on a buried self the other was as yet unaware of.

Back in his bedroom, he found Lydia fast asleep. She'd taken off her shoes, pulled a blanket over her. Chris sat down on the bed. "Lydia," he said quietly. "Lydia."

"Oh hi, Chris." She smiled up at him, groggily, contentedly. "Where's Craig?"

"He left. He went home." He wasn't going to say, We both forgot about you.

She only looked at him; he could see her trying to figure out exactly what this meant. Her eyes were dreamy, dilated with sleep.

"He left a while ago. You were sleeping. It's too late for you to go home. Go back to sleep."

"Where are you going to sleep?"

"I'll just lie down here beside you." He slipped off his shoes as she pulled the blanket aside for him. Fully clothed, he rolled in beside her. She put her arms around him, and he responded, holding her tight. It was like putting his arms around her brother.

They kissed. Her mouth tasted like old alcohol and cigarette smoke. Was that how Craig's mouth would taste? It surprised him how she was so shy with him, letting him put his hands everywhere but hardly reciprocating. He thought he'd understood from previous evenings that she'd be happy to make love to him. Was he once more only vain and stupid? Or was she just too sleepy? He worked his hands up under her skirt, pulled down her panties. She was her brother. He ran his fingertips across her brother's pubic hair. He cupped her brother's smooth buttocks. But it was also her. They kissed so they wouldn't have to say anything.

He entered her, whispering as he did, "I won't come inside you." It made her laugh. But he didn't come. He pumped inside her for a few minutes, then pulled out. It satisfied nothing. She wasn't her brother, of course. She was Anatole's best friend. He felt only panic, as if in a momentary confusion he had thrown everything away.

She was asleep before he could speak a single word to her and in the morning when he woke she was already up, swallowing a handful of aspirin tablets. They were ironic with each other as they arranged themselves to face the day's massive hangover. "We could do this again sometime if you wanted," she mentioned, looking not at him but at her reflection in the mirror.

He sat on the side of the bed, head pounding, in full panic. "Do what?" he said.

Chris knows Anatole would die if he ever found out about that night. Their relationship has reached a comfortable plateau of apparent friendship—after that single night of honesty between them on Anatole's sofa two years ago, they've never quite approached the same dangerous intensity. Whatever his relief at their truce, it also disappoints Chris a little, how Anatole seemed to lose heart after that night. He can't decipher the reason for that retreat, but he feels the loss. If he wants Anatole's love, it's only so he can keep it at bay. He wants it the way he wants to be noticed—but he also dreads it, dreads the consequences for Anatole if, beneath the uncharged intimacy of their current friendship, the anguish he suspects is there still smolders, like those underground coal fires that linger for years beneath quiet Pennsylvania towns.

Whatever lies between them, his action with Lydia has been a betrayal. He is certain of that. Anatole has trusted him with his love, and he's betrayed him where it would hurt the most. There's no other way Anatole would be able to understand it if he were to find out. He and Lydia have never spoken further of it, and Chris is sure Anatole doesn't know a thing. Still—how can Chris expect her to be better than *he'd* be under the circumstances? He can imagine it with stinging clarity—late one night, culmination of some unimportant squabble they've had over the phone, one hurt escalating to the next, she'll blurt it out. She'll have to. "Well, he *slept* with me, Anatole—Chris Havilland *fucked* me."

It's too good not to use.

His fate: He sees it for an instant with absolute clarity—the sunlight only enhances it. He'll be the catalyst in some final uproar that will devastate Anatole. He can't believe, sometimes, that it'll come to this, that he'll be the cause of it. He'd like to think he doesn't matter that much. But he suspects the truth. It's because Anatole loved him that he had to betray Anatole with Lydia.

He'd give anything to take it back, but if he's learned anything, it's that very little can be taken back. So it lingers. Every moment the three of them are together, every moment Anatole and Lydia are alone together: it threatens.

Lydia is unsacking the wine she's brought. "It was on sale, three ninety-nine. And I brought some bread."

"You'll never believe the bread," Anatole says.

Chris looks at the dark round loaf.

"Pesto bread, with walnuts."

"My God, sounds wonderful. We're *having* pesto. We'll O.D. on it. They had fresh basil at Adams."

Mismatched plates on a blue checked tablecloth. Wine and bread, antipasto—they become holy acts. The Last Supper must have felt this way.

"Sun-dried tomatoes," Lydia admires. "Yum. They're so expensive."

Chris shrugs. He lives simply, in order to be as luxurious as possible within that simplicity.

"Sixteen ninety-five a pound at The Market Place," she says. "Can you imagine?" She spears one with her fork. "Such a treat for the peasants, Chris."

"We try," he tells her mildly.

Anatole interrupts them. "Oh my God," he says. He jumps up from the chair where he's sitting and runs his fingers through his hair. "I completely forgot. I knew there was something, Big News of the day. You'll never guess who I saw."

"We never will, no," Lydia says.

He pauses appropriately, then speaks with gravity. "Our Boy of the Mall."

"Are you kidding?" Lydia grins with complicity. It leaves Chris out, he feels angry with both of them for perpetuating this fantasy well beyond its half-life.

"I'm sure it was him. I was driving out by K-Mart, and he was walking on the sidewalk. I almost ran off the road. He was with about three girls. They were all laughing and talking and he was walking in the middle of them, like they were surrounding him, you know, his disciples or something, and he wasn't saying anything. At least I couldn't tell that he was. They were talking and laughing and he was looking *very* serious. I kept looking in the rearview mirror to see him as long as I could. I drove around the block so I could see him again, but he wasn't there when I got back."

Lydia teases. "Anatole, you let him get away! That's not good."

"But it was him. I know it was him."

"Well, he probably lives in Poughkeepsie, after all," Chris says. "It's not *that* surprising."

"Chris, you'll depress me if you say another word," Anatole cries. "Let me savor it."

Chris smiles, but he feels vaguely distressed. Perhaps it's only because he hasn't seen this boy and so doesn't know what they're talking about. But even if he had, he'd leave himself out. It's just something that goes on between Anatole and Lydia, and he doesn't allow himself to have any part in it.

"I want to tell you both about my dream," Anatole announces. "I think maybe it prophesied the Second Sighting."

He pours himself more wine, then begins.

"There were a lot of us. Both of you were there. Other people I didn't recognize but in the dream I knew who they were. We were standing on the shore of a lake—the ground was completely white, the lake was blue like a lake. A big lake, you couldn't see the other side. And there was a water plane—what do you call them? An aquaplane. Anyway, we were waiting for this plane. Somebody was saying something about how they'd dropped the atomic bomb on Syracuse. They were evacuating us to somewhere. And then in the distance there was this flash of light, and we knew it was another atomic bomb."

"Syracuse," Chris laughs. "They probably *should* drop an atomic bomb on Syracuse."

"When I woke up," Anatole says, "I felt this complete emptiness. I'm always having atomic bomb dreams."

"So what does that have to do with Our Boy of the Mall?" Lydia wonders.

"I don't know," Anatole tells her. "It just seemed like there might be some connection."

"Sometimes it's just really scary these days," Lydia admits. "I mean, about everything."

"I can't remember dreams," Chris tells them. In the only dream he can remember, a recurrent dream, he is filled with an unbearable tenderness and hopelessness. In the dream he is making love to Anatole.

They've driven to Rhinebeck to feast on sushi; in the aftermath of their binge—they've spent unbelievable sums on sea urchin with quail eggs, California rolls, abalone—they land at Bertie's around midnight. Wednesday night is Punk Night—the dance floor's full of slightly scary-looking kids who make Chris, at twenty-six, feel old. Already a generation is springing up to replace him.

Anatole can't take his eyes off Chris, who's dazzling in white: he looks so vulnerable against the tide of punks, and Anatole's in love all over again. He can't help it: every evening he's with Chris, part of him keeps hoping against hope that somehow, they'll end up in bed together. He never mentions it to Lydia, or to anyone.

Tonight Chris is withdrawn, making much of his cigarette, flirting with it, a flirtation that excludes everyone else. The music dazes him. He allows its heavy beat to inhabit him, as if his heartbeat is no more than another kind of drumming. He likes watching people dance; they become parts of a mechanism that has nothing to do with him, they don't threaten or move him.

Lydia nudges Anatole. "Who's Chris watching?" They joke privately about Chris's indifference, how he's always ready to be seen but is never interested in seeing. Through the jostling bodies she can't see who it is. But it touches Lydia to catch Chris suddenly alert to a face in a crowd; he's usually so self-contained, so reticent about giving too much away. A kind of selfishness. She'd like to know him, know where he's failed, what he's won—but he's careful to avoid giving it to her. Even when his penis was in her, that one time, he didn't come; he withdrew, leaving nothing of himself behind.

His wants, his frustrations take place in private.

"Lydia, dear, it's plain," Daniel once told her. "It's like animals when they're wounded. You never see dying animals. They hide themselves away. They have this natural, I don't know, discretion."

Chris is unaware of being watched. He's not even watching the boy anymore, he's moved back inside himself. The boy interested him just for a moment. Dancing with himself, he seemed perfect. Whirl of blondish hair, thin arms, preoccupied look. Lifting a vial to his nose, he took a whiff of popper. Chris feels futile. What can anything lead to? He doesn't want to be close to anybody. He's known too many people in his life, and too disastrously, to want to know any more.

A break in the pattern of dancing, a rent in the solid wall of the crowd. Anatole grabs Lydia's arm. "Oh my God," he says. "Look."

Lydia sees instantly who he's noticed. She's a little amazed to find she hasn't really stopped thinking about him all week, hasn't stopped hoping she'd see him again. You never see boys like that again.

Suddenly she's intensely aware of needing—of all things—to pee. Great, she thinks. "This beer goes right through me," she tells Anatole. "Don't do anything rash till I get back." In the bathroom the graffiti reads U.S. Out of North America. When she comes back, Anatole's talking to the boy. They lean against the bar, they've known each other for ages. Anatole's talking animatedly, gesticulating. The boy laughs, takes a step back, tumbler in hand. Something Lydia always marvels at in Anatole: he looks a little goofy, a little gawky— but he has this talent, he knows how to meet anybody. There's a certain remarkable inadvertence to it. He just takes chances, and they work. She's listened to him talk to strangers. The sentences seem random, observations flung in panic and tempered by a wit that's always a little off. He laughs a lot, nervously, almost a giggle—at himself, it seems to say, at the ridiculous shyness of human beings. Perhaps that's what puts people at ease with him. They feel a sort of comfortable superiority to him, but also have to admire him for the way he surrenders himself, undergoes whatever humiliations are involved in making a new acquaintance.

It looks as if he's put this boy under his spell. He's bought him a drink. The boy drinks unsteadily—he's already pretty drunk, Lydia can tell. And there's something about him—he's been letting strangers talk to him all night, buy him drinks. He's used to that, comfortable with it. Deftly he maneuvers in and out of tricky situations without getting caught. At least, that's what she feels, watching him talk to Anatole. She takes a deep breath—there's always this moment that just kills her but that she loves, right before she meets somebody she really wants to meet. The last moment I'll not know him, she thinks—

and cherishes it: the memory of the boy sitting on the Main Street mall eating a frozen chocolate bar. After this it's all going to change.

"Anatole," she says, going up to him, putting her hand familiarly on his arm. The tone of voice says they haven't seen each other in days.

"Oh Lydia," he says. "Meet Leigh."

"Hi," Leigh tells her. His smile is shy, skittish—at the same time blatant and flirtatious.

Antole's annoyed. She's moved in so quickly. He's still not sure, after these few sentences, what he thinks of Leigh. "You're a good dancer," he's told him. His first words, going up to him, touching him boldly on the shoulder (thrilling: his shoulder fragile, delicate, as if his bones are hollow—a bird's bones, the kind of bones angels have); Leigh turning, his look asking, Am I supposed to remember you from somewhere? "I was watching you. I admire good dancing."

"That? I was stumbling around, basically."

"I like the way you stumble around. Can I buy you a drink?"

Leigh might be eighteen, he might be seventeen. He might be twenty. Anatole can't tell. It makes his spine prickle, there's something so pure, so corrupt in the way Leigh handles his glass easily, swirls the Johnnie Walker Red, gulps it down. "Ahh," he exaggerates—it's wonderful. Anatole tries to take in every detail of Leigh's face. Youth's a miracle to him, a boy's face more perfect than, well, than anything else he can think of. He wants quickly to memorize it in case it disappears. The part of him that despairs is already sated: all it wants is to get home quickly and masturbate about Leigh before he forgets what he looks like.

This is the best, he thinks. Right now. Whatever happens from now on will only darken this.

Leigh's vague with the two of them. "Yeah, I'm from around here. Poughkeepsie, you know." It's as if he's not sure, or he's making it up. He could be intensely dumb, or have a refined, extraordinary intelligence.

"It's hard to talk here," Anatole says. "The music's always so loud." Bronski Beat's "Small Town Boy" is playing for the third time of the evening.

"I like it. Cool bar. I like the people. You come from Pough-keepsie too?"

"Honey, some people think we *are* Poughkeepsie," Anatole says. "What do you do?"

"Moi? Hairstylist, Reflexion—"

"Don't know it."

"It's on the Main Street mall."

"I never go on Main Street," Leigh says. "I haven't been there in months."

Oh, Anatole thinks. Fine. That's the way we'll be, then.

"You should come sometime. Come by and I'll give you a haircut. Free."

"I just got my hair cut."

"I like it. Really I do. I never compliment unless I mean it. You can trust me on that. Where'd you get it?"

"This girl gave it to me. A friend. I don't remember her name."

"It's not professional?"

He can tell it's not professional, though it's not bad either.

"No, she just did it one afternoon."

"Well, it's nice-looking."

Leigh shrugs. He turns to Lydia. "And so who are you?" he asks—utterly, Lydia thinks, without curiosity.

"Just a friend of the deceased here," she says.

Leigh's got no reaction to that. "It's hot in here," he notices. He rubs a hand under the collar of his white T-shirt, examines the beads of sweat.

"See?" He shows them. His fingers glisten with droplets. His T-shirt clings to him.

"You *are* sweating a lot," Anatole confirms.

"I was dancing up a storm out there," Leigh reminds him. "Any-way, I hate hot weather. I can't wait for winter."

Lydia watches. The way he moves, there's a confidence, an elec-tricity. Something invites you to reach out and touch him, stroke his wrist, put your arm around him. The sort of boy you want to whisper a secret to, your lips against his downy ear. There's also something crazy and disconnected about him.

"We could go somewhere else," Anatole says. "I've got liquor at my place. And a regular medicine cabinet. If that interests you."

"Okay." Leigh looks around—he doesn't want to miss anything.

Chris is leaning against the bar. He's not been watching Anatole or Lydia or the boy. He's not been watching anything. He's just been letting the room affect him as it will. All these people are parts of a machine. The mechanism that controls them is the music.

"Come play with us." Anatole is jubilant. "This is Leigh." They march past, Anatole and Lydia, with Leigh between them.

Chris looks at Leigh. Something inside him says, quietly, a kind of fateful certainty, Oh.

Outside, it's rained. The night is thick, it rises from the pavement like fog. There are no stars, only the sulfur glow of the city's streetlights.

In Anatole's apartment they fling themselves down on sofas, in chairs, on the floor. They've all drunk too much. Still, Anatole brings out an armload of different liquor bottles, gin, vodka, scotch, bourbon, deposits them on the coffee table.

"Such an impressive array," Lydia approves. She reaches for the gin, pours herself a glass. "Ice cubes, dear?" she wonders.

Meanwhile Leigh is slapping Echo and the Bunnymen on the turntable. He turns the stereo up loud—"Oh wow," he approves.

The neighbors, Lydia mouths, pantomiming a twist of the volume knob downward as the music begins to boom.

"Fuck the neighbors"—Anatole appearing in the doorway, bearing ice, dropping it into glasses. Usually he's careful, even paranoid about his neighbors; but tonight he feels like celebrating. This is a moment of fate, return of the prodigal son; what was lost is found.

"So this is how people in Poughkeepsie live." Leigh is cool, taking stock of the apartment. "I always wondered." He walks around comfortably, picking up various objects to examine—an old perfume bottle, a chinoiserie plate, a porcelain vase. He's a thief, a connoisseur, a curious kid. He's completely at home with himself, moving like a dancer who knows his body. That's what impresses Anatole; he can't keep his eyes off him. He can't believe this boy's actually inside his apartment.

But now that they have him: what to do? Anatole still knows nothing about him. Is he straight, is he bi? Could he be gay? Anatole wants Chris and Lydia to leave so he can find out; he's also terrified that they might actually do that at some point. The evening will have to end, after all—somehow. When the time comes, will he lose his nerve?

Lydia wonders if Leigh regrets having left Bertie's, where something might actually have happened. But he seems content to be exactly where he is. Of all of them, he's the most at home.

Chris sits and smokes in silence. Sips at a scotch, leafs through the new *House and Garden* he's picked up from the coffee table. He tries to focus on the magazine's featured excerpt, Billy Baldwin's autobiography. "Edith, without knowing what she had been doing on her European buying trip, had picked out the most ravishing suite of Louis XVI furniture that I have ever seen in my life." He tries to ignore Leigh, but it's difficult. His presence fills the room like the strong scent of exotic flowers. Chris is amazed at this boy's drunken composure, his quick smiles, the way he flicks his head back now and again to get that lock of hair out of his eyes. He watches as Lydia and Anatole circle Leigh like sleek beasts of prey.

The music is very loud. Leigh especially seems lost in it. Anatole and Lydia talk to him as if they're competing for his attention, even though it's Echo and the Bunnymen who have his whole attention at the moment. He could be anywhere—he's exactly as he was at Bertie's when Chris saw him sniffing popper.

Suddenly something Anatole says seems to draw him back. He looks around, as if already he can't remember how he got here, who these people are. "What's your names again?" he asks them. "I read a book once that had an Anatole in it. It was a book for kids. I don't remember the name of it. It had pictures." He's busy balancing his wineglass on his knee, screwing up one eye to get a fix on it. "Fuck," he says as it almost spills. "I bet the carpet's expensive. I bet you'd of killed me."

"Hardly. It's more old than expensive. Pakistani," Anatole explains. It makes him feel old as well. He has no idea what to talk to this boy about. They belong to different worlds, no matter how many current albums Anatole may own. He has no idea what this boy might really want to talk about. If he even wants to talk. Is talking an adult thing? He's in a panic, he hates himself for having grown up and out of whatever this boy still knows about. And it'll get worse and worse, he'll be a fat old queer who jerks off behind the window curtains while watching the boy next door mow the lawn.

A higher wave of drunkenness seems to surge through the room, sweep them farther out to sea. They all feel it; suddenly they're all much drunker. All at once—it happens so quickly no one's sure what provokes it—Anatole's brought out a set of crayons. He and Lydia sit on the sofa, with Leigh between them, and they draw on his T-shirt. Perhaps he's asked them to autograph it.

"Tabula rasa," Lydia says.

"Tabula what? Don't talk dirty," Anatole admonishes.

Leigh simply sits between them, smiling, his eyes closed—clearly he's very, very drunk; he'll have to stay here tonight; he won't be able to make it home, wherever that is. YOU DRINK YOU DRIVE YOU DIE, Anatole writes in black, big block letters above Leigh's heart. Shoot Raygun, Lydia writes on his right sleeve. Beneath their touch Leigh is delicate as a deer, ready to bound away at any instant, held trembling in place only by his own curiosity to see what will happen next. They handle him gently, hands clambering to caress him into being. U.S. Out of North America, Lydia writes. It makes Chris laugh abruptly.

"That's really funny," he tells her. "Did you make that up?"

"It came to me."

Leigh's laugh is kidlike, shy, also calculating. Chris doesn't take part; he watches how this boy lets these avid strangers, these adults touch him. He's luxurious beneath their touch like a cat who's being rubbed down. It alarms Chris. He remembers—it surfaces without warning, something he hasn't thought of in years—he was five or six, visiting relatives, playing with a cousin of his, a little boy of two or three, in a school bus that was parked in a vacant lot next to his relatives' house. Chris had climbed up into the bus; now his little cousin wanted to climb up in it too. Chris sat in the driver's seat; with both hands he grasped the lever that opened and closed the bus's folding doors. The little boy—he was wearing just a diaper—tried to hoist himself up. The step was high, barely within his reach. Just when he was halfway into the bus, balanced on his stomach on the bottom step, his legs dangling, Chris pushed the lever and closed the door. It caught the little boy right at the waist. Trapped, he squirmed, he shrieked in surprise or pain. Chris pushed the lever tighter. He pushed and pushed. Then he opened it a little only to close it again, even harder. He wanted to push so hard that the doors would cut the little boy in half.

Pushing the lever made his penis get hard in his pants. He swooned with a strange excitement he'd never felt before. He felt an overwhelming tenderness and love, trying to squeeze the doors shut so tightly they'd slice that little boy in half. But he wasn't strong enough. He couldn't cut his cousin in half. He released the doors. The little boy wasn't hurt. He stopped crying in an instant, and clambered on into the bus. He wandered up the aisle, touching each of the seats, singing. Chris felt—he feels—abandoned, forlorn. He wanted—something. He didn't know what he wanted, and he still doesn't know.

But watching Anatole and Lydia draw on Leigh's T-shirt, this is what he thinks about. He realizes, with some surprise, he's as drunk as they are. His mind drifts, unmoored. With an effort he focuses on the room, the three of them seated on the sofa.

"What're you doing over there?" he asks Anatole, who's busy at work with the crayons. Holding three or four in reserve in his fist, Anatole concentrates on a spot along Leigh's left rib cage, just under his heart.

"Just a sec." Anatole slurs his words.

"His masterpiece," Lydia says.

Leigh has tilted his head back on the sofa. Eyes closed, legs stretched straight out. His long, almond-tanned throat is exposed, as if he's offered himself for sacrifice.

"Voilà." Anatole flings the crayons up into the air, lets them fall. They're all too drunk to care about anything except beauty. Chris manages to get out of his chair. He stands over Leigh—who looks dead, or asleep. On Leigh's T-shirt, under his heart, Anatole's drawn a perfect cartoon portrait of Leigh, colored it in, bright yellow hair, red lips, flesh-colored flesh.

"That's very good, Anatole." It *is* good, even uncanny how Anatole's caught him, his cartoon good looks. There are a million boys out there like this boy. Somehow it all just happens to coalesce here.

"I don't know about everybody else," Lydia says, "but I have to go home. I can't believe I'm supposed to be at work in"—checking her watch—"Yikes, do you realize I have to get up in four hours? I'll still be drunk."

"At least you won't be hung over."

"I don't want to still be alive come noon."

"That's when it'll hit," Anatole agrees grimly. "Take lots of vitamins. Do you want me to get you some vitamins?"

"I have some at my place." She laughs as the dark empty policed streets unspool themselves inside her. She realizes how truly drunk she is. Drunk deep inside, in her soul. It's because this evening's made her panic. Now she can't even think about it. All she wants to do is get home. Let Anatole do what he will with this Leigh: she's not going to be an accomplice to statutory sodomy. In the morning, she thinks, she isn't going to like all this very much. It's going to taste a little bitter.

"Can you drive?" Anatole asks, anxious for her to say yes.

"We'll drive slow. I'll steer, Chris can push the gas pedal."

Leigh's unconscious. His mouth has fallen slightly open. He's vulnerable to roving lions, hyenas, vultures.

Anatole's thrilled, terrified, thrilled. Anything might happen. He wants to thank all sorts of gods he'll invent just for the purpose of thanking. There's something chaste and pure, very holy in his terror. Up in the heavens the gods are laughing with great roiling laughs, the stars are spinning in a darkness that has no ceiling.

"Call me first thing," Lydia tells him. She and Chris look disheveled in the wearying light of the hallway.

Anatole. He has what he wants. It's not his. He wanders around the apartment stealthily, he's a thief who's prowling. His whole life balances on this single moment. He'll find out, he thinks. He'll know whether all these years of waiting will come true.

In an armchair he sits across from Leigh and watches him sleep. The boy's untouchable. If Anatole touches him he will disappear. And Anatole doesn't want to touch him. He wants the moment to last forever—like a reflection in water, the least movement will fracture it. The room goes in and out of focus; unless he concentrates, his image of Leigh blurs to double. He becomes aware of the stereo needle clicking in the final, endless groove of the record, where it was allowed to lapse.

He shakes himself, takes a deep breath, then goes over to the sofa and sits down beside Leigh. Gently he touches him on the shoulder, massages his shoulder.

"Leigh," he says quietly. "It's time to go to bed."

"What?" Leigh is groggy, a little child after a nap. He looks around wide-eyed, rubbing his eyes with his fists. "Oh," he says. "Uh. Where is this?"

"It's okay, it's my apartment. Chris and Lydia had to leave."

"I should leave too."

"No. It's late. You should stay here."

Leigh settles his head on the back of the sofa and starts to pass out again.

"Come on, I'll help you to bed."

He helps Leigh up. The boy's docile, lets himself be led by the hand down the hallway to the bedroom, the big double bed that used to belong to Anatole's grandmother. "We'll crash here," he says, as if it's an ordinary thing. He tries to be as unalarming as he can.

Leigh kicks off his loafers, slips his T-shirt over his head. His chest is smooth, nipples brown as pennies. A feathering of light hair under his arms. He unzips his jeans and slides them down, almost falling in his attempt to free himself of their embrace. His eyes are closed, he is dreaming this, dreaming these actions, this being. Anatole stands breathless, afraid to move. Then quickly, Leigh is beneath the sheets, his body surrendered, his mind sunk too deep for harm.

Anatole collapses into a chair and puts his head in his hands. Suddenly he wants to cry, the world is so huge and empty. He thinks of his childhood—how once he was a little boy who had a mother and a father. He feels completely alone, the way people who are about

35

to die must feel alone. There's nothing to tell him what to do next. There's nothing except this stillness here in the middle of this night that may never reach the other side of its journey through the desert, the mountains, wherever it is the dark night journeys.

It always surprises her, how from one hangover to the next she can really manage to forget. It's not possible this can be survived, is it? Meanwhile she says, "No, I think that looks right. It's *supposed* to be kind of blousy."

The woman looks at herself skeptically in the mirror. The corners of her mouth turn down in a moue. "I guess," she says. Her hair is dark red, her skin dried and pulled tight over her cheekbones. Too many beaches and sailboats. "Ever get in that mood where nothing looks right anymore, where you just can't *tell*?"

"But you should believe me," Lydia says. "It looks really nice. You'll see when you get it home. It'll be your favorite thing to wear this winter." She moves from one word to the next the way a rock climber moves, cautiously, looking for handholds to pull her through—while below, the abyss of her hangover gapes blackly. Her body alternates surges of hot and cold, mostly hot, a prickling in her skin, a welling in her stomach. For a moment she feels sure she's going to vomit, but then that's replaced by the throbbing behind her eyes. She can't believe she does this to herself.

"You don't look so good," Janet confides to her after she's rung up the sale, and ushered the woman out with a difficultly achieved "Have a nice day."

"Things got a little out of hand. I was out late." She and Janet are allies, they cover for each other's hangovers.

At noon Lydia rings Reflexion, but Anatole's not there. "He canceled all his appointments," Daniel reports.

When she reaches him at home—he picks up the phone on the first ring, as if he's waiting for a call—his voice is hushed, panicked. "I'm so glad to hear your voice," he tells her. "I was going to call you at the store."

"You're still alive?"

"I haven't decided. Actually, you know, I don't have a hangover. That's one of the four hundred and twelve signs, isn't it?"

"You always have a hangover, Anatole."

"True. Well, that's the nice thing about being an alcoholic. No matter what you do to yourself, you can't really make it much worse. Actually, I do feel a little the worse for wear."

"Um." Lydia doesn't quite know what to say next. "Dare I ask? How's Our Boy of the Mall?"

There's a pause. Suddenly she's afraid. She doesn't know what Anatole is going to say. It hasn't occurred to her that she might be jealous of Anatole.

"Oh—Leigh." Anatole tries to sound nonchalant. "That *is* what the child said his name was, isn't it?"

"You don't remember?"

"There are certain things I don't remember, no. Anyway, Leigh's out cold. He snores, but it's adorable. I don't think I want him to wake up. He really looks like Prince Charming."

"So wake him with a kiss. That's the way it's done."

"Lydia," Anatole asks, his voice childlike and grave, "what happened last night? I mean, exactly?"

"Don't ask me. I can't even remember driving home. That's the scary thing. I remember leaving your place, but I don't remember anything else. I hope I dropped Chris off at his apartment. We didn't do anything too terrible at your house, I don't think. Why?"

"Lydia, I feel awful this morning. I feel really scared. I don't know what's going to happen when this kid wakes up in my bed. I mean, we didn't *do* anything. We just went to sleep. We both just kind of fell unconscious. I couldn't go in to work today. But I'll let you know what happens. I'll give you an update if I'm still alive. Are you seeing Chris at Bertie's later?"

"Probably."

"I might be there. Who knows?"

"That's right," she says. "Who knows what might happen?"

He puts down the phone gently. All morning he's felt the incredible fragility of physical objects. It's part of the dream he's moving in, both awful and strange—like being suddenly holy, touched by God's fire and so removed just a little from the mundane comforting things.

Waking up sometime in the stingy light of dawn, raising himself on his elbow to gaze at the boy: not touching him. The way a cat's nose, quivering, will sniff right up to a surface but never graze it. Memorizing the details of his face—rim of eyelashes, sweep of nostrils, parted lips, various inessential blemishes in the impeccable skin. When he'd drunk his fill from the inexhaustible well of the boy's appearance, he got up and went into the bathroom, where, sitting on the toilet, he closed his eyes and re-created the boy's features and masturbated. Afterward, he felt completely empty, ashamed, scared. Making his way back to the bed he slid in beside Leigh carefully, sleeping for a couple more hours till daylight made it impossible to lie there anymore.

Then roaming the house—it's not his anymore, there's this other presence there, everything is contingent on that other presence, which till it wakes is completely mysterious. What will his reaction be? It won't be the first time Anatole's picked up trade with unfortunate reactions the next morning. He's learned to deal with that. That doesn't account in any way for the incredible anxiety, the trembling and flutter of the heart he feels as he waits to face Our Boy of the Mall by the haggard light of day.

It's possible there's nothing back there in his bedroom, the boy's vanished into air the way angels do. It's one in the afternoon, surely if he was alive he'd be stirring by now. So Anatole makes his way down the hallway, through the half-closed door. The boy is there. He's breathing, little puffs of warm air from his open mouth, there's a film of light sweat on his neck. Curled on his side like a question mark, he's thrown off all the covers, he's wearing nothing but briefs and a morning erection whose presence his posture nearly, but not quite, conceals.

Anatole stands in the doorway gazing at him, drinking him in. It feels forbidden, a shameful liberty. But then, Anatole doesn't care whether he takes shameful liberties. He's twenty-five. He's always been convinced he won't live past fifty. His life's half over.

Leigh's eyelids flutter, he's aware he's being watched, as sleepers are always aware. Perhaps Anatole is in his dream, perhaps his presence in the doorway is shaping whatever happens in Leigh's other, realer world. "Ohh," he murmurs, then opens his eyes till they're slits to let in the unwelcome world. "What time is it?"

"It's not too late. How do you feel?"

"I'm dead," Leigh says simply. "I died in my sleep." He rubs his eyes with the back of his hands, they're bloodshot, dilated. He looks at Anatole and grins broadly. "I've forgotten your name," he says. "I'm not even going to ask how I got here."

"Anatole. Make yourself at home. Want some tea?"

"That'd be great. I'm starved."

"I'll make breakfast, then. You go shower, whatever."

Making breakfast: with infinite care, Anatole fries bacon, cracks eggs into the skillet, eases them onto plates, their yolks perfect, unbroken. It's as if they made love, he thinks, as if they're lovers. Does it make any difference that they're not, that nothing happened? He's relieved, somehow. If they had, wouldn't this moment, right now, be by all odds terrible, frightening, not to be endured? Close call. Perhaps it's better—to share breakfast with Our Boy of the Mall instead of having made love to him. What would making love to him have gained? A momentary illusion of connection followed by recriminations that would have destroyed whatever truth the illusion might have sustained.

"I like feeling at home when it's a home I don't even know how I got to." Leigh stands in the door, a towel draped around his waist. The water's darkened his hair, spiked it. He points to breakfast. "That looks yum."

"Come, partake."

"Let me put on some clothes first." And with that he disappears—but then is back, almost instantly, in jeans but holding his T-shirt up like an artifact.

"Strange," he comments. "I thought I dreamed this."

"We got a little carried away," Anatole admits.

Leigh looks at the scrawled phrases as if unsure whether he likes what he sees. His sketched face on the white cotton seems to bother him. He screws up his own face in distaste, but then shrugs as if to accept the desecrated T-shirt as part of whatever it is that goes on.

At the table he eats parsimoniously, picking at the egg yolk with the tip of his fork, pushing his toast around, breaking it into smaller bits without really swallowing anything. Like a little child he sits with one leg drawn under him. The way he handles his fork, it's almost as if it's too big for him.

Anatole tries desperately to think of things to say to him. It seems wrong to be blunt, to ask, Who are you? Where did you come from? All he can do is accept whatever appears to be true at the moment—that you are whoever we want you to be, that you came from nowhere, that you only just arrived. Anyway, Leigh looks as if he's in a bad mood. He'd have to be, wouldn't he? Waking up in a stranger's apartment, not knowing what he might have done last night?

But Anatole doesn't know these things. He knows nothing for sure. Let's be ironic, let's be cool, his instincts tell him.

"Do you do this often?" he asks.

"Do you?" Leigh looks at him with what might pass for sardonic amusement. The air is drying his water-darkened hair—imperceptibly, moment by moment that Anatole can't stop, can't even see, it resumes its former, lighter color. "I thought people stopped doing this after a while. I mean, I thought it was something kids do. You know, like drink too much, stay up all night."

"Hey—nobody grows up in Poughkeepsie. You keep thinking something might happen."

"It never does, does it?"

"No," Anatole says, "it never does. But you keep hoping."

They look at each other, quite seriously, across the table. It's extraordinary. Leigh holds a triangle of toast halfway to his mouth. We've arrested each other in something, Anatole thinks with a thrill. We understand each other. Then Leigh takes a bite from the toast, looks away, the moment's gone.

"So what about you? Do you go to school? I don't know a single thing about you, Leigh." He wants to say, I've slept all night in the same bed with you and I don't know a single thing about you, but he isn't sure that would be wise.

Leigh shakes his head; his hair tumbles down over his forehead—

◀   40   ▼

Anatole wants to brush it back with his fingertips. "Don't believe anything I say about me," Leigh says. All at once the serious moment's back between them. "Don't believe anything anybody says about me. Okay?"

"Sure." Anything Leigh wants. "What *can* I believe, then?"

"Only what you see. Not what you hear about me. Only what you see me do. Promise that. Then we can be friends."

"I'd like to be your friend. I'll promise anything."

"I don't want to sit here and talk to you about me, because you won't find out anything that's true that way."

Perhaps Our Boy of the Mall's smart as well as beautiful. Perhaps, Anatole thinks, he's beyond intelligence. What will Lydia have to say about all this? Will she believe anything he tells her? He almost resolves to lie about everything. Otherwise, he's not sure what he'll say.

The ritual of breakfast has accomplished its task—it's kept things at bay a little longer.

"So what now?" Anatole asks. "Want a beer? It's the only thing for a hangover."

The idea seems to take Leigh. He hops to the fridge. "I like beer in the afternoon," he says. "Now all we need's some music."

He's completely at home, completely in control. Anatole can only marvel.

In the living room, where Echo and the Bunnymen have been spinning all night, the needle clicking in the endless final groove, Leigh relieves the record of its futility, lifts the needle back to the beginning, back into the life of music. Anatole walks around clicking off the lamps, whose bulb light is wan in the hazy afternoon sunlight. The beer helps to buoy him; it blurs the edges of his hangover. Leigh has settled luxuriously into an armchair. He cradles his beer, smiles up at Anatole with enigmatic friendliness.

All day Chris has been the shell of himself, sluggish as business on this Thursday the nineteenth of September. Waking early in the humid dawn that promises a difficult day, he lay between the sheets a few minutes and took the kind of stock of himself he often takes after a night of heavy drinking. A little hollowness, a lightness of the soul, a vacancy somewhere vital—otherwise he seemed to be okay.

He was wrong, of course. There're two kinds of hangovers, he's learned, slammers and creepers. Today's is a creeper, the kind that's much worse by midafternoon than at midmorning. By five in the afternoon, he will need another drink or, he thinks, he's going to pass out.

But for a moment early in the morning everything was okay. He couldn't remember the night before, he couldn't remember Leigh. Then it came back, and with a sickening feeling that it had all been wrong, ugly. Our Boy of the Mall—so that was him, that was what the fuss was all about.

Funny. He can hardly remember what the boy looked like—he has only an impression of fragility, of fine-tuned, profligate grace, like a Donatello bronze studied in some forgotten art course, perhaps: it's more a sort of motion he remembers, a few chance gestures—a hand used fluently, a shrug, nothing more. But his voice—he hears his voice. Anything Leigh said, he can't remember—he didn't strike Chris as particularly talkative or even particularly articulate; mostly a compendium of "you know"s and "I mean"s. But the tone of the voice has lodged in him—it's airy, flippant, ironic, transparent—you can see right through it to a sort of nothingness. The equivalent of a shrug, it throws everything away.

Last night Anatole drew a picture on the boy's T-shirt. What it meant was that they were all three sitting there sketching pictures of him in their heads. And he'd be able to become each of those, wouldn't he? There's no body there at all, only the potential for—for what? Chris hears Leigh's voice as it changes coloration, accent, provenance—effortlessly, all in a hopeless effort to conceal its killing insubstantiality.

He's spent the day shifting the heavy-metal albums from a shelf on the wall to a bin at the rear of the store. This fall rap and hardcore are in, heavy metal and reggae are out. Meaningless distinctions. As a way of staying afloat, of not yielding to the waves of hangover that threaten to drown him, he concentrates on each album—Ratt, Motley Crue, Quiet Riot, groups he has complete contempt for: they remind him of the dreariest moments of high school, afternoons when he'd wander over to Ned Thompson's house and smoke dope in a basement that had been converted to a game room—dark worm-eaten plywood paneling, black-light posters of Led Zeppelin, Alice Cooper. Of all the various selves he's been, this is one he particularly dislikes—that lost kid who might have been lost like that forever; who, in fact—there's no guarantee—might after all *have* been lost. Flipping through the album covers, he hates the way heavy metal, like Anatole, is essentially religious, its satanism only a frustrated embrace of the Christianity it so desperately wants to outrage.

Is he jealous that Anatole's slept with that boy? Is that what's disturbing him? He doesn't want it to, he doesn't think it does—but then he knows he can't be sure. The time before he lived in Poughkeepsie, when he lived in Ithaca in that house with John and John's sister Michelle: looking back on it, as he can seldom bring himself to do, he detects only a litany of lies stressed over and over as the truth. Even now it sickens him, the betrayals he perpetrated that opened the door to events, accidents—whatever they were. Chris can't, even three years later, bring himself to think about them.

It was an evening in July, John was back from Pittsburgh after a month spent away, in exile, trying to allow Chris and Michelle some space in that big empty house that was finally neither big enough nor empty enough to accommodate a brother and sister both in love with Chris, who in turn was in love with both of them. And with John's return, the unspoken strain, the reproach that had led John to flee in the first place: it wasn't John's fault—it was simply his presence. How to explain that, how to come to terms with it? But they both felt it, they both knew what the problem was. If Chris was going to be sleeping with Michelle, there was no way John could continue to live in that house.

Sitting out on the front steps—John saying, "I've got to go. You know that, don't you? I've got to disappear from here."

And Chris—"You've got to disappear from here." He felt he'd never lived through any moment so hopeless, and he wanted to tell John he loved him—but he couldn't because he didn't love him anymore. He'd decided—that was how it had to be. He used to love him and now he loved Michelle. Nothing else that happened now could count between them.

John sat on the steps pensively rubbing his bare ankles.

"Sometimes, Chris," he said, "you make me feel like I'm a piece of shit. You know that too, don't you?"

"I know that too," Chris said. "I guess I'm trying to make you feel that way." He'd never been so deliberately cruel in his life, and it hurt more than it thrilled. "It's impossible," he went on. "You know it's impossible, don't you?"

"Nothing's impossible," John told him. "I only know what I know."

"I can't love you." Chris was suddenly adamant: it was the one thing he knew for certain. "Whatever you may think," he said. "I thought I loved you, but I didn't. I was coerced."

Somewhere in the big house behind them Michelle would have been reading a book or watching TV, oblivious to everything she was winning and at the same time losing at that very moment on the front steps.

John didn't say anything. He stood up, the dark-haired graceful impossible boy Chris had fallen for as he'd fallen for no one else in his life. He couldn't look at him without that familiar pang he hated himself for.

"Bye," John said lightly, almost a whisper it was so insubstantial.

"What exactly is that supposed to mean?" Chris asked.

"I said 'bye'. That's what you want. That's what I said."

Chris winces to remember. Remember, he warns himself—you have to remember. Whatever you think you feel, you may not actually feel it. You may just think you feel it because it will help move you in the opposite direction from what you really feel but are mortally afraid to encounter.

Hangovers do this to Chris, so that he's relieved when five o'clock releases him to the safe harbor of Bertie's and a scotch. He's even a little drunk by the time Lydia gets there at a quarter to six. She settles into the booth, looking harassed, rummaging through her purse for a cigarette he holds his lighter out to ignite.

"So the wounded troops reassemble," he observes, lighting a cigarette for himself as well. She looks at his empty tumbler.

"*You're* on the road back, I see."

"Medicinal purposes." He toasts her with the empty glass.

"Well," she tells him when they've both been served, "I'm sure you're just dying to find out the latest on the Anatole front."

An old joke he remembers from some history class in one of those universities he flunked out of—World War I, the situation on the Prussian front is serious but not hopeless, on the Austrian front hopeless but not serious. Anatole as an Austrian front: he smiles bleakly and says, "I shudder to imagine. Please try to remember: I'm not as interested in Our Boy of the Mall as you and Anatole are."

"Of course you aren't. But sometimes you pretend curiosity so well, darling."

"Tell me everything," he says wearily, "since you will anyway." He's posing with his cigarette again. It annoys him about himself— he's sure Lydia must see right through it, to what it betrays. But he's so fraught today he doesn't know what else to do. What he really wants is to go home and collapse on his futon, stare at the blank ceiling, pretend not to exist for a while. Only there *is* this awful thing gnawing at him, the idea of Leigh is a splinter that's gotten stuck inside him and hasn't quite let him go all day long. He wants to hear everything, everything.

"Actually I have *very* little to report. He called in sick today. When I talked to him, Our Boy of the Mall was still passed out dead. I gather nothing particularly exciting happened. I think they both just blacked out last night."

"Our Boy, as you call him, was well on his way there when we left, if I remember."

"Chris, dear, he was the only one?"

Their banter, such as it is, somehow makes it easier for them. Lydia likes it that for once she and Chris are on equal footing. It brings back that short-lived time—a heartbreaking memory for her— when they were closer, she and Chris: before Chris, so to speak, turned his back on her.

"I thought he might be here," she says. "He said he might show up."

"Bearing trophies, no doubt."

"If I didn't know you were impervious to everything, Chris, I might think you were jealous."

"Jailbait boys just don't interest me. You know that."

My, she thinks, we've arrived at this quickly—we're awfully volatile this evening: Our Boy's had this effect, at least. She takes up the challenge. Her voice is flat and matter-of-fact—a stance she's rehearsed before, in private, usually with much ice-cold gin.

"I don't know anything about you, Chris. You won't let me. I don't have to remind you."

"Okay." He manages a smile, though it seems clear to Lydia that something pains him more than usual. "Then I'll just tell you. For the record: I'm *very* skeptical about this whole thing. I think Anatole's going to get hurt bad. I think it's going to be embarrassing."

"That's pessimistic."

"Come on, Lydia. You saw that kid. He's not going to be a savior to anybody, least of all to Anatole. And that's what he wants. Somebody to save him from himself. Well, nobody saves anybody from anything. Anatole can be such a silly faggot sometimes."

"I'll tell him you mentioned it."

"He already knows it. Lydia, we're grown-ups, this Leigh's a child. What are we supposed to be doing messing around with him? What can we possibly do except damage him?"

"I refuse, Chris, I *absolutely refuse* to be as dire as you are. Since when are you so fastidious? Everything doesn't *have* to end up in disaster, even if it *is* glamorous to think so."

"Oh, I'm being glamorous?"

"Of course you are. You're always glamorous."

It makes him laugh. He lights another cigarette, even though the one lying in the ashtray before him is only half smoked. "Yes, of course I am," he tells her bitterly. "I'm merely glamorous. I don't have any moral fiber."

•   •   •

"Anatole."

"Lydia. I thought you'd call."

Just the tone of his voice tells her something's different, something's changed. He's moved through something that's left its mark on him. He won't be the same.

"You'll be happy to know I'm completely recovered, Anatole. Chris and I had a therapeutic session. Really, gin and tonics are the only cure. I thought you'd want to know that."

"You're such a fount of obscure knowledge."

"According to Chris, scotch works equally well."

"Is he there?"

"We just had dinner. We thought about you. We gossiped mercilessly."

"I'm sure it was all the truth."

"Give me a hint. Let me know."

He laughs—a dry, abrupt laugh. The thing is, Anatole realizes, he has no hints to offer. The afternoon's unfurled itself so complicatedly, he doesn't want to talk about it with Lydia. He doesn't know where to start—even worse, he doesn't know where it will end or even what it looks like at the moment. For the first time in their friendship, he finds himself wanting a privacy from her. For the first time he resents her familiarity with his life.

"Or maybe you can't talk now," she surmises. "I understand how it is."

"Leigh's not here," he tells her.

"You've been sitting there by yourself and you haven't called? Do you want me to come over? Is everything okay?"

"I don't know how to say it. Everything's wonderful, Lydia. Really, it's wonderful."

"Is it true love?"

"I think so," he lies.

She's silent for a moment. "You know, Anatole?"

"What?"

"You should probably jump on the next train for Chicago. Savor what happened if it was beautiful. It won't be this good ever again."

Her words, meant as gently as possible, sting. They reinforce the extent of his lies.

"He's coming back," he tells her, relieved he can at least offer this as proof of the "wonderful." "He's just gone out to bring over some things."

"Things?" Lydia sounds suitably impressed.

"Well, like some clothes. Lydia, you won't believe this."

"Try me."

"He's moving in. We're going to try living together for a while."

"That's quick. So it really was a big success?"

Anatole feels he needs to back down just a little. "He's just going to stay here a few days," he amends. "He doesn't like where he's living. It's some house with these girls that are getting on his nerves."

What he doesn't say is that when he found out Leigh was having problems where he was living, he offered his apartment, offered it several times before Leigh picked up on it and said, reluctantly at first, "You mean I can really sleep on your sofa a few days till things work out?"

"That's great, Anatole. I'm happy for you." Lydia tries not to sound forced—though she shouldn't have to, she *is* happy for him. "Our Boy of the Mall. You've hooked a catch, face it. You'll be famous. Go on and gloat if you want to."

But Anatole doesn't feel like gloating. There's nothing to gloat about. He only feels a grave stillness in him, like a pool of dark water no stone can ripple. At the same time he feels on the verge of everything—it's like walking right toward the precipice, holding your breath, stepping over the edge and expecting to be in free-fall, only you're not—the precipice turns out to be one step farther along, always one step farther.

"You sound strange, Anatole. You don't sound like yourself. Are you sure you're all right?"

"I'm all right, Lydia. I'll talk to you later, okay? Too much has happened. I have to think."

When he hangs up the phone he's overcome by the feeling: already this is intolerable. Obviously Lydia thinks he's had sex with Leigh. Obviously he's allowed her to think that. Obviously he's already trying to live two separate self-contradicting lives, which is clearly nothing more than a species of insanity. But he just can't bear to let her know that nothing's happened. It seems too much like a defeat, a humiliation—even though he knows it isn't. But he doesn't know how to say to Lydia—it should be simple but he just can't do it—we spent all afternoon drinking beer, Leigh and I, and he's just a friendly, relaxed, fearless kid. Lydia won't understand. She just won't get it. How to intimate to her that the question of sex never even came up? He realizes he can't tell her because it wouldn't make any sense. After everything has been led up to with such fanfare, to see it all turned aside into a different path entirely—how to account for that?

Every week or so—it balances in a domestic way his ritual biweekly dinners with Chris at the Milanese—Anatole spends the evening with Lydia at her mother's house. Mrs. Forman will cook manicotti, meat loaf, simple meals. Later they'll drink coffee and scotch, sit up late and talk. Her husband died fifteen years ago; with Lydia on her own and Craig in school, she lives alone in the neat little house she's lived in for thirty years. She grew up in Brooklyn, a second-generation American Jew. The first time Anatole met her—he suspected he was being brought home as a "date" to placate her—he couldn't think what to say, so he spent the whole evening asking her questions. What was it like to grow up in Brooklyn? What were her parents like? Did they speak English? Where did her family emigrate from? But she shrugged, and said a little brusquely, "Poland, Russia. Who can say?" Similarly to the question about the pork chops she served that night: "Leave my poor pork chops alone. Do I ask you to go eating fish on Fridays?"

"When I was little, my family *did* eat fish on Friday," Anatole admitted, "till the pope decided it was okay to eat meat."

"The pope decided that? The pope does the family menu?"

"It was sometime in the sixties. The pope was always deciding things."

"So everybody started eating meat on Fridays, which just the Friday before if they'd eaten it they'd have gone to hell? Did it feel different?"

"Well, that wouldn't exactly send you to hell. But yeah, that's sort of what happened. It's a complicated religion."

"Religions," Mrs. Forman sniffed. She had no time. It set her aside from her neighbors, endeared her to Anatole, who felt the same things, but in his heart of hearts was still afraid that if you really didn't believe it all, then what was left?

The only vestige of the faith of Mrs. Forman's fathers is that she buys Israel Bonds. She buys them in Lydia's name.

"Don't waste your money, Mom," Lydia tells her. "It won't help. Let rich people support Israel."

"Don't tell your mother what to spend her money on. I go to sleep at night and think, Every penny I send is a bullet. It makes me go to sleep content. How do *you* fall asleep, daughter?"

"You wouldn't want to know, Mom, really you wouldn't."

"Lydia never sleeps," Anatole says. "It's one of her beauty secrets. She read about it in *How to Find a Husband*, volume two."

"Oh you." Mrs. Forman taps his knee to reprove him. It's a habit of hers, a habit he likes.

In fact, he likes many of her habits, the way they become her. He likes that she hates—positively is terrified of—public places, crowds; that she's never set foot on the Main Street mall and doesn't intend to even though he invites her constantly—dares her, is more like it—to visit him in Reflexion, to see for herself what he calls the Salon de Scandale. Agoraphobia, she calls her disability. She reads books on how to overcome it—they're often lying around the house, on end tables, wedged between the sofa pillows, books with titles like *You CAN Master Phobias* and *Diet to Overcome That Fear*. Her doctor long ago prescribed Valium to help her Master Her Phobias and Overcome That Fear—she likes the Valium too much, however, to overcome the fear it's meant to overcome. As a consequence, there's always this residual vagueness about her, this retreat even when she's being sharp-witted.

He likes it that she's also a hairdresser: it's what she took up after her husband died as a way of supplementing the pension she got from Western Publishing Company, in whose purchasing department he'd worked for twenty-two years. She operates out of her basement, her clientele's limited to the other women of the neighborhood: the work she does and the work Anatole does belong to different worlds. Still, they're allies in a world that fails to understand the raptures and heartbreak of human hair. Each is always shocked by the things the other inflicts on his or her clients; the two love to trade stories, over coffee, of special dyes or perms—stories that make the other cringe. "You two," Lydia will say, as they giggle together: the way they're always trying to one-up the other with some shocking account.

What Anatole most likes about Mrs. Forman is what, given her advance press, initially surprised him the most—a liberality, a certain winning sympathy she shows with the unexpected, the unproved. He'd been coming around regularly for several months when Lydia reported a bit of mother-daughter dialogue:

MRS. F: Anatole's not interested in young ladies, is he?

L: He's interested in their hair.

MRS. F: That's what I thought. Well, that's fine. Life's hard for everybody.

It continues to mark an important moment for Anatole, given his relations with his own family—who, though they live in Pough-keepsie, refuse to have anything to do with him anymore. It's one of those wounds he's learned to live with. Every year for five years he's sent them a Christmas card, an appeal for the renewal of a son's ties, but every year it's greeted by silence. He's tried to understand their pain, their bafflement, but can't really, and as time goes by it only makes him angry to think about it. In recent years he's more or less given up any hope of being their son any longer. Only occasionally does he brood.

It all began trivially enough—he was at his family's house for dinner, he and his mother were lingering at the kitchen table over a last cup of coffee. He'd been out of high school two years—living on his own, working at Jonsef's, mastering the arcana of the trade, taking supplementary courses at Dutchess Community College. It wasn't that he announced he was gay—rather, he alluded to it, as if it were common property, accomplished fact: nothing to be startled by. Certainly he didn't expect any great reaction—he'd known about himself, it seemed, forever; he naturally assumed everyone else knew too. So it just slipped out, as by the same token he saw no reason it shouldn't just slip into his mother's consciousness and that could be that. But his mother caught him up short. "What did you say?" she asked sharply, as if he'd tried to cheat her in making change. Perhaps he'd gotten too used to the impression that she never really listened to anything he told her.

"I said," he repeated deliberately, "there's this guy at work I have a crush on. He's cute, he's wonderful. Don't you think it's time for me to have a boyfriend? After all these years?"

"Don't talk like that, Anatole. You sound like a fairy or something."

"Well, of course I *am* a fairy or something. We all know that, Mom." He was still not taking the conversation all that seriously, until he saw his mother's look. It was as if a wall descended between her and him, in an instant they were no longer mother and son but deadly enemies.

"No, Anatole, no, no, no," she said to him, enunciating each word equally, injecting the full pure value of negation into each word. Her eyes narrowed into an expression of—hatred, there's no other way he can describe it to himself. The kind of hatred that could only have been building against him slowly, unconsciously over the years, and just now, with his words, was able to break into air and light and acknowledge itself for what it was. This was his mother: she'd carried him in her body, she bore him, she loved him.

At first he thinks it's a joke. "Mom," he says, grinning, reaching out to touch her wrist, to smooth over the gap—but she pulls away, knocks over her chair as she gets up, runs from the room.

Then it hits him—it's not a joke, it's real, it's happened and he can't take it back.

"What was that about?" His father looking into the kitchen from the den, where he's been watching television.

"Beats me. You'd better go talk to her."

He feels as if he's just signed his death warrant. He gets a beer out of the refrigerator and sits at the kitchen table to wait for the ax to fall. From the other side of the wall he can hear the dim, silly sounds of "Family Feud." The show's come to an end, the title theme's fiddle music that drives him crazy begins to play. He knows he should do something other than sit quietly, sipping beer—it almost seems callous—but he can't. He's paralyzed.

He remembers his father whipping him once when he was a child, with inexplicable fury, the leather belt hissing through the air to fall in loud stinging slaps across his bared bottom—all because he wouldn't eat mayonnaise on his bologna sandwich one Saturday at lunch. His father, who smelled of paint and turpentine, clothes splattered with the color of the thousand rooms he'd painted in his life, paint in his hair, under his fingernails, so that no matter how thoroughly he showered it was always there, a kind of residue of the big adult world that made Anatole fear his father as somehow tainted, unable to get entirely clean or pure.

His father takes a long time. When he does come back he walks stiffly, heavily, a man who's been shot and takes five or six last steps, a stricken look on his face, before pitching forward. He doesn't sit down, he stands in the doorway and says in a strange wooden voice, an almost unearthly voice, "Anatole, Anatole, how could you have said such things to your mother? Do you know how you've hurt her? Can you understand that?"

"Dad, this is crazy." It comes out as a disbelieving half laugh, shot through with jitters: how can the world be so absurd as this? He's amazed that he's even dared to forget that something like this might happen. He used to remember it all the time, used to be careful not to let it slip. Now, when it's too late, he remembers his dad watching the television news, a gay rights march in San Francisco—thousands, tens of thousands of men filling the avenue as far back as you could see, hundreds of thousands with banners and placards, and his father saying angrily—he always talked back to Walter Cronkite during the news—"Oh come on, Walter, why do you have to show us that garbage? They should all be shot. Every fucking one of them should be shot."

"Dad," Anatole pleads, "this is nineteen eighty."

"I don't care if it's twenty thousand and eighty. I'm not going to have a son of mine parading around here telling his mother he's a fucking fairy. I'm not going to have my sons grow up with their older brother the faggot."

"Dad, this is ridiculous."

"Look," his father says. "Just go. I don't want to hear another word. Just go now." His father's voice is controlled to the point of breaking. His father is about to cry.

"Okay, okay"—Anatole suddenly trembling, suddenly scared as much for his father and his mother as for himself—their hidden lives he'll never discern, their fears. "I'm going," he says.

He stands in the doorway. "Remember, Dad," he says, "I love you and I love Mom. I'll call you in a few days. We'll talk, okay?"

"There's nothing to say, Anatole. Save yourself the dime. I hope you're proud of ruining this family for us."

"I'll call," Anatole says.

And he does, but they won't talk to him. He visits, but they won't see him. It's just like that, irrevocable as death. There's nothing he can do. "When I think about you as my little boy," his mother tells him the one time he gets through to her on the phone, "all the things I did for you, it just makes me sick. It was like everything was rotten all the time but I couldn't see it. It just makes me sick to my stomach, Anatole, to think that my own son would want to do this to me." His mother, who'd shielded him his whole life from his father's shadowing presence; who put her arms around him when he came home from school in the afternoons; with whom, after the dishes were cleared and his little brothers had disappeared into the other room to watch TV with his father, he'd sit at the supper table and chat, banter, as if they were best friends, mother and son, as if they understood each other's hearts.

He resigns himself. The years pass, five years now. Gradually they fade from him. He hears occasionally, from the acquaintances they still have in common, how they're doing—that his dad's retired; his mother still works religiously at the bazaars at Holy Trinity. Sometimes he imagines driving past the house, how he'll glimpse his little brother Colin, incredibly grown up since Anatole last saw him, out mowing the lawn; or his father standing in the driveway talking to a neighbor.

But Anatole never does drive by—he feels as if he has no right, as if he never had any right.

It colors everything. Every time he goes to Mrs. Forman's, he thinks of it. Sometimes it seems to him that everything will end this same way, inexplicably, a suddenness born of malignant magic, a curtain that crashes down without his ever having had the chance or foresight to realize that it was coming. Somewhere inside himself he expects Mrs. Forman to cut him off without a word, unexpectedly, just as he expects one day to call Chris and find that Chris is no longer speaking to him for reasons he hasn't foreseen nor can fathom. He resigns himself to the truth that the world is capricious and treacherous beyond his ability to understand or control it in any way. When he's with Mrs. Forman and Lydia—or with Chris at their ritual, biweekly dinners at the Milanese—he often offers up a secret thanks, a prayer: We have this now; tomorrow we may not have it, even the next minute we may not have it, something unexpected and terrible may impose itself between us—but right now we have it and it's good, it's what counts.

Tonight Mrs. Forman has cooked meat loaf, mashed potatoes, a salad of greens and fresh onions. It's the kind of family food Anatole loves, the kind he grew up on. "So I don't have to be ashamed?" Lydia had asked him the first time he came home with her for dinner. His reassurance was absolute. "Don't worry, dear, I'm in heaven."

Afterward, after strawberry shortcake, they sit outside in lawn chairs. Bats swoop low, a water sprinkler's hissing over in the next yard. As the light fades, night seems to rise from the damp grass. And there's a breeze, a feeling the weather's going to change, the heat's going to break. Always there's that first moment when you know summer's over. Anatole forgets it every year, every year it touches him like a gentle reminder of time passing. He feels it tonight, an invisible wave that passes across the neighborhood, not breaking but just surging mildly forward.

They can't see one another, the dark has closed in on them entirely. It's peaceful to sit in darkness. For the moment Anatole feels safe, he feels protected.

"We're very thoughtful tonight," Mrs. Forman observes. "But

I'm glad you came by. The house feels so big and empty. There're too many rooms."

They all know it's Craig she misses, Lydia's brother, who in the summers is home from college, who just went back for his junior year two weeks ago—a handsome, athletic-looking boy who lounges about in flower-loud shorts and sneakers without socks, drifting in with a beer in hand, drifting out to go on a date in the orange VW bug he spends hours washing in the driveway with a hose and a bucket of endless suds. He and Anatole are on a friendly footing—though he intimidates Anatole, he's so well adjusted to the world through which he moves. Sometimes one of Craig's girlfriends will also be there for supper—he moves through them so quickly, they're all so alike, blond and giddy, that Anatole no longer bothers to learn their names; Craig must have had ten in the five years Anatole's been an honorary part of the Forman family.

Every year when Craig goes back to school, Mrs. Forman relives the death of her husband. One loss echoes the other, and for weeks she doubles her dosage of Valium, wanders the house in a delirious calm.

"You should be flattered tonight, Mom," Lydia says.

"Oh?"

"That Anatole here's decided to grace you with his company. He's been very scarce recently."

"What—you've been hiding out, Anatole?"

Anatole can only smile—benevolently, enigmatically: too bad it's too dark for them to see. Things have been just a little off all evening—their friendship's shifted into a different key. Lydia's miffed with me, he realizes. It's barely visible, she conceals it almost perfectly, but he can guess its roots. It's a question of Leigh. For a week now this boy's been living in his apartment, for a week now Anatole's been existing at a subtle but tangible remove from Chris and Lydia, stopping in at Bertie's after work for a quick drink but then heading home to "cook dinner for Leigh," as he puts it. He knows they're making fun of him for it—they even do it to his face. But it's a domesticity he positively revels in—he pretends he's embarked on the love affair of his life, that the boy of his dreams is really living with him as a lover instead of a lodger. He enjoys the corrupt thrill of suggesting to Chris and Lydia that this affair is fraught with unspeakable passions, nights spent in athletic lovemaking better left to the imagination. He's become, suddenly, elusive—a quality he's always been drawn to in others, but also driven crazy by: it's odd, it's even comic for him to find himself participating in it—as if he really has become a new person in the space of a few days, a person with qualities hitherto inaccessible to him.

He looks back with a kind of amazement—also a tinge of regret, even guilt—to think that just a week ago he was nightly confessing everything about his inner life to Lydia. Now he wouldn't even know where to begin.

It's like a dream, profound and resonant but finally without meaning—days at Reflexion, his mind all the time back at his apartment, anticipating the evening, when his and Leigh's bodies will occupy together the same cramped space of rooms. While at the same time the dream takes place in and around the ordinary, necessary things: earlier today he's gone to the Audi dealer to put his car through its sixty-thousand-mile checkup—he's disgruntled to have to spend three hundred dollars on a fuel pump, a water hose, brake shoes. . . . It's hard to believe that these two Anatoles, the mundane one and the one an angel has touched, occupy the same space in the world. But driving back from the dealer in his expensively serviced automobile, he sees the hills across the river and thinks, seeing himself as if he is nothing more than a character in a movie (the radio's on, Tears for Fears' "Everybody Wants to Rule the World" is playing), how this time last year—or even this time last week—he couldn't have imagined the sort of magical state he's in now. The sunlight's golden, a harvest sunlight, it rests on the far hills, drapes their wooded slopes. The car for an instant seems to float in light, a vessel bearing him toward the earthly paradise of the Hudson Valley, and he thinks how he's happy, happy . . . and then all at once he's sadder than he thinks he's ever been, the thought of Leigh depressing him because he knows it's all a lie, a game he's pretending, when really there's nothing between them at all, when really Leigh's just a kid he's taken in who doesn't even understand the first thing about what's going on. He feels alone, even more alone than before, when there was nothing, when there was only him and Lydia and Chris. And these days he can't even turn to Lydia for her bracing consolation. He's too embarrassed by what he takes to be the authenticity of his present emotions.

It's the same old story: how it seems entirely possible, though not likely, every night when he goes home that this may be the night he and Leigh really will make love. As always, the world's impossible to read. The simplest acts are signposts pointing in too many directions at once. He'll be making dinner, Leigh will saunter in, put his hand on Anatole's shoulder, look into the skillet at the green vegetables and tofu he's stir-frying. His touch is at once electric and neutral. Confronted by such a gesture—and it occurs two or three times an evening—Anatole's simply helpless. He knows that in some sense he's nothing but the classic soft touch, that for all his naïveté Leigh's nothing more than a canny hustler. But another part of Anatole, knowing all this, wants simply to follow it to the end, see where it'll go.

"What *about* you, Anatole? Earth to Anatole." Lydia's voice is amused but impatient.

"Sorry," he says. "I was thinking. My brain's hyperactive tonight. I'll have some more wine. More, Mrs. Forman?"

"Thanks." She holds out her glass. Usually she doesn't drink this much after dinner, but she seems to have felt an edge to the evening as well.

"See, what's happened is, I'm letting this guy I met stay at my apartment," Anatole explains to her. "It's just for a few days, till he finds a place to live. But it's a little unsettling."

"Oh, you love it, Anatole," Lydia accuses.

"I do sort of, but it's still unsettling. Good things can be just as unsettling as anything else."

They're only voices in the dark. It allows some kind of impersonality, a shield behind which each can hide. It's like confessing truths over the telephone or, Anatole thinks, in the confession box.

"This boy's *really* cute, Mom. Anatole's keeping him locked away. He's cast a spell over him."

"You should bring him over for dinner," Mrs. Forman suggests.

"I'm not sure you'd like him, Mrs. Forman."

"Anatole, if I like most of the people I like, I can like anybody."

"Touché."

"Anatole won't even let me *near* him," Lydia complains.

"He's probably smart that way, Lydia. It's love." Mrs. Forman sighs. "One day you'll understand these things." One of Mrs. Forman's complaints about Lydia is that she's never been truly in love. She's had all sorts of relationships—that year she was at Bard any number of boys traipsed through. But she's never been *in love*. "I like you, Anatole," Mrs. Forman tells him. "You know about love. You believe in it. My own children—well, it's the great failing of the new generation of Formans. They have affairs right and left, I can't even keep track of them—but do they fall in love? Do they give themselves a chance? No. It's flit off to this person, that person. Never the one person."

"Mr. Forman was the one person?"

"Dan was the one person, yes," Mrs. Forman says gravely. "I knew the first time I ever saw him. I never wavered."

"When was that?" Anatole always wants Mrs. Forman to talk more: she fascinates him, he feels they're alike in subterranean ways, and he's always trying to track down the things they share.

"It was in the main office of the Jet Messenger Service on West Forty-second Street in Manhattan. I was secretary there—I'd dropped out of college because I wanted a job, I wanted to be able to buy new clothes. My job was to dispatch messengers. One day there was this new boy, they told me he was studying at CCNY Downtown, majoring in business, he was going places. He needed money to put himself through. Oh, he was fine-looking that morning. He was wearing a white shirt. He had such a smile."

"It was love at first sight?"

"Well, you might say I had to work on him a little. He lived near me. I used to wait in the evenings to ride the subway till I knew he was leaving. He was such a gentleman. He'd ride with me on the old Culver line, and then walk home. It was so sweet of him. He could have taken the Sea Beach and saved twenty blocks. A young man wouldn't do that for you these days."

"He saw you home every evening? That's great."

"I hated the subways. All those people, all that rush. I was always a nervous wreck."

"Love on the subway. It's wonderful," Anatole tells her. "I really like that story." He'd do that for someone he loved, wouldn't he? If he really loved them, if they were the one person, wouldn't he do anything?

"The subway. When he got the job with Western, I didn't even know where Spapiksie, Poughkeepsie was. I thought it was in New Jersey. It seemed so far away from everything."

"But you hated New York, Mom. You hate crowds."

"One day I'll move back," Mrs. Forman asserts. "See if I don't. The doctor says I'm getting better. He says I'll be cured soon. When that—"

There's a thump; Mrs. Forman's voice says, "Shit."

"What's wrong?" Lydia asks.

"I knocked over the wine. I was going to pour more."

"It's just as well," Lydia tells her. "We should go. And you should stop drinking. You're starting to slur your words."

"No, she's not," Anatole says—though he's started to notice it, in the last couple of minutes, as well. "You're completely lucid."

"Of course I'm completely lucid. I'm always completely lucid. You might say, I'm hopelessly lucid." But when she goes to stand up from the lawn chair, they have to help her. "My legs gave out," she laughs as they steer her, holding her up by her elbows, into the house, to her bed. Anatole sits in the living room and has a scotch while Lydia undresses her mother, puts her to bed. He feels calm. He thinks about Mr. Forman, how there must have been a single instant when she first saw him, and he saw her, and after that life could never be the same. He wants desperately to believe life is like that.

"Okay, that's done." Lydia emerges from the bedroom.

"She'll be okay? She's cute when she's drunk."

"She makes me so mad." Lydia walks around the house turning off the lights, locking the doors.

"Mad?"

"I hate it when she does this. It's so embarrassing." They drive the empty streets.

"She was just enjoying herself, Lydia. She probably doesn't get that much of a chance. Anyway, it was a wonderful story she told. So romantic."

"It wasn't wonderful. Couldn't you tell? She hounded Dad into marrying her. She chased him like crazy. Carrying on, getting him to ride the subway home with her every night because she was afraid of crowds. My God, that's twenty blocks he walked home. My mother's a manipulator, Anatole. She's completely selfish."

"You're so cynical. And about your own mother."

"I *know* my mother too well, Anatole. There's too much of her inside here"—she taps her head—"for me not to know her. Anyway— looks like you have company." She slows, pulls over to the curb.

"I guess Leigh's home."

"You're not going to invite me up, are you?" She looks at him with something of a pout. In the orange streetlight, she looks completely unattractive to him.

"No," he says. "No I'm not. Sometime, though. I'll have a little brunch or something. You and Chris and me and Leigh. How does that sound?"

"Is it possible I don't like you as much as I used to?"

It makes him shudder, go cold in his heart. "God, I hope not. I know I'm being strange. Give me a few days, I'll be myself again."

"You'd better be." She flicks him a good-night kiss and then he's out of the car, the car's vanished down the still street. He looks up at the lights in the windows and thinks—it's the old familiar prayer of thanksgiving—Leigh's up there.

Leigh's up there. He's back from Denmarc, the restaurant where he waits tables four nights a week. Anatole's been there before, a brunch with Daniel; he found it pretentious—but he likes it that Leigh's working there. In his uniform of black trousers and white cotton shirt he looks like a schoolboy at a European academy. He'd be head of the school, he'd be adored by the other schoolboys, Anatole fantasizes.

Sprawled on the sofa with a beer, Leigh watches MTV. "I've been sitting here twenty minutes, I haven't seen a single thing that was interesting. But here I sit."

"See? It's the perfect product," Anatole tells him. "You don't want it, you tell yourself you don't want it, you even hate it, but you go on buying it anyway."

"I'll turn it off. But first I want to see who the next group's gonna be."

"It's hopeless." Anatole sinks down on the sofa beside him. "Had a good day?"

"A shitty day."

"What'd you do?"

"I'm in a bad mood. I went to Noah's Ark and did shots of scotch with Julie."

"Who's Julie?" Anatole's always afraid to learn anything new about Leigh. It threatens to disrupt the image he's distilled in his mind.

"Somebody from that house I moved out of. I don't even like her. You know, sometimes I think I'm crazy. I had this dream last night where I was having sex with her. It wasn't unpleasant, but I don't like her at all. She's manipulative. I don't trust her."

Anatole feels a chill clench itself around his heart—this intrusion of a past he can know nothing about except in fragments. He wants Leigh to himself, he realizes. He needs him living here in this apartment with no past, nothing hidden, everything simply ineffably accessible to the eye and ear. At the thought of Leigh out drinking with this girl, his security of possession—for the moment I have this, and it's good—threatens to disappear. He wonders bitterly how he has any right to feel possessive—he's known this boy for a week, he's done him the favor of putting him up for a few days, that's exactly as far as it goes: everything else takes place only in his head, his overexcited imagination. Still, he does feel possessive. He feels it's some sort of infidelity for Leigh to be out drinking shots of scotch with this Julie.

It comes to Anatole clearly. There's no way he can hold Leigh. Favors don't count, friends don't count: it's something else out in the world that matters, something that has to do with advantages and gain. Already he sees Leigh slipping from him. If I were more courageous, he thinks, if I were more selfish, I'd be able to hold him, I'd impress him, I'd entertain him, I'd manipulate him easily. This is what life is about, after all, this is why Julie, whoever she is, will win. It's only a matter of time till Leigh's won away—if not by Julie (and really, she's not so much a threat as a forecast), then by someone else. Anatole's never felt more precisely the extent of his failure to live. He's been a moment, a point of transition, nothing more. In a year Leigh won't remember a thing about him. He won't have made a mark.

"They're all lesbians in that house anyway," Leigh says suddenly. "Do you mind if I get violent for a minute?"

"No, of course not. Violence is my favorite pastime."

With a single fluid motion Leigh takes the beer bottle he's finished and flings it against the far wall. It shatters, leaves a mark on the wall, the stain of a last swallow of beer. The noise is explosive in the late-night stillness.

He shrugs. "I don't feel any better. See, they hated me because I didn't turn out to be what they thought I was going to be. That's why they wanted to throw me out."

"What did they think you were?"

"A male lesbian, something like that. A sister. They're all fucked up. I mean, they don't even *know* they're lesbians."

"I'm not sure I follow all this."

"It's not worth explaining. Explaining would only make it worse. My brain just sometimes goes around in circles. Do you have anything else I can break? No, I'm just joking."

Though he's suddenly on his feet, prowling as if he really does want to find something, a porcelain plate, an antique candlestick. Anatole's never seen him volatile like this, unless it was a volatility contained in the frenetic way he danced at Bertie's that first night.

When Leigh walks past the telephone, it rings as if on cue. He picks it up instantly. "No," he says, "Anatole's not home right now. No. You're right, we *are* a bit out of hand up here, aren't we?"

"That was your downstairs neighbor," he announces when he hangs up. "She says, 'Why, oh why do you have to make so much noise on a weeknight?' She says she's going to file a noise complaint."

"Oh great. You and I'll both be living in that house with the lesbians."

"They weren't really lesbians. Anyway, I'd rather sleep in the gutter than there. *I'd rather sleep in the gutter*," he shouts for the benefit of Anatole's downstairs neighbor.

Shh, Anatole pantomimes, though he's not really nervous. Somehow if it's Leigh who's making the noise it seems all right. It's celebrative. Poor woman, he thinks—if only she knew, if only she understood. There're always people looking the other way when the miracles take place, people who want only a good night's sleep when the stars are dancing, comets falling, the angels leaning low out of midnight with their trumpets, their cantatas of longing.

Leigh's picked a copy of *House and Garden* off the coffee table. "Can I toss this?"

"Why not?"

It hits the wall with a clatter of unfurling pages. "Not very satisfactory. Let me see"—he looks around—"Don't you have anything I can *break*?"

"I'll see. In the meantime, more beer?"

"More beer. Yes, yes, yes. Or is there scotch left?"

"There's scotch."

"Like, I want to get ripped. I feel like flying off the handle. Do you ever feel like that? I mean, like hurting people for no reason. Yelling at the top of your lungs."

"Maybe you're right, Leigh. Maybe you have gone crazy."

"I warned you. You know, I was in Colorado once, there was this place where there were sand dunes. The wind picked up the sand in the valley and blew it against the mountains, so it piled up there, huge dunes. They went for miles, you could go out in them till you were completely alone, just piled-up sand and nothing else. So I went there and found this dune and stood on the top of it and yelled my head off. I mean, like, really yelled, the way you're too inhibited to ever yell with people around, even when you're completely angry. It didn't change anything. I had a sore throat next day, my friends thought I'd caught a cold."

Anatole's never heard this much about Leigh's life before. "You're so talkative tonight," he tells him.

"Remember, don't believe any of this tomorrow."

"Can I believe the broken beer bottle?" They sit on the sofa and share the scotch bottle, passing it back and forth between them.

"You can believe that, sure, I'll let you believe that. Anyway, it left a mark. You *have* to believe it, right?"

"I have to believe it."

Anatole feels drunk as they sit close to each other on the sofa. Their arms touch, their hands as they share the scotch bottle touch. Leigh's nails are long and shapely, the backs of his hands hairless; the sun has colored them the color of honey. Their legs touch. Leigh's fit of restlessness has passed, he seems resigned, even content. Anatole's glimpsed enough fissures in Leigh's personality to allow him to guess there's never any real ease there. Still, for the moment, he enjoys the illusion of content, a feeling of perfect intimacy.

The record they're listening to has lapsed. "You choose," Leigh commands. Already he's worked through Anatole's collection, already he's at a loss for anything new to play. Anatole kneels, flips through the albums, finds an old Psychedelic Furs issue that has one of his favorite songs ever, "Love My Way," a song whose voice his own singing voice matches perfectly in timbre and pitch—as Chris once pointed out to him when he sang along with it. Coked up, they were flying along the Taconic toward New York, Chris a relentless, implacable driver, taking the mountainous stretches at eighty even though it was snowing out. The radio was playing "Love My Way," and to contain his nervousness, his exhilaration—the lightning will strike—Anatole sang along.

"Anatole," Leigh says. A moment of absolute stillness between them, a pact of some kind. Perhaps Leigh detects Anatole in the momentary throes of a memory. The best moments of their week-old friendship consist of such pauses in the ordinary texture of activity. They invite something; perhaps they dare it. This time Anatole hesitates for an instant, still kneeling before the stereo turntable, then gathers his nerve to say simply, "I think we should go to bed together tonight."

He turns around to find Leigh looking dead at him.

"You don't really know anything about me, do you?" Leigh says.

"No, I don't. I never know anything about anybody till it's too late."

"I respect that." Leigh looks plunged into moodiness. He grimaces, draws his knees up and wraps his arms around them, rocking back and forth as if in deep thought, or in pain.

"If you knew anything about me, Anatole, I'd disappoint you."

"Try me."

Leigh shakes his head sadly.

"You knew I was gay, didn't you?" Anatole asks him.

"I knew I was taking a chance."

"And you went along with it?" He wants to ask, You moved in here in spite of or because of it?

"I figured I could take care of myself. And I can. Look, Anatole . . ." He pauses to think, his brow furrows in something that passes as much for remorse as for thought. "I don't want to sleep with you. That's that, okay? If you're just after my ass, tell me and I'll leave. If it's something else . . . well, otherwise, everything's the same. Just tell me which."

"Everything's the same, Leigh."

"Then let's don't talk about it anymore. It'll depress both of us. It'll just make both of us angry."

Anatole sees some chance receding before him, and he reaches out to try to grasp it as it fades. "I wish sometime we *could* talk about it," he says.

Leigh shakes his head slowly—it's more for his own sake than for Anatole's; this conversation's burrowed him deep into himself. "I'm too confused about too many things," he says. "I'll say things I don't mean. I'll talk myself into things I don't want."

It's Anatole's turn to respect. "Okay," he says. "Okay."

The Psych Furs album has reached "Love My Way." Anatole's flying along the Taconic next to Chris Havilland. He's sitting on the sofa next to Chris, this same sofa. Nothing changes, it just unfolds. Sitting down beside Leigh—"Love my way," Richard Butler sings, his voice rough-edged with longing—Anatole takes the scotch bottle from him, takes a long swallow. He doesn't say, "You've sort of changed my life." He's older, he doesn't say things like that anymore.

Till the song's over, they say nothing. Leigh seems to realize the song's importance as well, its forlornness. Perhaps he has his own memories. At last he breaks the morose silence.

"Look, Anatole, we could sleep together. I mean, like that first night. It's a big mattress."

"Right, it's a big mattress," Anatole says.

Under the blankets Anatole's laid down because of the coolness of the evening, that first hint of autumn in the air: Anatole feels Leigh's hand brush his thigh, a touch light yet warm like sunlight.

"You know," Leigh says, his voice quiet, composed, "like, I could give you a handjob." He settles his palm over Anatole's crotch, kneads it gently through the soft cotton.

"No," Anatole tells him. But Leigh only laughs softly.

"Well, well, well," he kids. "So it was already hard for me. You pervert."

"It was already hard," Anatole says quietly. He feels himself falling, free-fall, the precipice reached at last, the abyss opening wide to receive him. Leigh works his hand down into Anatole's underwear. "This isn't the first time, is it?" Anatole asks him. "I mean, you've done this sort of thing before."

"I've done everything before," Leigh says wearily. He knocks Anatole's exploratory hand away lightly. "Just don't touch me," he tells him. "I'll make you come, but just don't touch me. That's the rules."

NIGHT MUSIC

In the middle of the dark building
there's an air shaft that plunges down to a narrow courtyard, and
someone's lined the floor and walls of the courtyard with brilliant blue
tiles. Leigh's looking out a fourth- or fifth-floor window down into
this courtyard that's more like a well than a courtyard, it's so narrow
and deep. Someone, maybe the same person who put down the blue
tiles, has strung a net of wire mesh to catch whatever might fall into
the airshaft, and over the years it's caught loose roof tiles, geranium
pots, tin cans, a variety of other debris.

It's a little like looking down into a deep swimming pool that's
had its water drained. The blue tiles glimmer vaguely in the dim light.
They fascinate him, these blue tiles—why someone would have put
them down there, because the sun never shines there, it's always in

shadow. But there has to be a reason, even if the reason is only that whoever put them down there thought they looked pretty.

Leigh doesn't think he dreamed that courtyard with the tiles. He thinks it may be his earliest memory, the apartment house where he lived as a small child. If he closes his eyes—as he does now in the dark room where he's lying in bed, drawn awake in the middle of the night as if for no other reason than to remember those blue tiles—he can see them so clearly, a photograph burned into his eyelids. But if that's where he lived as a small child, he can't remember anything else about it at all—which is why he sometimes thinks maybe he did dream it, and that's why it's so vivid, more vivid than anything else, because it never really happened.

Sometimes he tries to think back as far as he can into his memories, and then it's like falling into a well, falling and falling, and if he falls far enough he'll hit bottom and the bottom will be those blue tiles.

There's always that moment when you wake in the middle of the night and don't know where you are, what strange city or room or bed; what stranger is lying next to you, the way people stay strangers even after you've gotten to know them; and those are the times when what you remember is more real than you are—you're floating on the surface of these vivid memories and they're the only things buoying you up.

This fascinates and terrifies him, he can't resist peering into it as deeply as he can. Tonight he can see those blue tiles shining though the other, closer things he remembers, the way the water makes the bottom of a pool shimmer and distort. Tonight he sees those blue tiles shining through a field. At first he doesn't know where the field is, he thinks it's somewhere he's never been before, but then he remembers—it's the field behind Billy's grandmother's house, and he and Billy are out there for the weekend. They're standing behind the barn in the field peeing, and he's telling Billy what his father told him a few days ago, repeating it word for word as if it's extremely important to be accurate about such a strange thing as this. He's telling Billy how when men and women do it the women spread their legs open and the men put their thing right in there in the hole women have. It makes him shiver to tell Billy about it, the same way he shivered when his father told him about it and the other facts of life. It makes him clammy to think about putting his thing in a hole like that, but then Billy says it feels really good to put your thing in somebody's mouth too, which is one of the facts of life his father didn't tell him about, and would he like to put it in Billy's mouth? He thinks what a strange thing that is, since your mouth is just another kind of hole, but thinking about it makes him get hard and when Billy lets him put his thing in Billy's mouth it feels really good, even though he doesn't come because he's not old enough yet, he's only ten.

Then it's some other year and he's in a parking lot with Billy, they're on their bikes. Billy's got a joint, and he says they should go to his house and smoke it because his parents aren't there and so it's fine. They sit on Billy's bed and listen to the stereo, turning it up all the way and letting Bunny and the Wailers blast the room. Leigh's never smoked dope before, though he knows Billy has. Billy says to take the smoke deep down in your lungs and hold it there, and then Billy does it to show him how. He lets the smoke out very slowly and then hands the joint over.

Leigh follows his lead, holding in the smoke for as long as he can even though he wants to cough it out, and then finally when he can't hold it in anymore he lets it out. Billy looks at him and grins, and says, Take another puff and hold it longer. At first it's hard to tell anything's different, but then he's feeling hazy and good and everything seems to be a little deeper and more colorful than it was before. He never realized how much the bass line on the stereo thumps when you're listening to good reggae, and it occurs to him this must be what it means to get high.

See, Billy tells him, looking sorrowfully at the joint, which is almost smoked up, I have this idea. I mean, where I get this stuff, I could get more and we could cut it with something and sell it. I know these middle school types who'd really like to get their hands on some stuff, and they won't know whether they getting some kind of deal or not. Anyway, they trust me.

It sounds okay, because the big thing for both of them is always that they have to get money, they somehow have to figure out how to get their hands on money and live some life that's better than this one they're living. So they make plans all the time—mostly daydreams, this is just Billy's latest daydream. But he always goes along with Billy's plan, whatever it is—he doesn't really know why, he just does.

He tells Billy it sounds like a good idea, and then Billy says, his voice dreamy and hazy with the dope, Yeah, it's a great idea, so why don't you come on and lay up here beside me? He gets up—a little unsteadily—and walks over to the bed, where Billy's sprawled out, and sits on the edge of it. He lets Billy cup his crotch with his hand because he knows Billy knows it turns him on. This is five or six times a week—not something they think about, it's just what happens between them. He feels himself get hard beneath Billy's rummaging hand. I'll do you, Billy tells him, then you do me, okay? They unzip and when Billy goes down on him, his favorite sensation in the world how that warm slick mouth clamps down around him, he comes almost immediately. Then he does Billy, even though he doesn't like doing it all that much—though he likes doing it to Billy, even when Billy shoots it off in his mouth.

Neither of them has anything except his sex—no money, no things; their families, such as they are, live in barracks apartments whose rows look exactly alike, a jaundiced yellow color, and though they've been standing there fifty years or so nobody's bothered to plant any trees—as if whoever built those apartments forgot them as soon as they were built, put them out of their minds as something shameful. Billy tells the story how once when he was really stoned he wasn't paying attention and stood there trying to get into the apartment, only his key wouldn't fit and he was completely paranoid his family had locked him out till he realized it was completely the wrong building he was trying to get into.

They both think this story is very very funny when they're stoned together—which they are more and more often, especially since Leigh's mother is sick now. All her hair has fallen out from the chemotherapy, she spends half the day vomiting and the other half in bed moaning low moans you can hear no matter what room of the apartment you're in. He can hardly stand to look at her, she looks so terrible, shrunk down to half her size, and even her voice has changed. Even though he knows it's crazy, he's sure all of them in the apartment are going to catch her cancer, his father and his sisters and him—either from her, somehow, or from the nearby toxic waste dumps that are the reason she got cancer in the first place according to the doctor. Though his father doesn't believe that—he says it was her smoking, which he tried for years to make her give up. But nobody can be sure about these things, and now she's smoking more than ever—she can hardly breathe and hacks the smoke out when she exhales, but she's always asking Leigh to run to the store and pick up another pack, she's run out. When he asks her why she doesn't stop, she looks at him and says, Why the hell should I? and that's the day he realizes it doesn't matter for her anymore, they've done everything they can do and there's nothing to help, so why the hell not?

When he tells Billy about that, Billy says he wants to visit her, so he starts coming by in the afternoons. He'll go in and sit down on her bed and talk to her a while. Billy must know she never liked him much, she thinks he's a bad influence Leigh should stop hanging around with—but that doesn't stop Billy from being nice to her. Leigh can't figure it out, till one day he comes into the bedroom, where Billy is sitting on the side of the bed and his mother's propped up on pillows—and they're smoking dope together. He can't believe it—he just stands in the doorway and watches, till Billy sees him and says how he read somewhere how doctors sometimes give people dope to smoke to relieve the pain when they have cancer. So he just decided to give her some if she wanted it.

It's not something he'd have ever thought to do for his mother in a million years, but Billy thought to do it for her. And after that whenever Billy comes over he brings a little plastic bag to give to her for free, a gift, so she can smoke whenever she needs to. They never talk about it, he and Billy, or he and his mother, and he doesn't think his father ever knows, because his father's the kind of person who's against illegal drugs no matter what. But he'll come home in the afternoon sometimes and there's his mother in her room smoking, and then he'll hear her spraying Lysol to get rid of the smell, and he knows it's only because of Billy that she ever felt like a person in those last couple of months before she died.

II

OCTOBER

Sunday morning, and Chris has been driving aimlessly around Poughkeepsie, putting off as long as he can his arrival at Anatole's brunch. Often on Sundays, when he can thing of nothing to do and the temptation to drink alone in the morning drives him from his apartment, he'll get in his car and just drift. Poughkeepsie's large enough to get lost in, small enough so you can't stay lost for long. There are islands of affluence, long stretches of squalor, boarded-up buildings, vacant stores, apartment complexes bleak as the military barracks he remembers from his transient childhood.

The morning's lightly overcast, the trees darkly saturated with summer. Sycamores have started to drop their brown-edged leaves, in lawns and unmowed lots signs of autumn have begun quietly to appear. He puts a tape in the tape deck and the whole city turns into a melancholy music video. The simplest things—flowers along a windowsill, a girl walking her dog—become poetic, sad, lost.

He's been down by the train station, Little Italy. He's been on Main Street above the mall, where even on Sunday mornings life is lived in the streets, as in South American countries. So Cheap You Can Afford to Pay Cash announces a sign painted on the side of a furniture store. In front of a West Indian restaurant there's a fistfight in progress. Two black men, both ancient and unsteady on their feet, attempt farcical punches at each other. One of them wears bright red sneakers. Chris is past before he can see what happens.

In front of their doorways, immense black women sit in folding chairs and fan themselves. Everywhere radios seem to be playing. Everywhere there are black children. Even their walking is musical.

On South Hamilton Chris drives past Anatole's building—Lydia's Chevy's already parked in front, Chris is half an hour late, but he can't force himself to park. He'll make one more pass around the block, then he'll go in. The prospect of seeing Leigh again—now that he's, apparently, Anatole's acquisition—depresses him. Déjà vu overtakes him: another city, another brunch four years ago, when he was a student at Cornell. His roommate John's sister was visiting from Oberlin one spring weekend, and John had invited friends over to meet her. Bagels and blueberry muffins, hard-boiled eggs, grapes. Afterward—playing volleyball on the lawn in back of the dorm, by the gorge. The way Michelle was hopeless with the volleyball, standing like a martyr as it shot toward her over the net, the way she'd take a cigarette break every three minutes, standing on the sideline with her hand on her hip as she watched her side lose.

The sense of not knowing anything about her at all. The sense of wondering how she could be connected with her brother, whom he knew too well, a year of sharing lives in the same small dorm room. They seemed completely different, brother and sister, as if raised in different countries speaking different languages. But then later, sprawled on the front steps, some intonation of her voice caught John's accent perfectly; it was uncanny how alike they sounded in that instant. And the way she took a cigarette from him, held it between forefinger and thumb—as if that gesture was in their blood.

That summer the three of them lived together—Michelle didn't want to go home to Pittsburgh, and there was nothing in Oberlin during the summers. A big house in Collegetown, that student ghetto across the gorge from the university's meticulous lawns—big and empty the way student houses are always empty: the living room with its four folding chairs, stereo and John's racing bicycle; the kitchen whose black and white linoleum tiles always made Chris feel inexplicably lonely; the refrigerator stocked with the vegetables he and John had shoplifted from the IGA down the street. With Michelle's arrival, they'd decided to go vegetarian and criminal in a single giddy step—though Michelle disapproved of their thefts. It was her stoic position that if they ran out of money they should starve.

That was the summer he and Michelle stopped the car one afternoon—they were high, they were giddy with each other's company, they'd been drinking champagne all afternoon at an outdoor restaurant—to make love in a field whose weeds concealed a perfect wealth of blooming midsummer wildflowers, flowers you could see only as you lay amid the golden stalks of weeds, a private bed for lovers—and Michelle suddenly had an allergic reaction, sneezing uncontrollably and at the same time laughing at the absurdity of it, trying to make love while sneezing.

Chris really dreads this brunch, he'd give anything not to go through with it. But he's come full circle around the block and now slides into place behind Lydia's car with a sense of weariness.

Lydia greets him at the door. "Church run overtime?"

"Welcome to the Cathedral of the Holy Brunch," Anatole chimes in. He hands Chris a Bloody Mary.

Leigh sits on a sofa, apparently engrossed in his reading of the *Poughkeepsie Journal*. Chris wonders, as he always wonders, What was going on here the instant before I arrived? He always fantasizes that he's caught people at something but never knows what exactly it is.

"You remember Chris," Anatole is saying.

"What's the salt point?" Leigh asks. Then lowering the paper—"Oh hi, Chris."

He doesn't remember me at all, Chris thinks. And he's disappointed; he's annoyed.

"The salt point?" Anatole asks. "I never heard of it."

"Well, it's heading this way. Or it was. Now it's hovering, whatever that means. So watch out."

"What're you talking about, Leigh?" Lydia sounds stern as a parent.

"I'm just reporting what it says. See?" He points to the lead on page three.

Chris could intervene, he could explain. But he won't. He feels completely outside the circle Lydia and Anatole have drawn around Leigh.

"It's probably nuclear weapons," Anatole assures him. "Everything's about nuclear weapons these days. Let's eat."

They settle around the big walnut table Anatole's spread lavishly with croissants, cantaloupe, his famous crab-and-avocado salad that Chris once pretended to love, and which in consequence Anatole serves all the time now. Pachelbel's canon, the only classical record Anatole owns, makes background music on the stereo.

He's really quite beautiful, Chris thinks, watching as Leigh butters a croissant. Though if you look at him too closely you'll break him, his features are so refined, the definition of his cheekbones so breathtakingly clear.

Anatole reaches out and tousles Leigh's hair as the boy forks crab salad onto his plate. It's a way of taking public possession of him. "You know, you're getting what my mother used to call shaggy," he says playfully. "What do you say? We could go over to Reflexion this afternoon, my treat. We could make you look really exciting. Provocative."

Leigh makes as if to fend off Anatole's touch—but his grin is amused. He doesn't like people to touch him, Chris notices—he shies away like a small animal that's been traumatized at some point in its little life. But at the same time he forces himself to let people touch him. Chris doesn't want to be moved, but in some small way he is.

"Have you ever imagined yourself with black hair?" Anatole's acting.

"I try not to imagine myself period."

Chris tries to figure it out. The boy's quick. Are they really lovers? Or has Lydia been right to suggest that something else altogether is going on, that Anatole is making it all up, staging a love affair that doesn't exist, and really he and Leigh are just what they appear to be: improbable, inexplicable apartment mates?

"I can see you with jet-black hair, blue-black, raven black." Anatole's getting carried away. But he must realize it, because immediately he sobers up. "So what do you think?"

"You'll ruin me," Leigh tells him flirtatiously. "I'll look ugly and you'll turn me out on the streets. I'll have to sell my body."

"Honey, you'll be a millionaire. Anyway," Anatole pauses, "dyeing's not forever." It's a line he's stolen from Daniel. "Be bold," he urges, touching Leigh's hair again (and again Leigh flinches, but again allows himself to be touched). "Experiment."

It worries Chris, the way they treat Leigh like a mannequin to be dressed and groomed. Or perhaps it's more like a statue in a shrine, the kind that's taken out of the niche once a year and borne through the streets on the shoulders of the faithful. Anatole's always been a cultist at heart, and Lydia, for whatever reason, has always been there to abet him.

But all at once Chris realizes the real reason for his disapproval of what's happening. Watching Lydia and Anatole swarm about Our Boy of the Mall, Chris sees something accomplished that's only gradually come about, the loss of a privilege he's let lie implicit in his relations with both Lydia and Anatole for the two years he's known them; a privilege he realizes now he's basked in without having done anything to earn. It damns him, he thinks—his comfortable acceptance, these past two years, of the central fact in their perfect circle of three: that both Anatole and Lydia have been in love with him. They've deferred to him, his presence has ratified them. Now it's gone; he can only marvel at his vanity, his self-deception. This perfect, accidental boy sitting across from him at the table—he wears a white T-shirt across which is written, in tiny precise letters you have to lean close to read, Life Sucks, Then You Die—displaces him neatly. Whatever he once was to them, Chris tells himself, he is no longer. They've passed on, he's been passed over. Where once he stood at the center, Leigh's replaced him, and he's on the edge with the rest of them, where Anatole and Lydia have always been.

Odd the things you realize about yourself only after they cease to be true. He remembers a line from somewhere; it floats, he can't remember where it's from, perhaps a movie—he can hear the voice that uttered it with perfect clarity, though he can't associate a face or a situation or anything else with it: "Age, my dear friend, age is the most corrupt of all." He feels himself, Sunday morning, the sixth of October 1985, move a perceptible step closer to that time when he'll no longer possess anything but the corruption of having lived.

"The salt point," he says aloud. They all look at him. It's what he might have said earlier, but didn't. "What Leigh said before. The salt point. It's what they call the place in the Hudson where the river changes from fresh to salt water. Where it stops being a river and becomes an estuary."

They're not really interested, even Leigh's uninterested—Chris has the feeling he's interrupted some other conversation he wasn't following. Nevertheless he forges on. It's something he has to say. "It's always changing," he tells them. "You can't exactly fix it, but it's there, a point. But it's never the same."

They all look at him, they sort of shake their heads. He feels foolish and indulgent.

"Yeah," Leigh says. "That's sort of what the newspaper said."

When the brunch comes to an end, it's as a set of signals passed wordlessly between friends who know when things are over. "Nice to see you two again," Leigh says as if withdrawing, receding into himself. "I'll see you around, I'm sure."

"I'm sure," Lydia tells him. "Be good, Anatole," she says as she kisses her host on the cheek.

"Stop by the record store sometime," Chris tells Leigh. "I'll give you a discount." It's said before he realizes he's going to say it. He doesn't quite want to relinquish Leigh, but neither is he quite sure what to do with him.

"I never buy records," Leigh says. "I never have any money."

"Anatole buys records. Buy some for him. Whatever you buy, he'll love."

"Yeah," Leigh says. But he sounds indifferent, and that disconcerts Chris. It makes him feel ill at ease as Anatole conducts him and Lydia to the front door, as he eases them out into sunlight.

"So . . ." Anatole collapses on the sofa in nervous exhaustion. Leigh sits in a straight-backed chair—he's made them both Bloody Marys; he looks, well, ineffable. "What'd you think? What's the post-mortem?"

Leigh laughs. His general silence throughout brunch has managed to conceal, more or less, his drunkenness. "There you go again," he observes. "You should relax, Anatole, really you should."

"Can I help it? My friends make me nervous. I'm just interested in your opinion is all. You know, like an objective point of view."

Leigh grimaces. "Well, if you have to know," he says. "I liked Lydia. She's interested in people. She wants to know them—not just about them, but actually know them. At least that's what I felt."

"And Chris?" Anatole asks uneasily.

"It's hard to get an impression of him. He's too careful about all the little things. He's always watching the little things, making sure they're just right, and he misses the big things."

It thrills Anatole to hear Leigh assess his friends so crisply, so skeptically: it seems to confirm that Leigh's special after all, that Anatole's not reading things into him.

He doesn't, though, necessarily agree with what Leigh's said. "Chris is hard to get to know," he defends. "But rewarding. While Lydia—you might say, she's diminishing returns. Don't misunderstand me. Lydia and I are like this. But—well, you can only go so far."

Meaning what? he thinks. That I can only go so far? Sometimes he's intuited that unspoken reproach in her friendship with him, but only now does he see it actually surface for a moment. He's sorry that what he's just said sounded so much like a challenge, because Leigh takes it up.

"I bet," he says, "in the right situation, you could go very far with her. She'd let you go very far. She's brave that way."

Again uneasiness. Anatole doesn't want them to talk about Lydia. So far he's been able to shape everything the way he wanted to, or needed to—he's impressed Chris and Lydia with his appropriation of Leigh, Leigh's acquiescence in that appropriation. Now for the first time he's alert to danger, things he may not be able to control. In a sense, he realizes, he and Leigh have gone as far with each other as they ever will. That's what frightens and troubles him, what accounts for this feeling of elegy. So they got drunk one night and Leigh gave him a handjob: it's happened only that once—next morning Leigh's only reaction was "Sometimes I drink too much and then I can't remember what went on the night before. Don't take advantage of me when I'm like that, okay? I trust you not to." There's nothing else there, what's happened is all that's going to happen.

Having without having: it's possible, isn't it, that that's worse than not having at all?

Maybe it's just having drunk too much too early in the day, but in the aftermath of this brunch Anatole feels very sad. He's put Leigh on the trail of his friends. Now anything can happen—and it will. He and Leigh have exhausted each other, they're looking for something else in each other they can't find. They'll never be able to go back; and Anatole feels as if something is ending, a period in his life. There are these moments—the connections that usually bind them fail, they have nothing to say to each other, they're just strangers, even faintly hostile strangers with very different, even incompatible agendas.

"Actually, you know, I should tell you," Leigh says. "I sort of hated brunch. I mean, it made me *very* uncomfortable."

"How so?"

"Can I be completely honest?"

"Please do." That icy feeling around the heart again.

"Well, I felt like I was being used just a little bit. Like I was on display."

"I . . ." Anatole's said his prayer of thanks that the brunch has been endured; now he's not sure he wasn't premature.

"No, don't apologize. It doesn't really bother me. I mean, well— it doesn't bother me. I just sort of thought that was what was going on. It made me a little uncomfortable, is all, and I just wanted to tell you that. Now," he says brightly, changing the subject, putting it all behind him, "what color are we going to make my hair? I've decided: I want you to dye it. I want to look completely different. I don't want anybody to be able to recognize me."

Midweek, Lydia's day off. She's slept till noon, spent the last two hours considering whether to go to the pet store in South Hills Mall and buy a dog, something expensive, spur-of-the-moment, an Akita or a Dalmatian. Her landlord would kill her, she'd have to keep it at her mother's, it's all too complicated to think about.

So she paints her nails carefully, with a sort of morbid attentiveness. She studies her face in the mirror: pouty cheeks, lips too thin, God her eyes are bloodshot in the mornings. She's tired of her hair, she'd like to do something really radical with it—like Marion the fag hag had the courage to do. Of course, Marion's not *speaking* to Daniel or Antole these days—she's telling everybody who'll listen how they made a fool of her. It must have been after the champagne and cocaine wore off and she realized it was no dream, her hair really was streaked eggplant purple and wine red. "They just toy with women, they're cruel to them, it's their idea of a joke," she accuses.

"So unstable, some of these girls." Daniel's philosophical. "And I was thinking of graduating her to the Patti LaBelle look—you know, *ironed* hair."

"Daniel," Lydia teases him, "sometimes I think you really *do* despise women."

"I despise the way men look at women," he tells her.

She pulls a strand of blondish hair down over her eye, then lets it go. Maybe she'll call Anatole and insist he make her over. However, the thought of Anatole these days leaves her somehow empty.

Lydia, she chides herself. It's so hard. She should work up the energy to go to Edwards Food Warehouse and buy groceries; she should take her car in and get the oil changed and see about that noise when she touches the brakes (it's a Chevy compact, it's a piece of junk); she should buy a card to send Craig for his birthday; she's paralyzed. The thought of venturing out, standing in lines at Edwards—the cashiers are inept, it takes forever, she'd be in a furious mood by the time she got to the front of the line: she'd rather eat nothing but a can of soup, a glass of milk for dinner, she'd rather fast. If she goes to Edwards, chances are she'll run into somebody she knows, some girl she went to high school with, who now has three kids, who'll pity her in a cowish sort of way. And I think *I* need to lose fifteen pounds, she thinks.

Craig she'll see in a week or so, he's home for fall break from BU, she'll tell him happy birthday then. And who knows? Maybe he'll take a look at her car: he's after all a magician of sorts with old cars, he bought his VW for a hundred dollars five years ago, it wouldn't even run, and now it's better than new. He amazes her, her brother, the way he lives so comfortably in a world of material things that conspire constantly to trip *her* up. She couldn't be more different from him, could she? And yet she once moved boldly through that world of things that only depresses and intimidates her now. Where did it happen, that failure, that giving up? Was it that year at Bard, or in New York? Could she muster the courage to go back there now? She longs for the City the way she longs for a lover, but every time she visits she's overwhelmed, she feels like a completely alien creature with no business there at all. Yet, if she'd hung on, if she'd been living there these past eight or nine years, surely she'd fit right in, she'd be a part of that world she so craves and is intimidated by now.

I'll surprise everybody, she thinks. One day I'll just go. I'll just pick up and go. I'll force myself.

She can't even force herself to go grocery shopping. Who, she thinks, are you kidding? So instead she lays out a sweater she bought yesterday and hasn't had a chance yet to examine—a gorgeous turquoise knit she got at the Up-to-Date for way more than she can afford, but you only live once.

The thought that there is gin in the freezer keeps flitting into her mind, but so far today she's resisted the temptation.

When the phone rings, it's salvation—unexpected, miraculous, as salvation always is. It's Leigh.

And not the first time, either. In the week and a half since Anatole's brunch, he's called three, maybe four times, never with anything in particular to say: "I didn't expect you to be home," he explained the first time. "I just saw your number in Anatole's datebook, and I wasn't doing anything, so I thought well, I'll just give a call." It was as if he were talking into space just to see what would happen to his words out there. Every conversation, he's nervous, chattery—but also confident she'll want to listen. He's very self-involved, she thinks, he moves into things with his eyes slightly averted—but that's okay. She's curious to see what'll happen. She likes his calls.

"Hey," he asks, "are you, like, doing anything? Do you have to go to work?"

"Um, not at the moment, no."

"Want to do something, then? Like maybe go on a picnic or something? It's just this idea I had. I mean, I'm kind of sitting around doing nothing—well, I sort of feel like getting out. It's so nice today."

"Is it? I haven't even looked out the window"—which is true, she hasn't gotten around to opening her venetian blinds yet.

"Oh, it's great out. It's warm, it's like summer. There's a little plane flying around. Listen."

Lydia listens. "I hear it," she says. "Outside the window. That'd be fun, a picnic."

"Come by and pick me up, okay? Soon."

At first glance she doesn't recognize the boy sitting on the front steps of Anatole's apartment. She hasn't seen him since the brunch, only talked with him by phone: his hair, as Anatole proposed, is black as a raven's wing, cut very short on the sides, developing into a moussed tangle on top. He sees her, hops up and strolls across the grass to the curb. He's wearing faded jeans, bright red sneakers, a black sleeveless sweater over a white T-shirt.

"I didn't recognize you."

"Like it? I felt like changing my life."

She studies him: it changes him, certainly—he looks less safe than before, darker, more out of control, capable of anything. She's not sure, all at once, she trusts him; there's no telling what may be going through a head with a haircut like that. Perhaps he really is unbalanced, crazy, a drifter. Come on, she tells herself. But the impression persists—through the buying of a stick of French bread, a wedge of Jarlsberg, a small container of button mushrooms, another of artichoke salad; through a stop at Arlington Liquor for two bottles of the $2.99 special, Les Douelles, a Bordeaux that's not half bad: Leigh's a restless, lost kid, this picnic covers all sorts of discontents. She's not sure she wants to go through with it.

She feels like a middle-aged woman out on a fling that she's having second thoughts about already.

"So what did I rescue you from?" Leigh asks.

"You wouldn't want to know. I was fighting off the temptation of ice-cold gin."

"Just another Wednesday afternoon, huh? I have to work later tonight, so I can't get too drunk. But a little drunk's okay."

"I see Anatole's educating you well: how to survive Poughkeepsie on a liter a day." She winces a little as she says his name. Unfaithful.

"You mean drink? I think I knew about that a long time ago. Certainly way before Anatole."

"It couldn't have been *too* long. I mean, how old *are* you, Leigh?"

"Oh, old enough."

"You're not going to tell me?"

"All I want is to be a rumor," he tells her, fiddling with the radio, interrupting a Madonna song in progress. He shakes his shoulders to the beat.

"I see why Anatole likes you."

"Anatole," Leigh says. He turns down the radio.

"What do you mean?"

"Nothing," he says.

They drive north on Route 9—past the Western Publishing Company, now closed, where her father used to work. Poughkeepsie thins into suburban clutter. Culinary Institute of America, housed in a defunct monastery. Opposite a drive-in move theater, the Roosevelt estate with ancient oaks in an unmown field. Hyde Park's strip of motels, McDonald's, antique stores. On the other side of town are the grounds of the old Vanderbilt estate, now thrown open for picnickers, stray lovers, vagrants like themselves. They take the winding drive till the compact limestone mansion emerges before them, complete with romantic vista of river and mountains as if wealth can indeed purchase beauty.

They park overlooking a long field that slopes steeply down to the river. From the glove compartment Lydia extracts a corkscrew, from the trunk a yellow beach towel; Leigh grabs the food and wine, and they settle down on the grass. They forgot cups, so they share from the bottle, holding it by the neck, tilting it back in big gulps. The landscape lies in the lull of an Indian summer. On the other side of the Hudson the maples are brilliant, even incandescent—light seems to fill them from the inside out. To brim, to overflow.

They eat peacefully, not saying much; they share the wine. She's hyperconscious of the presence next to her of his body. What's he thinking? He fascinates her: surely he didn't call her up just because he wanted to go on a picnic. He seems both content and happy at the same time.

She can't believe how much his haircut changes him. It's as if Anatole's put his mark on him. It's corrupt. She's not a romantic like Anatole, she's impatient to do more than merely decorate the shrine with haircuts and new clothes—she wants to cut through those rumors Leigh likes, childishly, to think of himself as. If she can do anything for him, she thinks, it's to bring him a little more into the world than he allows himself. She wonders if that's what lies behind the seeming aimlessness of his phone calls to her—he's feeling hemmed in by all those things that make Anatole Anatole. She flatters herself that he sees in her something that will ground him where Anatole leaves him floating. Nobody really wants to be a rumor, after all. Not even Leigh. There's always something at the bottom of everything.

Their silences are not so much eloquent as blank. It's too much: Lydia's seized by the need to cut through to the heart.

"Talk," she tells him.

"It'll ruin the view."

"I'm nervous without talk. Say anything that comes into your head. What you're thinking right now, this instant."

Leigh sort of laughs, not really a laugh so much as an acknowledgment that this is where a laugh should take place. He's opened the second bottle of wine and hands it to her for the inaugural swallow.

"I'm thinking how things must look strange," he says. "I mean, you and your friend Chris must think all sorts of things about me."

"We always think all sorts of things. I wouldn't worry too much."

"It's just that at that brunch . . ."

"Yes?"

"Well, I felt uncomfortable. Usually I never feel uncomfortable, but I did. It made me ask myself questions."

All at once she's sure of it—whatever Anatole thinks, Leigh's not gay in the least, he's as straight as he can be. If he and Anatole are lovers, it's in Anatole's overheated imagination only. She's never been so sure of anything.

She takes another long swallow of wine. It gives her a certain courage. She begins—and it surprises her, how long it's been since she felt this—to feel possible again.

"Leigh," she tells him firmly, "I want to know what those questions are. You can't just play with me. Maybe with Anatole—he likes being played with—but I'm not Anatole."

He stares into the distance, the picturesque river that winds between cleft hills. "Fair enough," he says. "You're not Anatole."

"I've never been able to stand not knowing where things stand. When I was in college," she laughs, "I used to just go up to people and say, 'I want to sleep with you' so there wouldn't be any ambiguity at all. How's that?"

"Well, I like it. It's challenging. At least you know what's what. I could never do that, it's so black and white. To me things always seem to flow in and out of each other."

"So there's no yes and no? Not even to a question like that?"

"Do I want to sleep with you? Is that the question? Yes or no?"

Suddenly, out of the blue, they've arrived at it, and it takes her breath away.

"That's the question," she enunciates precisely. She looks at him and waits. He doesn't say anything, he doesn't look at her. Where a plane has appeared out over the Hudson, circling, doing loops and barrel rolls, he contemplates it. It violates the placid landscape.

"Cessna," he says at last. "You can tell by its configuration. It's something I know, the shapes of airplanes. I think it's the same plane we heard earlier. Obviously it's following us." She doesn't say anything, she doesn't want to let him get away with a single thing. He's silent for a moment. "Maybe he's just looking for the salt point," he jokes. "Actually, you know, the reason he's doing all his tricks out over the river"—it's his voice talking into space to see what will happen—"is so if he crashes, he'll just crash into the river, he won't kill anybody else."

The answer's no, it must be no. She's not so young anymore, he's—what?—ten, twelve years younger than she is. It was stupid to bring it up. "So how do you know so much about flying?" she asks, about to burst into tears.

"I just know, is all." He turns and looks at her. "Do you know what I feel like? I feel like getting really drunk with you this afternoon. I feel like shrooming or something."

"Are you playing with me? Is that what it is?"

"No," he says. "That's not what it is." He jumps to his feet. Gesticulating wildly, he runs down the slope into the center of the field. "Here we are," he cries, motioning to the Cessna, taking off his sweater and T-shirt and waving them as if they are signals of distress. "Down here. We're down here. See us?"

But the Cessna only continues to circle.

Leigh stands there, not so much a figure to scare crows as to beckon doves. Finally he gives up, loping back up the steep slope. "You never know." He collapses beside her on the beach towel. He's out of breath. He wipes his chest with his shirt. "I've got the shrooms right here with me. I was down on the Main Street mall this morning, I bought them. I went by where you said you worked, I thought you might be there. I thought you might like a little present." He takes a small plastic bag from his pocket.

"God, it's been so long since I shroomed," she tells him, accepting the bag, hefting it. "I must've still been in college. Not," she adds self-protectively, "that that was the Dark Ages or anything."

"What do you say—you want to?"

"Why the hell not?" she says resolutely. Why the hell not? If things are going to be complicated, if they're going to be surprising and convoluted, then let them. She'll follow wherever.

Leigh divides the brownish powder, they ingest it in silence, looking into each other's eyes as if it's some ritual. Leigh smiles. "Good," he says. "I love shrooming. It's a great way to get to know somebody. Hey, I have an idea. Let's take the mansion tour."

It suddenly seems, absurdly, the thing to do.

"Put your shirt on," she tells him, "and off we go."

She begins to feel the old, once-familiar heightening of the edges shrooming can bring. As if autumn hasn't charged the trees enough, now they seem to pulse with some inner fire. And the sky, the sky is breathtaking, a pool of bottomless blue with only the flyspeck of the circling plane to mar it.

Tours are on the half hour—they're lucky to catch one that's forming up. The leader's a tiny old woman who introduces herself winsomely as Florence. Her open, shiny face glows with tiny broken blood vessels beneath the surface of her cheeks. The Hyde Park chapter of the DAR provides the volunteer guides, she explains, clasping her hands in front of her and smiling beatifically. Against the blue of her dress, her diamond brooch glitters with a life of its own.

"Please refrain from touching anything," Florence requests as they stand on the front steps. With a big key she unlocks the massive front door.

"Anything?" Leigh whispers, rubbing Lydia's arm furtively, provocatively.

Inside, the mansion's gloomy and ornate. With reverent awe Florence catalogs the materials—green marble from Italy, Santo Domingo mahogany in the study, Louis XV furniture in the Gold Room, Louis XIV in the dining room. "Parties had to end by midnight," she explains as they view the roped-off drawing room, "because Mrs. Vanderbilt disapproved of dancing on Sundays."

"I do too," Leigh says, a loud stage whisper to Lydia. "Saturday night for dancing, Sunday morning for the long slow sweaty fuck."

Florence stares at him wonderingly—she must've heard. "Now

we'll proceed upstairs," she continues, barely discomposed by it. "The bedrooms," she announces, "are located upstairs."

"Yikes," Leigh says. "So soon."

"Leigh." Lydia has to warn him—others are looking at them with alarm. Ordinarily she'd think Leigh's behavior boorish and stupid, but now she can hardly keep from laughing at the predicament Leigh's putting them in.

"You may touch the banister," Florence tells the group as they head up the stairs. "It's covered in crushed velvet."

Oohs and aahs from the tourists.

"Wow." Leigh touches the velvet then holds up his hand to contemplate it. "You could get a hard-on touching that velvet."

Lydia can't help herself, she lets out a whoop of laughter at what Leigh's just said. To be caught up in this tour seems the funniest thing anybody ever dreamed up. And the house—the big pretentious house seems incredibly silly, all she can think of is these two dour old people doddering about, falling asleep in armchairs, never saying anything to each other. Mrs. Vanderbilt reading religious tracts, Mr. Vanderbilt studying agricultural manuals—Florence has informed them that Mr. Vanderbilt's favorite pastime was raising cows.

It turns out Mr. and Mrs. Vanderbilt had separate bedrooms, his in the brooding style of a Bavarian hunting lodge, hers next door effete and faded, a copy of Marie Antoinette's bedroom at Versailles. There's even a balustrade around the bed—it provokes giggles from the tourists. "It's so when she falls out of bed during sex she won't roll down the hall," Leigh eagerly informs the crowd.

"Young man, please," says Florence.

Clearly no one knows quite what to do with them—but far from being mortified, Lydia's exhilarated. "Don't worry," she tells Leigh. "It's just a play. All these people here are actors." And afterward, after Florence has cut short the interminable tour for (Lydia suspects) their sake, they stand in the waning sunlight with the Shawangunks heaped like sleeping whales across the river and it seems that that is exactly what they've so masterfully negotiated—a play whose lines everybody else knew by heart, but that she and Leigh had to improvise hilariously from scratch.

After such a success before a critical audience, they laugh and laugh, they cavort in lengthening shadows, play tag and havoc among the leaves gardeners have raked into neat piles along the lawn. Leigh tackles her, they go down, giddy, tumbling over and in and out of each other. Leigh kisses her on the cheek. Leaves lace his hair. With her hand she brushes them away, running her fingers through his fine hair, feeling the curve of his skull.

On the way back, Leigh drives—Lydia surrenders the wheel, she just doesn't feel capable. She feels instead out of this world, clear and free. Anatole might be light-years away, now it's just she and Leigh. He's right: shrooming's a great way to get to know somebody.

Coming into Poughkeepsie they drive under the imposing skeleton of the abandoned train bridge. Fire-blackened, it looms above the old houses of Delafield Street. "I wonder," Leigh muses, "if you could get up there."

"There're no tracks up there, I know that much. You have to balance on the girders. It's dangerous. People go out there to jump off."

Leigh turns the car abruptly up a side street.

"You're not thinking of it, I hope?"

"I just want to explore a little. I want to see where the bridge connects." They try to keep the long span of the bridge in sight as the street rises to meet its level. In the lot of a gas station gone out of business and boarded up, Leigh parks. The bridge has come to rest in the slope of the hill. "We'll follow the tracks," he says. "We'll see what we can see."

"We're not going out on the bridge," she tells him. "It's just what we need—to get arrested."

He smiles certainly, then turns and scrambles up the embankment. The train bed's still clear, the tracks rusted. They walk down them—it feels nostalgic, like walking down a path that leads back into someone's forgotten childhood. She'd never be doing this if she were in her right mind. Still, all she can do is follow—Leigh walks along confidently, jauntily, as if it never occurs to him for an instant they might get in trouble. He's young, she's old. Fuck it. All she thinks about these days is whether something'll get her into trouble.

Who cares? There was certainly a time when *she* didn't: and she was a better person then. It's what Leigh brings back to her, it's his gift of new life.

The ground's started to fall away, they bridge Washington Street at fifteen feet or so, then before they know it they're on the big bridge proper. The tracks end abruptly, there're only the two parallel steel struts, wide as a narrow sidewalk but that's all. Wide enough to walk single file on. She takes the north leg, he the south, they venture out over the disappearing ground. In no time they're a hundred feet up. Lydia can keep walking if she just concentrates, if she doesn't look down. They don't talk, each of them intent on just walking, one careful step at a time. Is Leigh as exhilarated and frightened as she is? Impossible to tell. He stretches his arms out like a bird balancing the moment before flight.

What if they're seen? Vague recollections come back to her: news reports from years gone by of people arrested for trespassing.

But it's growing dark, the quick nightfall of autumn. When's the equinox? Is it soon, or has it already passed—the year balanced on a single point, nights exactly as long as days—if she just thinks about that balance, she'll be all right, she'll stay steady.

There's all sorts of junk on the bridge you have to be careful to step over, that could trip you up if you aren't looking.

It must be a mile out to the water—they've gone only part of the way. The town looks impossibly small below them, veiled in dusk, romantic. Lights are coming on. It's not her town anymore, it's a town foreign and enchanted as she imagines European towns along the Rhine.

Leigh's gotten twenty yards ahead of her.

"I can't believe," she calls to him, giddy, transcendent, "I've lived here my whole life and never been out here. It's amazing. I remember when it burned. My dad drove us down so we could watch the smoke pouring off it."

The first stars appear, clear precise points of light. She shivers, there's a chill breeze up here above the silent river. Because suddenly, they're out over the water. There're no lights below them, no shapes of roofs or outlines of streets, there's nothing but the trackless face of the river, a pervasive murmur below them, the stealthy, nearly subliminal movement of the Hudson's flow.

Somewhere on the bridge something is knocking against something else, a hollow, lonely sound. Leigh's stopped dead in his tracks. He stands listening. "It's just us," he says. "We could be astronauts walking in space." If they stretch out their hands, they can almost touch across the empty space that separates them, but not quite. "I can see why people jump," Leigh muses. "It's so tempting. I almost feel like—"

With a sudden motion he slips down, sits with his legs dangling over the edge. It makes Lydia's heart stop. "Don't," she says. "I'll kill you if you jump."

"Don't worry. Someday, maybe. For the fun of it, to see what it's like. But not now."

Not now. Now. She becomes aware of it: here I am right now, right now I'm standing two hundred feet above the water, balancing crazily on a piece of steel three feet wide, nothing to hold me up but my own sense of balance and—and what else? When she was walking, it was fine, her movement gave her something to hang on to. Now even that's gone. She has the most peculiar, terrifying sensation— she's about to fall over, she won't be able to maintain her balance. How to tell what's balance when there's not a single reference except the sky above, the river underneath? Leigh's vague figure. Who is this boy that he's tempted her out here to this impossible present tense? She has the panicked impulse to lie down on the rusted girder and hold on for sheer life.

"I'm terrified," she admits to Leigh.

"Really? I feel great. I really feel like free-fall or something."

"Let's go back."

"You want to?" He sounds disappointed. "I wish we had a six-pack out here."

The mushrooms have almost completely dissipated in them, their fantasia overwhelmed by the greater reality of the dead bridge. The walk back's a slow spooling of a thread that's been unraveled as far as it'll go. Each step brings her closer to sanity. Soon they're strolling along the tracks through the woods, it's as if they were never out there. They walk close, their arms touching. She's hyperaware of his body.

"Nobody'll believe us," Leigh says, with a note of disappointment.

"I don't think we should *tell* anybody. They'll think we're crazy." She wants to keep the amazing adventure just between the two of them. It seals something between them. Whatever happens, even if they never spend another instant together, Leigh'll have to remember—years later, when he's forgotten everything else—how one evening he walked out on the old Poughkeepsie train bridge with her. It's a kind of immortality they'll share, a minor victory of sorts against—well, against whatever it is she drinks ice-cold gin in the middle of the night to keep at bay.

And yet—she can scarcely believe that ten minutes ago she was telling herself that this is *now*, this exact moment of the present balanced above the abyss, the absolute insanity of perching hundreds of feet in the air on an abandoned, unsafe train bridge—when now they're walking safely. But toward what?

Leigh echoes it. "What next?" he wonders.

Somehow, she feels this is only the beginning. "I, for one, need a *drink*," she says. "I feel all shaken up."

He looks at her—it's as if he can't quite believe only walking on the bridge has rattled her, as if he's looking for other causes. And perhaps he finds them.

"We could buy champagne," he says, "we could go to your apartment. I've never seen where you live."

"My apartment's a mess. It's not like Anatole's." She speaks the name freely, almost defiantly.

"*You're* not like Anatole."

Of course, when they get there, it's not quite as much of a mess as she'd feared. Toss a few things here and there, and the living room's basically straightened up. "I'll find some glasses," she offers. "I'm not letting you near the kitchen. Some of the dishes have been in that sink since before you were born."

He sits compliant on the sofa. She remembers the first night how he roamed Anatole's apartment, hungry, looking at everything. He's completely uninterested in her things, he doesn't look around at all. It faintly disappoints her. She's confused, rinsing a couple of champagne flutes she hasn't used in so long they're covered with a film of dust—it's the kind of day she'll have to sit down and *think* about later.

While he uncorks the champagne, she brings out a dope pipe, some good pot she's been saving for—well, for nothing so auspicious as this.

They smoke, they drink, he keeps springing up—some tension coiling inside him, he has to release it. He flings himself around the living room, manic, given edge by the pot, the champagne.

"I'm in such a good mood," he bursts out with. "Everything seems so *fine*."

"I hate to bring this up, but didn't you have to work tonight?"

"Shit. I completely forgot." He throws himself down on the sofa again, his body touching hers familiarly. He ponders for a moment. "It'll be okay," he announces. "They love me there."

"Everybody loves you, Leigh."

"Not everybody," he says.

"There're exceptions?"

He frowns. "Notable exceptions. But I don't want to talk about that. Let's talk about who *does* love me."

Fondly, he rubs her thigh with his hand.

"Is this playing again?" she asks.

"It hasn't been playing for a long time."

She doesn't say anything. She rubs his slender, child's arms fondly. She feels old, weary, corrupt. When their lips come together, she lets him kiss her, his tongue nimble and warm in her mouth. He tastes of pot smoke and champagne. In between kisses he's laughing, as if in amusement at himself, at them, the things that happen.

What Lydia thinks of is this: the Cessna, its view of river, mansion, hills; yellow beach towel on a golden spread of lawn; two figures, human beings, too far away to be distinguishable in identities or actions.

A rainstorm's moved across the city: Lydia lies in bed and listens to its aftermath, how sounds—the whirr of tires, the dripping of water-drops in the downspout—seem to carry farther in the stillness after rain, as if a way's been cleared for them. She imagines being able to hear sounds from all over the city—not only the occasional, after-midnight traffic on the arterial, but the forlorn sounds of the fountains on the Main Street mall as they splash through the long night, the lapping of the Hudson against the piers of the suspension bridge, the gaunt abandoned train bridge.

She hasn't been dreaming, it must be the sound of the rain that's wakened her. She finds herself thinking about a boy she once knew at Bard, Danny Rothenburg. She'd had a crush on him for months—she'd see him walking across campus, or sitting on the steps of the library—but she'd never really met him, she'd never talked to him. Then at a party they were at together, she followed him out onto the porch when he went to smoke a cigarette, and sat down next to him, pretending to be drunker than she really was, and leaned her head against his shoulder, and he put his arm around her, thinking she was cold or something, and she responded, and before she knew it they were kissing, before she knew it they were back at his place in his bed with their clothes off and he was fucking her.

He didn't know who she was. He didn't know she'd watched him for months. Danny Rothenburg. He had curly dark hair, he wore denim jackets, old jeans with an American flag sewn on the back pocket. Later they sat around in his room and smoked pot and listened to a Jackson Browne album and made love again. They lasted about three weeks, the two of them. It was spring, blossoms everywhere, a season of petals raining down on sidewalks, lawn, steps: that's what she remembers. She can't remember why they stopped seeing each other; perhaps Danny already had another girlfriend, perhaps she met someone else she thought she should sleep with. It bothers her that she can't remember. Her life's fading from her, patches of darkness are beginning to appear in the texture, gaps in the storyline. Try as she might—it's like having a name on the tip of her tongue—she can't remember. And she hasn't thought of Danny in years. It hurts, somehow: lying in the middle of the night ten years later, she misses him, she doesn't have any clue to whatever happened to him, if they were to meet by accident, say, on a street in New York, he probably wouldn't even remember who she was.

Of course she wasn't in love with him or anything like that, it was a way to prove herself capable of something. That was important to her back then.

Back then; well—she gets out of bed to pour herself a tumbler of gin—this is now, and nothing's easy. I'm thinking about Danny Rothenburg, she realizes, because I don't want to think about Leigh. It even makes her shudder as she moves through the chill of her dark apartment and gropes in the freezer for the frosted bottle. It doesn't seem possible—how moments can break like a wave, unexpected, then recede so completely that the shore, all its flotsam, is exposed to the whole world. She feels particularly naked—the gin goes down like a sliver of ice, she can feel it spread through her, highlighting her insides like an X ray. She shivers and sits down on the floor, in the dark.

Everything's tangled with everything else. Anatole's going to die, she said to Leigh after they'd made love. He can't ever, ever know about this.

"I'm always cool, Lydia," he told her, his voice betraying hurt. A pall seemed to fall over them both, a regret. "I'm cool about everything." And then he was gone, because it was past midnight and Anatole would expect him back from work.

She hates the panic she feels. Has she lost Anatole for this? Is that what she wants? Part of her thinks: she's put up with Anatole for too long, she's played his game, now let him play hers. All those nights talking about *his* crushes, worrying about *his* love life. Somehow, she thinks, hers always disappeared into the cracks, hers weren't worth talking about. She feels resentment—how she's always been so careful not to do anything that would hurt him, how she's never said a word about Chris, not even a hint—no matter what it cost *her*. Suddenly she's worked herself into being furious with Anatole. He goes his own way, never thinking twice about her, about her needs or wants— he's really, when you get down to it, callous, insensitive, completely self-centered. And she's martyred herself to him. That's what it is, really, a martyrdom. He's been safe, he's part of that whole retreat from real life that started in New York. Well now, all of a sudden, here's Leigh—all of a sudden she's standing with him high above Poughkeepsie, in the gathering night, on the wreckage of a magnificent bridge.

His tenderness with her, the care he took with her body, as if it was something to be treasured, something beautiful, even miraculous—she hasn't felt anything like that, she has to admit it, in years. The memory of it makes a thrill as strong as gin slide through her. Still, she doesn't know what she wants to happen anymore. It can't work out, can it? They'll make love, they'll grow tired of each other, Leigh will disappear—ten years later, will it have been worth it? Will she wake in the night and miss him?

She thinks about the salt point, that mysterious, elusive moment of change Leigh read to them about from the newspaper: how this rain will push it farther from Poughkeepsie. Or is it closer?

The rainstorm eddies over the sleeping city, pensive—pausing to reconsider, double back, its motion random as memory. What do storms forget? What life that has passed them by do they seek to renew, to challenge, to accuse? It's enough that they encompass whole landscapes, mar dreams, connect sleepers in a design that's never clear, never complete.

A rumble of thunder jars him from a dream, he lies in a sort of stupor while lightning—so distant it yields no thunder, only a sort of grumbling—flits in ghastly strokes about the room. For a few minutes he can't tell what's going on, whether it's a continuation of the dream he's in, or whether, perhaps worse, this is what waking's like. The news comes to them at twilight. They're standing on the front lawn, darkness is falling, only more quickly than it does in actual life—a downpour of darkness. They can barely see each other. A man in a bowler hat rides an old-fashioned bicycle slowly up the street, and Anatole thinks, calmly but sadly, oh, right, he's read about it being this way, the nuclear winter, here it is. Bombs have been exploded over New York City, this is the fallout. And he can feel it as it falls, it pricks his skin like grains of sand—

He's sweating, icy, prickling sweat. Beside him, mouth open, breathing sweetly, Leigh sleeps his easy sleep.

"You *talk* in your sleep," Leigh kids him sometimes. "You cry out sometimes."

"I dream about the end of the world," Anatole tells him.

"Oh God, you should know what *I* dream about," Leigh says. "Then you wouldn't complain."

Anatole raises himself on his elbow and studies Leigh. They've slept together like this twenty even thirty times, he still can't get over the torment. It's as if an angel lies down beside him every night—if he were to reach out to touch it, to prove to himself it really is there, that God really has sent this sign that the world means something, then there'd be nothing there. It's part of the bargain—you have to believe, and the instant that's not enough—well, then there's nothing. He finds himself remembering stories the nuns told him in elementary school—Fatima, the children in the field who saw the Virgin Mary sitting in the branches of a tree. As a child he believed all that, then as an adolescent he could no longer believe it—now, lying beside Leigh, he wonders if he finally understands. How they must have known it was only a hallucination they were seeing, a body that wasn't really there, that existed only in their imagination, in the part of them that wanted to see a vision so intensely that it *had* to happen. And even knowing it was nothing but an accident of tangled branches, noonday sun, they couldn't move, they had to watch God's Mother sitting placidly in an apple tree. They fall on their knees, miracles happen anyway, cures are performed, the shrine is built.

Our Boy of the Mall.

Anatole can't stand it. He can't stand saints, shrines, the Virgin Mary, miracles. He lives inside them, he can never free himself.

Careful not to jar Leigh's sleep, he glides from the bed, wafts out into the living room to sit among the debris of beer bottles and water crackers and Jarlsberg and kippered herring Leigh feasted on when he got home from work. "I'm starved," he said. "I'm famished."

"Where were you?" Anatole asked, regretting it the moment he said it.

"Oh, around. Out on some errands, then I met a friend for a drink."

"You didn't work tonight?"

"They called earlier, they didn't need me tonight."

Anatole sits in the armchair Leigh curled in to consume his snack. Was he just imagining, or did Leigh seem different? Anatole likes to think he's supersensitive to the boy's moods, that he follows them avidly. Usually Leigh eats so little, he dabbles in his food even when Anatole takes him to expensive restaurants like Le Pavillion, and La Trattoria across the river in New Paltz: What brings it on, this sudden hunger? What despair or triumph? Or is he only hungry? Anatole hates these moments when Leigh's life extends beyond him into territories he can't follow. It tells him how little he can know about anything. It isolates him in the old futility. And he can't stop it. Every day Leigh lives fills him with more and more that Anatole can't know about him.

A long low rumble of thunder, a shudder convulsing the hills that hem the Hudson into its valley. In the distance, sirens rise and fall, almost peaceful in their fatalism. Things that aren't really there, but that make all the difference. It seems to Anatole that if he could think that through thoroughly enough, he could figure out something important.

The two Puerto Rican boys are nervy, restless—they stalk the room like animals newly caged up. Chris is nervous too, he smokes to hide it, leaning back against the battered bureau, arms crossed, as aloof from the boys, the filthy room, as he can make himself. He watches them, these teenagers he's picked up. Dark-haired, slender, they could almost be brothers. They claim they're eighteen, but Chris is sure they're no more than sixteen. They're cool but skittish with him, and he admires that. Kids like these are infinite in their cool. It becomes a kind of dead-end wisdom—but who says wisdom has to lead anywhere?

They don't know what he wants, he isn't their usual kind of john. He impresses them, in some way. Perhaps, after all, this is his best milieu. He hasn't had time to wear thin, he's all appearance and assurance. To these boys he seems perfect—though even they can detect that it's a perfection going slightly to seed. A year ago, two years ago, he was at his peak. Already the decline's set in. Young as they are, they can barely distinguish signs of decay, easily forgettable, but once you know they're there, they're there.

He's always able to pick up the best-looking hustlers. They flock to him. Were he to come down more often, he'd perhaps be legendary.

In the small room the two boys strut and preen for him. They thrust out their hips, they run their hands over their smooth stomachs. These are actions that have become habitual with them. They no longer notice what they do—their bodies just react to being in a room with a john.

They wear dirty jeans, dirty T-shirts, brand-new white high tops. Their thin brown arms are covered with track marks they make no effort to conceal. The prettier of the two has a tattoo on his left arm: an ornate cross, entwined with roses.

They don't know what to do next. Money talks. They're waiting for Money to say something.

"You guys friends?" Chris asks. He doesn't know their names, he doesn't want to know. They were hanging out in a doorway when he walked by—he caught the eye of the one with the tattoo, the really attractive one. He slowed to see if one would ask him for a light. And he did. Chris has done it before. He knows what will happen. The script is limited.

They shrug at his question. Sure, they'll be best friends if he wants them to be. Any fantasy you want, man.

"I like friends who make out," he tells them matter-of-factly. His voice doesn't belong to him. It's a voice he's heard somewhere before, that he's imitating. It's precise and measured, the voice of a bad actor in a forgotten film. They glance at each other. "Go on, make out," he tells them. "Just pretend I'm not here. Pretend like it's a movie." They hesitate. Then the taller boy grabs the other boy by the head and kisses him on the mouth. It's rough, even angry. Neither of them likes doing this, Chris can see. But they do it. They do a passable job of faking a romantic kiss. Their hands move over each other's bodies, cupping buttocks, massaging stomachs, rubbing crotches. They don't like this at all, but their bodies like it. They both have hard-ons whether they like it or not. Kneeling, the taller boy gently, almost tenderly unzips the other boy's jeans. He reaches in and pulls out the boy's cock.

"Go on, suck it," Chris tells him. Hesitating, he touches his mouth to its tip. He opens up and lets it slide in. The boy grips his shoulders, throws his head back and closes his eyes dreamily. His black hair falls down into his eyes. He's far away. Perhaps he imagines it's his girlfriend blowing him. Perhaps he only imagines being dead.

The kneeling boy becomes more active. His mouth makes squelching sounds around the standing boy's cock. He grips the backs of the boy's thighs.

"Okay," Chris says, "okay, that's fine. Now get undressed."

The boy seems relieved to have postponed this just a little longer. Awkwardly—and yet they are graceful as untamed animals—they undress. Their cocks flop about, excited, blood-gorged, living a life of their own.

They stand at uneasy attention. Chris inspects both of them but he doesn't touch them. "Now make love," he says. "Like you mean it."

He feels nothing. Just that these are two bodies like his own with which he has a distant affinity. They reek of sweat as they grapple, embrace, as they sixty-nine on the sagging, putrid bed. Their scent fills the room the way a fart fills a room. It's just a spectacle—these cocks plunging and withdrawing from avid mouths. The boys can't help themselves. They're excited, they spill into each other's mouths with groans and shouts. In spite of themselves, they've done an act of intimacy, something that feels almost, to Chris as he watches them, like love.

Once every couple of months he does this—feelings of mortality, of futility, eventually overcome the careful pattern of identical days. He sanctions these corruptions, these participations in death, as the rent he owes for his continued existence.

He's moved in spite of himself at these grapplings on the bed. Not excited: he doesn't have even the stirrings of an erection. He feels a sadness and emptiness beyond anything he usually encounters. He feels clinical, distanced; no qualms about the act he's sponsored and provoked.

It makes him feel like a ghost. He drove all the way to New York City on a Tuesday afternoon for this.

"Don't you want nothing?" the younger boy asks him. He's slipping back into his clothes. "I'm not no faggot, but like I'm telling you, nobody does it the way I do it."

Chris shakes his head. He unfolds two twenty-dollar bills from his back pocket. "Get out of here," he tells them.

They dress quickly, alert with each other—did these two boys really just make love? It seems incomprehensible to Chris that he can have financed an act of tenderness in the world so brutally, so peremptorily as this.

They're just kids. They're happy they've gotten the money so easily. In fifteen minutes they'll be shooting up in an empty lot. In five years they'll both be dead. Chris feels tender, he feels hopeless and indifferent toward that. What can he do? He likes the idea they'll be dead soon. He respects them for that.

When they've left, he stands at the window and stares out through the grimy pane down at the intersection of Lexington and Twenty-eighth. Traffic moves in the street as if nothing has occurred. People walk by, purposefully or aimlessly. An old black woman, wrapped in enormous filthy shawls that nearly obscure her, fishes in a trash basket for tin cans. From somewhere comes the sound of a jackhammer. He hasn't noticed it before, but now in the emptiness of the room its sound is somehow fateful, inescapable. It starts, stops, starts again.

He moves from the window to the bed. The covers are tangled where the tricks wrestled in their lovemaking. Their come hasn't dried yet, the dingy fabric's still damp in spots, as if someone has splattered wax from a candle on it. He shudders. Do they change the sheets from one occupant to another in these rooms that rent by the hour? He feels filthy, though he's touched nothing, he's kept himself clean. It's not that he's afraid of AIDS, certainly not with the obsessive sort of fear that haunts, say, Anatole—in fact, when he thinks about the disease, he finds something compelling in the idea of it. Don't fight it, the body tells its defenses—whatever it is, marauding virus, insidious cancer, allow it in, give it a home. Let it define you however it will. No longer will the body remain immaculate, aloof in the isolation of its immunities. It's a physical metaphor, AIDS. The best die from it, the bravest. Trapped in the terrified ego the rest of the world knows as Chris Havilland, he's immune. He's given up being touched by anything.

You're absurd, Chris, he tells himself, straightening the covers of the bed, careful not to touch the boys' spilled come. Somehow he feels better having witnessed all this and lived through it. It quells the things that panic him—the recollected sound of Leigh's voice through all these days, the thought of Leigh and Anatole together. Things that can only come to nothing.

The jackhammer's stopped again. Like an echo the stale radiator below the window comes to life, clanks feebly two or three times. The room feels like a tomb, a mausoleum of dried semen, tears, the tender wastes of human futility. Shutting the door behind him—the room, those boys cease to exist in that instant—Chris feels grave, he feels moved by the meaninglessness. In the dingy lobby, a stricken sorrowful old man sits in the phone booth. He doesn't pick up the phone to dial, he only sits as if waiting for some call he knows will not come—as if he has sat there waiting for days.

He drives back on the Taconic, keeping the Mitsubishi at an even eighty, making the two-hour trip in an hour and fifteen minutes. He's home before dark. The bareness of his apartment soothes him. He likes the cream-colored pictureless walls, the bright maple floors. He likes it that it's impossible to reconcile this cube of light with that hotel room in New York. It tells him that his life remains ordered, that he really can maintain this island of calm regardless of the price extracted. He remembers the first day he saw it—the rooms completely empty, a summer afternoon, sunlight filling the space. It looked huge, overflowing with light. Since then it's never looked so beautiful, so—well, life-affirming. The first piece of furniture began to clutter it. The day he moved in, he watched the apartment get smaller and smaller. Since then, he's thrown out as much as he can. Still, it's too much. Even if he removed everything, his presence alone would clutter it.

Downing a Quaalude with a glass of wine, he lies on the floor and stares at the ceiling. The CD's been programmed for "Loving the

Alien"—an infinite loop, music to fade by: if he died tonight, whoever found him would find that song as well. A requiem. Somehow it comforts him, the post-heroin sadness of David Bowie's voice as it wafts leisurely over the hollow rhythm of drums and marimba.

Sometimes a song will trigger a single memory, elusive as the scent of a flower—the more you try to catch it the more it recedes. It's early April, he's barefoot, he's dancing. There's no music, only the lawn behind Cornell's Risley dorm, that lawn that spills carelessly to the lip of the gorge. He's dancing, and John starts dancing with him. Someone tells him afterward—"You were wonderful, you were so convincing, you two, I was absolutely sure there was music only I couldn't hear it." It terrifies him to have somebody tell him that about him and John.

He hadn't intended to have sex with John—it was just one of those things that happened, John sitting one night on his bed, knees pulled up to his chin, hands massaging his calloused dancer's feet. "I'd like to sleep with you," John told him simply. "We could be really close friends."

"No," Chris said. "I'm sorry. I'm not into that."

"I could seduce you," John coaxed. "It wouldn't be your fault."

John always wore a rolled blue bandanna around his forehead, to keep his long dark hair out of his eyes. Chris didn't know what to say. Sometimes he'd be walking across campus and glimpse his roommate from a distance, his lithe body in tight black pants, black winter coat with a costume jewelry starburst pinned to his breast, and he'd think, My God, my roommate's beautiful.

"What do you say? I really like you, you know. I'm in love with you."

And he started to undress. "Don't," Chris said. But he didn't do anything to stop him. With a kind of wonder—is this me, is this happening?—he watched the slim body emerge from its clothes. When John was naked, he began to undress Chris. Chris allowed himself to be caressed into an erection. John pulled them close, and kissed him on the mouth. "I don't think I want to kiss you," Chris told him. John drew back and looked at him.

"What do you want, then?" His hand continued to play with Chris's penis—Chris sighed and said, "I don't know, John. What do you want me to want?"

Without a word, John slipped down and took Chris's penis in his mouth.

It makes Chris angry and sad to remember—how the next morning, in a blizzard, he took a long walk, miles past the Cornell plantations. He knew he didn't want to be a part of this, he knew it would be an intolerable situation.

"Nobody can know anything about us, okay?" he told John. They lay in each other's arms. "It's got to be a complete secret. The instant it's not, it'll be like it never happened. I won't even acknowledge who you are. That's the rules."

John looked at him sadly, but with a hint of humor—as if it were a challenge. "That's the only way I can keep you?" His finger circled Chris's nipple—Chris felt an unspeakable emptiness, a longing.

"That's the only way."

"It's the rules, then."

Much as he wants to erase it, that winter and spring he'll never forget. He loved John because of the way he moved through the world, the way be drank Campari in the afternoon and smoked clove cigarettes, the way he'd put Palestrina and then the Velvet Underground and then Balinese gamelan on the stereo in the course of a single evening of study and lovemaking. He loved John because John had found a squirrel's tail once and had tacked it to the bulletin board over his desk, where he also had a quote, his motto, which he'd typed out from Ned Rorem's diaries, his bible: "The child says: when I grow up the important part will begin. As a grownup he says: those first lost years were the important part."

Then that spring John's sister Michelle came from Oberlin to visit for the weekend.

Disappear, disappear. Sometimes Chris feels like the monk who's sacrificed everything to a vision that fails to come clear: years pass, he's still waiting, praying in the cloister garden, so rapt in prayer that he doesn't notice the vision when it finally appears before him.

• • •

"Another morning in the city of dreams," Anatole observes for the benefit of Leigh and Lydia as they emerge from Grand Central into the impressive crowds of Forty-second Street. And as if to confirm exactly that . . .

"You're looking marvelous this morning," a slender young black man, purse under his arm, hair flattopped Grace Jones–style, mentions deftly to Leigh as he walks past. Leigh only smiles—apologetically. Anatole touches him lightly on the shoulder when the man is gone. "Everybody's sizing you up," he whispers playfully in his ear. And it's true—men that pass ignore Anatole and Lydia to send a quick appraising glance up and down Leigh's figure. It delights Anatole to be walking in the company of such a golden property.

Lydia comforts Leigh. "Don't worry, we'll protect you."

Leigh seems not quite to know what to say—he basks in the attention and is embarrassed by it. He puts his arm around Lydia and kisses her lightly on the cheek. "Am I sending off the right signals now?" he says.

"You can run but you can't hide," Anatole tells him, patting him on the cheek, happy to show off like this to Lydia.

In a little restaurant they pause to reinforce themselves with bagels and coffee. That's where it happens—a tremor, in itself fleeting, but with widening repercussions. It comes out casually: at first Anatole doesn't get what they're talking about, he thinks it's a picnic they're *proposing*. "Sure," he says. "Sounds fun."

"No," Leigh tells him. "We've already *gone*. It was last week." Anatole blushes, the way he does when he says something stupid; he also feels the familiar-awful sting of ice around his heart.

"Yeah, Leigh called up, he was bored," Lydia hastens to add, as if she's afraid he'll even get a hint of the wrong idea about the whole thing. "We just drove out to the Vanderbilt mansion. It was nice. Real spur-of-the-moment."

"She was surprised," Leigh says. "Since usually when I call I don't have anything to say."

Since usually when I call . . . Anatole doesn't want to hear any more. He hasn't known any of this. It alarms him terribly; he doesn't get into moods, or at least he likes to think he doesn't (Daniel has a different story), but this plunges him into blackness.

He pushes his cup of coffee away, though Leigh and Lydia don't notice, they're too busy—as he sees it—noticing each other. He sits in stunned silence while they banter desultorily about this or that—he doesn't follow, his mind's off on its own spiraling path.

Lydia teases, tapping him on the wrist. "Finish your bagel, so we can go."

He doesn't say anything. He gets up and walks out of the restaurant.

"Hey, Anatole," they both call after him, but he keeps walking. "Here"— Lydia thrusts cash on Leigh—"pay this." And she runs after him.

"Anatole, what the hell's the matter? What's this sudden ice treatment?"

Anatole can't even speak to her. He lets her walk beside him. "Slow down," she tells him. "We'll lose Leigh. He's paying."

"Maybe we *should* lose Leigh," he says, stopping abruptly and looking at her. "Would you like that, Lydia?"

"Don't be stupid, Anatole. What—are you upset because we went on a picnic? Is that what it is? You're getting bent out of shape over *that*? Leigh and I can be friends too, you know. He's not your property. Anyway, *he* called *me* up."

"*Why*, Lydia?" Anatole asks, gripping her by both arms, trying to figure out from her expression exactly what's behind her. He knows, for an instant, why it is he hates women. But now Leigh's with them. "Everything okay?" he asks, so cheerful (it's impossible, isn't it? and yet here he is) that Anatole has to let go of Lydia's arm.

"He just got disoriented," Lydia tells Leigh. Her tone's sly, a little triumphant. "The City's always a shock to his system."

"I'm all right," Anatole tells Leigh. "Let's forget it."

So they walk. They take the subway downtown, they walk the Village a little aimlessly, a little adrift. The mild sunlight of late morning disappears into the chillier overcast of midafternoon. Anatole realizes how lost he feels in the City, what an unfriendly face it turns toward strangers who have no place to go. The streets seem alive with people whose style just shames him. Usually he's not self-conscious, but today he finds himself looking at his passing reflection in every plate-glass window, annoyed how unchic he looks. He hates his haircut, his clothes seem silly, a failure. He's got Poughkeepsie written all over him. Lydia, likewise, seems sadly lacking. Only Leigh fits in, moving into this new setting with nearly perfect ease. Over faded jeans, high-topped Reeboks, he wears a harvest yellow T-shirt many sizes too big, it goes practically to his knees. RELAX, it says in big black letters.

He hates it that he said yes so easily when Leigh suggested yesterday, out of the blue—Leigh lounging barefoot on the sofa, watching a Tarzan movie—"Let's go to the City, let's take Lydia, she'll be fun." All because he felt guilty about not having spent much time with Lydia these past few weeks. Never think you're secure, he reproaches himself, because you aren't. In an instant you can lose everything.

It irks Anatole how, subtly, the conversation as they walk seems always to be taking place away from him. He always seems to be a step or two behind Lydia and Leigh, he doesn't hear what gets said, he's always asking "What?" and having it repeated. Surely it's only his paranoia—that they address their remarks to each other and not to him.

You're overreacting, he tells himself. So they've gone on a picnic, so they talk to each other on the phone. He doesn't want to be in the mood he's in, but he can't help it. Every time Leigh touches Lydia playfully, every remark he addresses to her—it seems charged with new, sullen significance. The advantage is all between Leigh and Lydia. It's your own fault, he accuses as he walks. You're the one who excluded yourself. But now he can't get back in.

An antique store attracts Lydia's attention: Windsor chairs, a table with a variety of plates stacked in display have been set out on the sidewalk. She and Leigh pause at the window to browse. He can't hear what they say to one another, but the small adjustments in their bodies—they shift toward each other like dancers—communicate an ease, a familiarity. These aren't strangers—they've spent time together, they know each other. Lydia's wearing a simple black dress, pearls, her peroxided hair looks slightly frizzed in the dead light of afternoon. The thought that Leigh might actually want to make love to Lydia wreaks havoc on Anatole's precarious sense of the world.

With half a dozen steps he could rejoin them, reenter their banter; but he stands on the curb, hands in his pockets, and watches them: they're strangers, he doesn't know them—they're just a couple he's glimpsed as he strolls a city street. Leigh looks back at him, a glance over his shoulder—they're going into the store, they disappear into it, out of his life, he'll never see them again, that couple who momentarily interested him. He could walk away and be free, they can hurt him no more than any couple glimpsed for an instant can hurt him.

"Anatole." Lydia stands at the door of the shop. It annoys him that she's raised her voice to call to him. Leave me alone, he thinks. He hasn't been this irritable since he was six years old. "Come in here. You've *got* to see this lamp."

He hates it that he can't yield, but he can't. He just sighs, shrugs his shoulders, shakes his head—it conveys weariness, boredom. "I don't want to go in there," he says. "Look around as much as you want. I just want to stand out here."

Framed in the doorway, she looks at him for a moment, her mouth thinning into a bitter line, then she turns abruptly and goes back into the store.

"Are you feeling okay?" Leigh asks gingerly when they rejoin him a few minutes later on the street.

"I've got this headache, is all," Anatole tells him. "Antique stores depress me."

"Anatole," Lydia chides him, "you *love* antique stores. We've spent literally whole days in antique stores," she explains to Leigh.

"Look, don't nag me, okay?"

It makes them both withdraw a little from him, lapse back into a camaraderie with each other. They were courting him back into their company, he realizes; they wanted things to be okay—but he's stupid, his jealousy imprisons him in this standoffishness like a palpable force. As they stroll—they've cut across Thirteenth Street, they head down Broadway—he continues to trail just slightly behind them. The city harrows him this afternoon, a nightmare labyrinth of grotesques.

Africans hawk watches, combs, sunglasses, umbrellas. A man standing on a corner sells leather bullwhips. In a crowded crosswalk he bumps shoulders with a woman walking the opposite direction. "Excuse me," she says in a loud, belligerent voice. He turns around—she's standing in the middle of the crosswalk, hands on her hips. "Excuse me, mister," she shouts at him. "Are you going to apologize or what?" He feels particularly fragile, vulnerable: for an instant he's ready to burst into tears. But he only walks on, ignoring her, catching up with Lydia and Leigh, who haven't heard anything.

"And this, you see, is Mecca," Lydia is telling Leigh. Anatole comes out of his stupor of jealousy to find them standing on the sidewalk outside Astor Place. "We should all get haircuts for souvenirs," Lydia suggests. "Daniel and Anatole want to turn Reflexion into Poughkeepsie's version of this. Right, Anatole?"

Beautiful kids line up on the sidewalk, outside the door, to wait their turn for a haircut. Just inside, a man Anatole's age directs traffic: whenever a chair's vacant, he directs the next client that way. It's an assembly line, these kids are being inducted into some funky army of the beautiful and damned.

All he can manage to say is, "I can't believe it. My day off, and you drag me to a haircutter's? Are you crazy? Let's get the hell out of here."

"I thought you liked Astor Place," Leigh says. Anatole waves his hand in front of his face, turns away. But he can't help eyeing two boys who've just come out of Astor Place. They both look about twenty. Dressed in the latest Generra gear, one has spiked, peroxided hair—a long filigree of silver hangs from his left ear. The other's jet-black hair's been shaved on the sides, left long on top; his ear's busy with five or six earrings that climb in barbaric, beautiful succession from his lobe halfway to the crest of his ear. Give me a dozen clients like that, Anatole thinks.

The streets are simply full of boys who challenge Leigh's beauty. This ain't Poughkeepsie: Leigh's clothes, apparently so cutting-edge, seem just a little off; the haircut Anatole gave him looks already unfashionable. Suddenly there's something touching, even pathetic about him in a way Anatole hasn't seen before: he wants to protect him from all this competition, the cool calculating beauty of these New York boys who always know exactly where the edge is going to be, not only this afternoon but tomorrow as well. He's no longer the impervious heartbreaking angel, Leigh: he's just another pretty kid in a city that loses pretty kids by the dozens.

Late afternoon, exhausted by the aimlessness of their daylong wandering, they come to rest in a cavernous, nearly deserted wine bar. Behind the bar, a cruvinet pumps nitrogen into a row of opened bottles. The wine list's staggering, so are the prices.

Lydia downs her first wine defiantly. "So what's the game, Anatole?" she asks wearily.

"The game?"

"I mean, all day today . . . Moping around. Throwing your little temper tantrum."

"Look, we don't have to talk about it." To Anatole it feels like an inexcusable breach of decorum to bring this up.

"I think we do." Lydia's adamant. "Leigh thinks we do."

Anatole looks at Leigh—who only shrugs, tries to smile amiably, staying on both sides at once. Is he bored, worried, uncomfortable? He's drinking two four-dollar glasses to each of their one.

Lydia's not to be deterred. Wandering around all day with no particular direction's exhausted her, her nerves are frayed. "It really pisses me off," she says, "that you think you can set ground rules about who can know who, and what the conditions are. What gives you that right?"

"I'm *not* setting rules. You can do whatever you want, it doesn't bother me."

"Oh yeah, sure. You'll just pout and make everybody miserable. You're very manipulative, Anatole. You're very successful at it. I'll give you that. You don't have any illusions in that quarter, at least."

"I didn't think I had illusions about anything." Anatole's mild.

Lydia laughs. "Come again? Anyway, that's not the point. I feel like you've been sabotaging our fun today. Doing everything you can to make it seem little. To make yourself seem like this oh-so-noble suffering martyr. It's not a fair position to put either me or Leigh in. I just think you should know that."

"Does Leigh have anything to say about this?" Anatole turns, hyperpolite, toward Leigh—then is sorry he's done so, Leigh looks so perturbed with both of them.

"I'm staying out of it," Leigh defers. "I'm just the audience."

"Can you see that this isn't my fight?" Anatole tries to clear himself, to salvage something with Leigh in case everything goes crash.

But it doesn't seem to work: Leigh stands up abruptly, militantly. "I'm going to walk around a little on my own," he announces. "I don't want to be here. This whole thing makes me very uncomfortable." There's no way to read the tone of his voice.

Suddenly Anatole knows with certainty—Leigh's going to walk out that door, he'll never see him again. He knew it would happen like this, he always knew—he's just surprised that it's here so unexpectedly.

"Don't go," he says. He reaches out his hand but doesn't touch Leigh at all. "We'll get off this subject, I promise. You're not the only one who's had enough of it."

"Look, I don't want to get involved."

"You *are* involved, Leigh," Lydia tells him flatly. "Like it or not."

He looks at her only for an instant. "I'm staying out of it," he reiterates. He's polite but firm. This is the way children are taught to say no to strangers: he's just seen Anatole and Lydia as the strangers they really are. He backs away with a reassuring smile still on his face. He wants out.

"Like I said," Anatole tells him—it's for Lydia's benefit too—"we've *finished* discussing it."

Leigh just looks at him. "No you haven't, Anatole." He sounds annoyed: Anatole's never heard Leigh sound annoyed with him, and it hurts.

"So what's happening?" Lydia asks briskly. She's always been an organizer: it's something Anatole despises about her. "You want to walk around a little? Give me and Anatole a chance to chat? We'll meet you in, say, an hour."

"Sure, fine. An hour. Where?"

"Here. We'll be here."

"I'll be back. If I'm not, well . . ." Then without another word

he's out the door, a stranger you glimpse never to glimpse again—
and looking angry himself, as if *he's* the one who's thrown a tantrum
that needs to be walked off.

My God, Lydia thinks, watching Leigh's back disappear, my God.
She's not sure what she's provoked with this attack on Anatole—but
it'll have to suffice; the day's been intolerable, she blames Leigh for
occasioning it, she blames Anatole for being Anatole. She hates that
she's caught in the middle, and she thinks how the whole thing's
impossible, how she should just get out now.

But at the same time she's defiant. Fuck it, she tells herself. This
boy she's made love to every day for the past week, this boy whose
body she knows intimately, every crevice and curve, just as he knows
her body—she shivers to recall how he rimmed her, his tongue rough
as a cat's, how he fingered her till she screamed with vertigo, that
emptiness fuller than anything, how he's spilled himself milky and
pungent into her mouth, Anatole's Boy of the Mall: she's not going
to walk around with him, Anatole or no Anatole, and pretend those
things didn't happen. She's just not going to do it.

"Okay," Anatole tells her. "Be brutal. Otherwise there's no
hope."

"Don't count too much on it anyway." It's odd: the instant Leigh
walks out the door, it's hard to be combative, they're friends again,
they understand each other. In an instant Lydia's prepared to forgive
anything. But then she remembers.

"I'm upset," Anatole tells her. "I won't lie. You know I don't
hide these things very well. I don't like my friends carrying on behind
my back, is all. I mean, I have no idea what you and Leigh, well, I
have no idea what's going on, but—"

"Do you want to know?"

"Do I?" He looks at her wistfully.

"Oh, Anatole, I don't know. I don't know why we keep on being
friends if this is all we can think of to do to each other."

"You and Leigh are having an affair," he says simply.

"We're having an affair, if you want to put it that way, yes. I'm
sorry."

"Oh, don't be sorry." As if to say, It's only my life. "These things happen. I've read about them in the newspaper." He smiles. She knows him well enough to know he's coming apart inside. Still, she likes it that he's upset enough with her not to make a scene. He has good qualities, if you can untangle them from everything else.

"It just sort of happened, Anatole. I wouldn't have let it happen if I'd known it would hurt you like this."

It makes him laugh. He pats her hand fondly. "Lydia, I can't *imagine* saying anything like that and meaning it. I really don't think you can either."

"Okay—I did know it would hurt you. But God damn it, Anatole, I have to live life too. I mean, it's not as if I went out fishing for Leigh. It was his idea. You might say, he seduced me."

She's aware how pathetic that image must look; she wishes she could retract it, but there it is. She thinks what they must have looked like to that Cessna as it circled, aloof as any observing angel.

Anatole doesn't say anything; he orders more wine from a svelte young waiter who seems utterly uninterested in the discord of their private lives. "Four dollars a glass. You know, we're spending a fortune here."

"Breaking up was never cheap."

"Here's to drinking away the fortune. I really don't know what to tell you, Lydia. I've been walking around all day today getting ready for this. I knew it was going to happen."

"Anatole—try to see this clearly. It was Leigh who made the moves."

"You just tangoed?"

"I never turn down the chance to dance. You know that. Besides, how do you think Leigh feels right now?"

"Really, I wouldn't have the faintest idea."

For once, she thinks, he actually looks somewhat handsome. It must be the pain.

"That's funny," she says. "Neither would I. Sometimes I wonder if I like him very much."

"Of course you do. You're in love with him."

"That's you, Anatole. My feelings are a little more complicated.

It's not fair, is it? I think I probably feel we'd all be better off if he didn't come back. If he just disappeared."

"Him too?"

"Him most of all."

She doesn't know how much to tell Anatole. She long ago gave up trying to be merely truthful, saying things as they came to her. Does she say, "Leigh talks about you all the time, about how sweet, how cool you are, how he's never met anybody quite like you"? Does she mention how he does this to the point where she occasionally suspects he's really more interested in having somebody to talk to about Anatole with than somebody to fuck? Though she's long ago come to her own conclusions—that when you get down to it, it's always fucking that matters, not talking.

"Him most of all," she says again, and she means it.

The bar begins to fill, the waiter ignores them for more novel patrons. An hour's passed, an hour and a half. We've said all we can to each other—this is what their silence seems to communicate—we've said all we can, we've arrived at whatever reconciliation's possible for the moment. Now it only remains for Leigh's return to upset the balance once again. If it were just us, we could be as we were before. We could clear things up with a talk, there've been misunderstandings in the past. But we can't be as we were before, because we don't want to be. That's what each comes to in silence. They want Leigh to come back, whatever the price.

And for an instant it seems he really is back. Anatole starts, glimpsing the familiar figure. But it's not him, it's another of those New York City boys, full of beauty and confidence. In fact—the coincidence arrests him—it's one of the boys that caught his eye at Astor Place, he's sure of it. The waiter shows him to the table next to where he and Lydia are sitting. "There'll be two of us," he says, his voice delicate, sweet—completely at odds with the barbaric panoply of earrings that thrillingly mar his ear.

There's always this purity about boys Anatole doesn't know, the ones he glimpses in supermarkets or on sidewalks and falls instantly in love with. Yet he refuses even now to believe that the only right thing to do, the only incorrupt thing, is to watch a boy like Leigh dance alone at Bertie's, feel the emptiness and loneliness, and then resolutely turn your back and let it go at that, realizing that life can never be any more than the sum of these turnings away.

That's what Chris would do. But he's not Chris, he can't withdraw from the world. The instant he turns his back on those moments there's nothing left, there's only the pain of loss the nuns used to tell him was the true meaning of Hell.

"Sorry I'm late." The boy with the multiple earrings has been joined by the other boy from Astor Place, the one with the silver filigree.

"Oh, you're not late. You're just in time. Did you see Sarah?"

"I talked to her on the phone. I thought we might drop by later. Or we could hit the baths."

The first boy covers the other boy's hand with his.

"We could hit the baths," he agrees, "whatever else we decide to do."

The thought occurs to Anatole: should he have warned Leigh in advance? Watch out for me, for us—you'll get in over your head. Though it's not clear who's in over whose head. That's the way Chris lives, warning everyone who gets close of the lightning that may strike. Never touch anything, never make a mark. But Anatole can't live that way. The world's too lonely a place: he has to touch things, he has to put his arms around them.

He understands, though, something about Chris he hasn't understood before.

"You're incorrigible," the first boy teases.

"No I'm not. I just know I'm going to die. That's all it is."

The waiter knows the two. "Did you see Bob?" he asks. They shake their heads as he sets glasses of white wine in front of them. "He was looking for you. He made his connection."

"Cool. We'll stop by. How much?"

"A hundred, I think."

"That's cool."

Anatole can't quite keep his eyes off them, they seem so alien and enticing. He has a fantasy—it occurs to him at odd moments, he enjoys it though at the same time it makes him uneasy, he suppresses it as best he can. What if Leigh died? What if he was killed? Anatole can't quite account—he doesn't *want* to account—for the poignant pleasure that thought wakens in him. It would have the virtue of making things simple, wouldn't it? Leigh would be his, no one would ever know whatever had or hadn't happened between them.

"Don't worry, they'll never close the baths," the first boy is insisting. "I mean, my God, what would we do?"

"I don't know. I feel like time's running out, somehow. It's like, I want to get everything in while I still can."

Sometimes Anatole wonders just where the elusive point is, where you stop being sane.

I envy him, Lydia thinks, watching Anatole as he alternates glances at the two stylish boys at the next table and at the door, waiting for Leigh—who's late, who should've been back half an hour ago. He fingers the stem of his glass nervously—she doesn't know what he's thinking, but thinks she can guess. She envies the rapt anguish of his love for Leigh, the tornadoes of feeling it unleashes in him—haven't they all been victims of that storm today? It's something that's always mystified, often provoked her about him, the way he's so willing to be swept away—lighthouse that invites the storm, its dangerous passionate waves. Whereas her life, whatever its adventures, its craziness, runs close to the ground, stays matter-of-fact, far inland.

She regrets that however much she likes Leigh, however much his body excites her, he's not an angel. He's just a kid with identity problems, a runaway, a bit of a hustler who's careful to let you know only what he wants you to know. She'd just as soon have sex with one of those two punks incongruously sipping glasses of expensive wine—though their conversation, filtered through the din of the restaurant, would seem to indicate they're interested in other things. Did she really hear the term *fist fucking*? Did one of them really just say, "I'm not sure my guts can take much more. I was bleeding this morning"? New York, as always, too much.

She remembers a conversation she had with Chris: Anatole's a cultist, he claimed. Watch him, you'll see. Then it seemed an arbitrary assertion, a bit of subterranean annoyance with Anatole finding its way to Chris's normally unblemished surface. Now she begins to wonder if it might after all be true, the source of some deep imbalance in him, and strength she has no access to.

She wonders what kind of perspective, if any, Anatole has on the world. He's a great awkward bird, swooping high into the dizzying air, then plunging, never certain of catching himself in flight before it's too late. And one day it will be too late. She can see that even now, as she sits here: she can all but see him in free-fall. It scares her, it scares her for his sake. It also, she feels, puts her to shame. She'll always have perspective, she'll never know his exhilarating, humiliating brand of flight. Poor Anatole: For me Leigh's a fuck. For him, the stars would sing, the heavens would open were he allowed a single touch. But of course the stars *don't* sing, the heavens are vast and impressive but empty, empty, empty.

When Leigh comes trailing through the door—it's six-thirty, he's an hour late; RELAX, his T-shirt commands—it's clear he's known they'll be waiting for him, that neither of them would dream, no matter what happened, no matter how late he was, of leaving without him. It's a gamble he's taken with himself, and he's won. The earring boys at the next table pause to size him up appreciatively, though he's oblivious of them.

He's only eighteen years old, Lydia tells herself with something like awe. He's got us. He's got all of us.

"It's shocking," Chris tells him. "I mean, think about it, Anatole. You're twenty-five years old. You should have some kind of inner resources. You should be impervious to somebody like Leigh. Aren't I right in finding this whole thing a little mysterious? Even a little embarrassing?"

They linger, sitting in the dim Milanese, over the remains of their meal. They drink espresso with sambuca. When the espresso's gone, they fill their cups with straight sambuca.

Putting the last week into words—it encloses it, tames the storm, all these wounding incidents begin to seem more like a story you might read than like something that can wreck your life. The evening with Chris makes Anatole long for what he sees as those simpler days, when he was first in love with Chris. Everything seems to get harder, not easier, with the passing years: he regrets not having savored his love for Chris to its fullest, now when he can't trick himself back into it, when the wrenching image of Leigh lodges in him and won't be shaken loose no matter what sort of mental contortions he undertakes.

"Do you think I'm crazy?" he wonders. "I mean, to let him go on staying at my place. Does it make any sense?"

"I think you're crazy, yes. But then, this whole thing seems a little unbelievable to me. You haven't exactly managed to explain *why* he wants to fuck Lydia but doesn't want to sleep with her at night. Or why he wants to sleep with you but not touch you. Can't you see that's a little strange?"

"I don't know what he wants," Anatole says.

"Sounds like he doesn't either. But what do *you* want? You really don't want him out, do you? Despite everything."

"No, I guess I don't."

Chris shakes his head. "People's lives are beyond me," he says. "I mean, how they even keep on living." He's angry with Anatole for allowing himself to be put in a situation that's so patently untenable, and out of which he can reap nothing but frustration and hurt. It depresses Chris that Anatole's needs seem so thwarted, so self-destructive.

"Leigh doesn't want out," Anatole tries to explain, as if that's any explanation at all. "I don't know what it means," he admits, "but I think he needs me. If that makes any sense." How to explain to Chris, how even to begin to convey the luminous tenor of their confrontation, his and Leigh's, that night they got back from New York?

"I guess you'll want to be spending tonight at Lydia's?" he asked Leigh. They waited in the Poughkeepsie train station for a taxi, Lydia'd slipped into the rest room for a moment, it was his first chance to acknowledge alone to Leigh that he knew everything.

"Why should I?" Leigh looking at him seriously, even puzzled.

It was something Anatole couldn't answer. "I don't understand," he said.

"Look," Leigh told him as Lydia approached, as simultaneously the yellow cab pulled up to the front of the station, "I'm going home with you. Unless you're kicking me out."

Anatole shook his head. "I'm not kicking you out," he said.

"What are you two conspiring about?" Lydia looking smug.

"Nothing," Leigh told her. "Let's go. Two addresses," he instructed the driver, taking complete charge of them both. "The lady's going to May Street, then we want to go to South Hamilton."

And how completely foreign and strange it felt, coming back to the apartment now that everything had changed. How they stood facing each other just inside the front door—too tense even to sit down. "I'm very tired," Leigh told him. "Days like this wear me out. But I want to talk to you for just a minute."

"Well, I think we *need* to talk."

"You know what I think about talking. You know how much I think talking's what got us into all this in the first place. I told you in the beginning you didn't know anything about me."

"But I did know, Leigh, I did know. Look, if you want to spend the night with Lydia—"

"I want to sleep here with you. It's important to me. Everything can stay like it was."

"I'm really confused, Leigh—I have to tell you that. I just don't know what to think about anything right now. I don't know what I want things to be. I don't know what I can stand for things to be. I just . . . well, look, you're welcome to whatever I have. I can't do anything else."

"Anatole," Leigh said quietly. And he walked over to him and put his arms around him, they embraced like that for a full minute, neither saying a word, bodies swaying ever so slightly as if in tune with their heartbeats, the pulse of their night. "I'm very tired," Leigh repeated, drawing away tenderly. "I'm going to go to sleep."

The waitress clears away the espresso pot, the sambuca bottle, she leaves their bill on a little plastic platter. "I don't expect you to understand," Anatole tells Chris. "If somebody told me all this, I'd think they were crazy too. A masochist. I'm really not into suffering, I don't like it. That's not why I'm doing all this."

"Then why, pray tell?"

"Because if I didn't I'd kill myself."

"Really?" Chris isn't sure whether to be ironic or concerned.

"Maybe. That's what just came into my head. I might believe it. It's as close to explaining things as I can get." It amazes Anatole, it moves him how tonight, for once, they've dropped their irony, their manner with each other, completely. It's the kind of talk he used to dream of having with Chris, straightforward and honest. Now here it is. You get exactly what you want, Anatole's always suspected, only when you get it it's no longer what you want, you need something else.

He wishes he could be in love with Chris again. At least Chris respected certain things, at least he kept the lines of demarcation clear. Chris would never have slept with Lydia, he'd have been too sensitive, too alert to the ways friendships allow vulnerabilities. He's trusted Chris in a way he can't trust Leigh. But he doesn't want Chris now, he wants Leigh—it's Leigh he'd give anything to be having this conversation with. It's a grim thing to realize, it tells him more than he wants to know about the heart's frailty.

"So where are you going?" Chris asks him as they stand in the parking lot.

Anatole shrugs. Leigh's out with Lydia tonight—they've gone to try an Indian restaurant that's just opened down on the South Road. He's told Chris that. "Home, I guess. I'll knit, watch TV, sit up late for Leigh. I feel like somebody's mother."

"You're so stupid," Chris tells him affectionately. "Come on, we'll go to Bertie's. You'll forget about Leigh."

"I *can't* forget about him when he sleeps in the same bed with me."

"We'll work on that too."

"I should kick him out, shouldn't I?"

"You should kick him out. It's a choice of saving you or him. I like you, Anatole, you're my friend: I don't want to see you go down with the ship."

It's somehow the tenderest thing Chris has ever said to him. It fills Anatole with a warmth that's partly just the wine, the sambuca, that's partly the sense that even now everything may not be lost. He's glad Chris isn't a part of this whole sordid escapade, for once the aloofness that so maddens him in Chris seems a saving quality. If he couldn't talk to somebody about all this, somebody who stood outside it all, objective and disinterested—and surely Chris is that—it would simply kill him. He'd die, if nothing else, of loneliness.

Bertie's is crowded, it's a Thursday night, Halloween night. The management's made lackluster attempts to acknowledge the holiday—there're a couple of pumpkins on the bar, their hollowness lit by unsteady candles; four or five people have gotten themselves up in costume, but the effect is more desolate than festive. Chris reflects—he hasn't been here much recently, none of them have. Strange to think they were once coming here in trio every night of the week—days impossible to retrieve now that it's everybody for himself. He feels particularly estranged from both Anatole and Lydia. Okay, he thinks, perhaps it's time for everybody to move on; nothing lasts forever, it's part of the physics of friendships, alliances, whatever it might be they perpetrated for a while among themselves.

Nevertheless, hearing Anatole spell out Lydia's involvement with Leigh affects Chris in ways he hasn't foreseen. He'd never let Anatole see this, but he can't clear himself of a sudden jealousy of Lydia. He surprises himself—how much he's upset by the mental picture Anatole conjures of Lydia and Leigh making love. Why? he asks himself, cringing from the terrible possibility that suggests itself—that the two times he's been with Leigh have touched him in some way, that there are times when he wakes in the middle of the night to think about him.

He remembers, from Anatole's brunch, how he offered Leigh—"Stop by the store someday, I'll give you a discount on some records." Nothing heightens his sense of his own absurdity more than to admit to himself that he's waited every day since then for Leigh to walk in the store.

All evening they loop back to the subject of Leigh.

"I don't mean to keep talking about him," Anatole apologizes. He twists restlessly in his seat. Bertie's is filling up, its usual mix of ambitious young IBMers and garishly dead-end punks.

"Go on, get it out of your system," Chris invites him. They've ordered double scotches, they sit at a table in the corner, where they have a vantage of the whole room. "The more you talk about him the less real he'll be. So tell me everything. He'll disappear before your eyes."

"What can I say, Chris? There're these moments when everything seems like it's almost ready to make sense: I can see my life clearly, everything's in a kind of place. Then the rest of the time it's all a horrible jumble, like in a nightmare where nothing fits together, there're just all these details but they're not connected to anything. It's waking up in the middle of the night and not knowing where you are. Do you ever do that—wake up and for a minute not only do you not know where you are, you don't even know *who* you are? You can't remember your name. It's like you don't belong to whoever that person sleeping there in the bed is, you look at that person the way you'd look at anybody, you see them clearly—and what you feel is pity. All you know about them is that they're in a bad way, that one day they're going to die, and you feel the kind of pity for them you feel for other people. It's not self-pity, because it's not *you* you're feeling pity for, at least you don't realize that at the moment, and then it comes back to you, your name, who you are, and you realize you're the person you've been looking at, you're the person who's going to die. Does that make any sense, or am I just rambling?"

"You're rambling, but I know what you mean. Do you want another drink?"

Anatole nods, Chris waves the waitress over. "I had something with Leigh, Chris. He felt it too—I think, in a way, he still does. In ways I'm trying to figure out. But there's more to him than Lydia knows; she thinks she's got his number, but she doesn't. That's what upsets me the most, she thinks she has him now just because he's sexually attracted to her. But it's more complicated."

"Lydia's always the practical one," Chris agrees. "It's her great limitation, if you want to look at it that way."

"I could tell her things," Anatole continues. "I could upset her whole way of looking at this thing."

"Then do."

"Should I? Should I go and wreck everything for her? It's not as if she's the only one who's had illusions. I made up all sorts of things—it's embarrassing, but I admit it—because I wanted Leigh to be one way or another way. What I can't stand, what drives me absolutely crazy, Chris, is the way Lydia wants to replace *my* illusions with her own, and then insist that her way of looking at things is the real way. I know things about Leigh she'll never know; we've had . . . well, we've had tender moments too. She can't touch those."

"Well, take that as consolation, then. It's terrible, we all live such separate lives. But if what you say is true, then she'll find out, won't she? I mean, she can't go on thinking Leigh's a certain way if he's not, just as you couldn't. It'll all come out in the wash."

"I know, I know. It's just that waiting for it's so unbearable, it makes me just want to die. I don't want to watch the way life happens."

"To life," Chris toasts. "You were content to let it happen when it was happening to *you*, after all."

"Oh, I don't know, Chris, it all just goes around and around in my head. Even talking about it doesn't solve anything."

What does solve it, at least for the moment, is a flurry at the door.

"Oh look," Anatole says, "isn't that Daniel? You know, sometimes you can't really quite tell. Daniel!" He waves eagerly; across the crowded bar Daniel sees them and makes his way over.

"You're ravishing,"Anatole tells him, caressing his arm. "Such a vamp." Daniel purrs and rubs against him. He's in black, a vintage forties dress with padded shoulders, around his neck he's looped and loosely knotted a long string of thick white pearls. He's done himself to the hilt: black sequined hat, matching purse, white elbow-length gloves.

"It *is* Halloween," he explains coyly. "I wanted to come out as something beautiful. None of this witch stuff for me. My God, don't we spend our whole life as witches? Let's be honest." He surveys the room with a quick appraising glance. "You know, I'm disappointed. I thought at least a few boys would be all tricked out tonight. It's so dead."

"It's not bad when you get used to it. Chris and I were having this lovely conversation."

Chris hates the mode Anatole falls into when he's around Daniel.

"You know," Daniel complains, "they wouldn't let my dates in at the door. They insisted on carding them, which was of course all she wrote. I'm sure because they were of the darker persuasion. I wanted to introduce you to them, but they've probably run off by now. They were so nice, they had such fabulous names."

"What names?"

"Would you believe Born True Allah and Supremely Blest Allah?" He pronounces them with a kind of magnificence. "They're not related, they just have the same last name."

Anatole guffaws. "You're kidding."

"Five Percenters is what they are," Chris says. "I'd be careful, Daniel."

"Is that some kind of lingo, 'Five Percenters'? Am I missing out on something kinky?" He plays with his rope of pearls.

"It's not kinky," Chris explains. "It's this cult. They all have the same last name so the government can't keep track of them. The boys are all Allah and the girls are Earth. They hate white people, certain kinds of white people more than others, I imagine. Like, you know, unnatural white boys."

"Such intimate knowledge of the lowlife. So I was in danger?"

"I wouldn't exactly invite them home with me."

Daniel's reflective. "I think that *was* part of the idea," he muses.

"And you *know* these people?" Anatole wonders. He clucks his tongue. "*Chris!*"

"They, how shall we say, avail themselves of Immaculate's head shop. They're always coming in and trying to pinch something or other. They've got this leader called Messiah who lives down in Newburgh."

"Newburgh." Daniel wrinkles his nose. "They *need* a messiah down there."

"I just wouldn't mess with them," Chris tells him.

"This girl *knows* how to take care of herself," Daniel brags. "Sorry to hit and run, as they say, but I want to cruise this joint before the ugly girls get all the cute boys." And he flounces off, a latter-day Lana Turner intent on the glamour of her dignity.

"I worry," Anatole admits. "He's going to get killed one day. He's got no fear." He remembers the week in August he and Daniel spent on Fire Island a few years ago, when they first knew each other and were sleeping together to try to figure out if they were really in love or, as the case turned out, just a little dazzled by the newness of their friendship, their partnership in Reflexion: how Daniel would go out tricking in the shrubbery stoned out of his mind, unable even to speak coherently. How that was the week they went through a thousand dollars in drugs. Anatole came back to Poughkeepsie a ghost of himself, he's never spent a week like that since—but Daniel's never stopped, he lives that way all the time.

Midnight nears, Bertie's has managed to become dense, lively, even festive. The video screen above the bar, tuned to MTV, runs silently, at odds with the music the speakers convey. The autumnal beach images of "Boys of Summer" are accompanied by Talking Heads' "Burning Down the House," Madonna finds herself writhing to the music of Depeche Mode.

A boy materializes from the dancing and comes toward Chris and Anatole's table. "I thought that was you," he says.

"Craig, my God, what're you doing here?"

"Home for fall break. I'm going back Sunday. So what's up?"

A sturdy boy, in khakis and a white shirt.

"Not much," Anatole tells him. "You know Chris Havilland?"

"We know each other, yes," Chris says dryly, as they shake hands.

"It was a couple years ago, right?"

"Yeah," Chris says. "It was a while ago." He hasn't seen Craig since that evening he ended up sleeping with Lydia; his memory of the boy's been relegated to the status of things he'd rather not think about. Craig's two years older now, he's not as handsome as he once was: the kind of boy, moderately attractive in childhood, who suddenly, almost accidentally, passes through a year or two of intense beauty in late adolescence before settling into something coarse and ordinary. He's grown beefier, he has the body of a boxer. Chris is a little ashamed of having once fallen for him: it makes him sad how everything changes, how ruthless the heart can be.

"So," Craig is saying. "What do you know? My sister's got her a boyfriend."

"So I've heard." Anatole's cautious. "You've met him?"

"It's weird. He's like, my age. I found him a little superficial. But, you know—to each his own, right? What do you think about it?"

Anatole has to smile. "I guess you're right, to each his own. I don't have much impression of him."

"He said he knew you."

"Did he? What else did he say?"

"Not much. He's not really that talkative. He and Lydia were going off somewhere for dinner tonight. They said they might come here later."

Craig looks around: all at once he seems awkward, as if realizing he doesn't really, without his sister's mediation, know Anatole that well.

"You been out to the house much?"

"Not much. Things have been pretty hectic lately. How's your mother?"

"Oh, you know. I worry. She's always taking Valium, she drinks too much. And she's all upset these days."

"Oh?"

"Various things. She got fixated on that ship the PLO hijacked a couple weeks ago. You know, that guy in the wheelchair they killed. She went out and bought two thousand dollars in Israel Bonds—which believe me she can't afford—one in my name and one in Lydia's, and you know what she wrote on the check? She wrote, 'Buy Missiles. Kill the Bastards.' "

"She shouldn't get all worked up. I like your mother, I should stop by and see her sometime."

"Well, like I say, I'll be here till Sunday. Maybe you could come over for dinner. Like Saturday night maybe."

"Sure," Anatole says. He can't think of anything he'd rather do less. "Give me a call."

"I'll do that. You know, this place is really hopping tonight." He leans closer, confidential—"Do you know that girl over there? The slinky one in black? I thought I saw her talking to you earlier." He points in the direction of Daniel, who's sidled up to the bar and is drinking what looks, from this distance, like a sea breeze, his favorite drink. He drinks it through a straw.

Anatole's about to explain, but Chris interrupts him. "No," he says on an impulse. "We don't. She just came by to ask us for a light."

"She's really pretty," Craig says. "I think I might see if I can get her to dance."

"I imagine she'd love that," Chris tells him. "She seemed like she was looking for some fun."

"Well"—Craig grins broadly—"she's not the only one. Wish me luck, guys."

"Why'd you do that?" Anatole wants to know when Craig's sauntered off in the direction of the bar.

Chris shrugs, lights a cigarette. "It's too long a story," he says. "It's Halloween." He can't account for the bitterness he feels toward Lydia and, by extension, her brother. He's angry he ever slept with her, he's angry her brother Craig tempted him, however unknowingly, into that betrayal. He wishes it would vanish. But it won't.

Anatole has to laugh. "I don't believe it," he says.

"Just watch," Chris instructs him. "Do you think Lydia and Leigh'll really show up? She'll kill us."

"I can't imagine they will. They're probably home right now fucking their brains out," he adds bitterly.

"Now, now." Chris pats his arm. "We weren't going to think about that, remember."

"This whole thing's going to make me kill somebody. I swear it is. I mean, I can't *stand* it. I just can't live this way."

"Consider yourself revenged," Chris tells him, gesturing to where Craig has apparently coaxed Daniel onto the dance floor. "Do you think he really doesn't know?"

"Daniel is very very good," Anatole says. "He can fool anybody."

"I guess so. Up to a point. What happens then?"

Anatole hides his face in his hands. "I don't even want to think," he says. "Lydia's going to find out about this, you know. It's going to be total war."

"Oh, relax, have some fun for once. You deserve it. The next round's on me." He pulls out a vial from his pocket. "And if you want to make a little trip to the men's room, it's on me too. Happy Halloween, said the spook to the goblin. Courtesy of my man Jonas."

It's midnight. The lights dim briefly, then come back up. There are whoops. Over explosive percussion, Whodini raps "The Freaks Come Out at Night."

Anatole takes the vial from Chris's open palm. "I owe you one," he says.

Chris watches as Anatole weaves his way through the crowd to the men's room. He feels very drunk, he feels implicated in everything Anatole's told him. Watching Craig and Daniel dance—they're hot, there's an electricity between them: Daniel, Chris presumes, is having the time of his life—he feels nothing but a desire to get back at Lydia. Not for Anatole's sake so much as for his own—a bitterness shapes itself against her, he hates the fact that his moment inside her has threatened for so long, a storm that never breaks. He finds himself blaming Craig for it, though he knows he really has only himself to blame.

"I'm a new person," Anatole tells him, sliding back into his chair. His eyes glisten, he grins. "As always, you're a godsend. I hope you saved some for yourself."

"Don't worry. I overindulged earlier. I'm still wired."

"Scotch and blow," Anatole muses. "It really is the best, isn't it?"

Chris only smiles, vaguely. "I think we should have another drink," he says. "I feel committed"—gesturing toward the dance floor— "to watching this little fiasco to its end."

While they wait for the drinks to come, Anatole returns to something he said earlier. He has to reiterate it, he has to get it right. He wants to make sure Chris has understood him. "About Leigh," he says. "What actually happens isn't necessarily everything. There're other things that are just as important."

"Like?"

"Like—what doesn't happen. What might have happened. Lydia doesn't understand that. She only understands actual things. I think maybe you can."

"I think maybe I can," Chris tells him honestly, as the waitress sets their scotches before them.

Craig and Daniel have moved off the dance floor; they stand at the bar, Craig appears to have bought Daniel a drink. Daniel sips through a straw. Craig puts his arm around Daniel's shoulder, kisses him on the cheek. Together they leave the bar, a perfect couple.

"Well well," Chris says. "Another one for the gipper."

"He'll kill Daniel when he finds out. There's going to be a murder. I *know* Craig. He's straight as they come."

"Did we do the wrong thing, do you think?"

"Who knows? I still don't understand why you said that, that we didn't know Daniel."

"If I said I did it because I hate myself, would that make sense?"

"No, it wouldn't. Nobody has less reason to hate themselves than you, Chris. You don't let the filth of all this touch you, you stay clean. You're the only person I know who has a clear conscience. It drives me crazy sometimes, but I admire it. You know I do."

Chris smiles a pained smile, shakes his head slowly. "Sometimes I like you so much, Anatole, I want to strangle you or something."

"What does that mean?"

"That I'm drunk. That I'm not a good person."

Anatole tries to think of some answer to that, but his brain's suddenly in a fog, and the moment eludes him. They both sit in silence, content within whatever momentary equilibrium the scotch and blow have allowed them. The next thing Anatole knows, Craig is back, pulling up a chair to their table. He settles into it defeatedly.

"I just don't get it," Craig tells them. He rests his elbows heavily on the table.

"You're back," Chris observes. "I thought you left with that slinky girl."

"I did. Fuck, I thought everything was working out. I thought she liked me."

"She didn't?"

"I don't know. I really don't get girls at all."

"Well, what happened?"

"Mind if I have a sip?" Craig picks up the beer Anatole's been using as a chaser; he tilts it back for a long, fierce swallow. "We went to my car and got in, and we were sort of, you know, necking, I mean, it was real passionate, she was about to give me a blow job right there in the parking lot, so I said, 'Why don't we go somewhere where we could be more comfortable?' "

"That sounds sensible." Chris is avuncular, detached. He's lit another cigarette to fortify his wit.

"She just sort of freaked out. She said how she couldn't, she wished she could but she couldn't, and before I knew it she was out of the car and running away. It's crazy. I couldn't even follow her. She just disappeared."

She disappeared into Reflexion, Anatole thinks. She's hiding out there. Anatole imagines Daniel wandering the spacious loft in the dark, touching the smooth, mysterious shapes of the hair dryers, their cool, unyearning curves of metal. He can't imagine what he must be feeling right now.

"I hate these cock-tease girls," Craig tells them fiercely. "I know about fifty girls like that at BU. They're all the same. Shit. I hate getting all excited like that for nothing. It upsets my cock, if you know what I mean."

"You mean it's jerk-off city tonight?" Chris still cool, icily ironic. He blows smoke through bitterly pursed lips.

His performance is so seamless, it alarms Anatole: it seems so devilish.

"Looks like it," Craig laments. "God damn it, some cunts I meet are enough to turn a guy queer."

"It does happen, I suppose," Chris tells him. "Want a drink?"

"I'm too depressed. I'm just going to go home."

. . . and jerk off, Anatole half expects Chris to add, but he doesn't.

"Does that boy have any self-awareness, or what?" Chris wonders after Craig's left.

"Poor guy. You were being mean."

"I was, wasn't I? I don't know what got into me. Shall we go?"

"We should. I'll pass out if I drink any more. It's been a great evening, Chris. It's done me good."

"It's done me good too. You don't have to believe that if you don't want." They stand in the parking lot and shake hands, a handshake that metamorphoses gracefully, a little drunkenly, into a long hug that leaves Anatole breathless.

"Good night," Anatole says, sad and amazed at the way things just go on and on.

When he gets home, the phone's ringing. It's Daniel. He's crying.

"Are you okay? Nothing bad's happened, has it?"

Daniel can hardly talk. He gathers himself together, his voice is shaky. "Nothing's wrong," he says. "That's just it. Oh Anatole, I met the man of my dreams tonight. This georgeous, sensitive hunk of muscle. We sat in his car and necked. I mean, we kissed and kissed."

"Sounds great," Anatole tells him. He feels awful, his heart breaks for Daniel, for the things people do to one another. "So why're you crying?" he asks.

"I had to get out of that car. I had to leave."

Anatole pretends to know nothing. "I don't understand," he says.

"Anatole, he said he was really attracted to me. He wanted to go to bed with me."

"So?"

"He never knew for an instant I wasn't a girl."

NIGHT MUSIC

All through sleep he's falling, there's nothing to catch him so he's falling free-fall until suddenly he's awake and what he knows is that waking is what catches him up from the falling. It's a clearing that opens in the forest—he's free to wander around in that clearing, and for a minute or two he knows that's all being awake is, is having a few minutes to wander the clearing. But then he forgets it's only a clearing and everywhere else is sleep, sleep is the forest that goes on forever.

They're driving out to Delta Lake, where they go on Saturday afternoons to smoke dope and drink wine. Billy's girlfriend Annette's with them, they're all stoned, they've been smoking earlier that afternoon and now it's dusk. They're in Billy's Dad's old beat-up truck, and Billy's said he's too stoned to drive and he doesn't trust Annette with the wheel, which makes her mad for a minute but then she's over it—so Leigh's driving and Annette's between them with Billy on the passenger side, and suddenly, because she's stoned or maybe she wants to get back at Billy for what he said earlier, she starts fooling around with Billy's crotch there in front of everybody—rubbing his hard-on with her wrist, working her hand down inside his jeans.

Leigh tries to concentrate on driving, but he can't help glancing over to see what's going on—which makes him start getting hard himself, especially when Annette unzips Billy's jeans and slides her hand down in there to pull him out. She closes a fist around it and starts these long slow strokes that make Billy sigh, like those sighs are being tugged out of him.

Leigh can't believe Billy's letting her do this to him with him right there, he guesses it's because Billy's so stoned and is just completely out of his head—but then Billy says We're going to get Leigh all jealous if we keep this up, so Annette reaches her other hand over and starts fiddling with Leigh too. He's already hard from watching her and Billy, and when she puts her hand on his hard-on he feels a melting feeling inside so he lets her go on with it. When he looks over at Billy to see how he's taking this, he sees Billy looking at him, this strange serious look, and Billy keeps on looking at him, not watching Annette at all—she's sitting there between them like she doesn't exist even though she's got both of them in her hands and is working them up and down with slow smooth strokes.

He wants to keep watching Billy's face, but he has to look back at the road too, so they won't run off into a ditch, but still he keeps watching Billy all he can, and he's sure they're swerving all over the road like he's drunk or stoned, which he is of course, but that isn't why he's swerving all over the place, it's because Annette's hand is going wild on his thing and he wants to keep looking at Billy's face while it's happening to both of them at the same time. Then before he knows it he's shooting off all over everywhere, they swerve way into the other lane and then back again, and in a second Billy's shooting off too and letting out this loud roar like it really hurts him. Annette just keeps pumping both of them—it sounds all squelchy, and suddenly he feels strange and sick, like they shouldn't have done what they just did. But nobody says anything about it, then or later—they just go on the way they are, and it felt good while it was happening so he guesses it was okay. But he can't forget that look on Billy's face when Billy was looking at him.

Another time he's with Billy at a bar downtown where you can get in under age, and these two guys walk up to them while they're playing pinball and start talking, and ask if they'll go with them and Billy says Where? They say How about over to the park, so Billy says Okay, sure, but it better pay, and they say Sure, of course it pays. The two guys are maybe thirty-five, forty, it's early summer and the fireflies are out, the park's filled with fireflies blinking like stars, and one of the guys says how it's mating season, which makes the other guy laugh like he never heard anything so funny. They smoke a joint behind a statue of some general with a sword, and Leigh's really stoned and not nervous at all, not even when one of the guys starts unzipping his jeans and pulling them down and before he knows it the guy's going down on it like crazy. He can see the other guy going down on Billy, and once again he and Billy are looking at each other that same way—just watching each other with this calm peaceful questioning look, and it's that same strange feeling when he comes of feeling sick and depressed. When the guy tries to stick his finger up his asshole Leigh grabs the guy's wrist and says he's not into that, and Billy must not be into that either, because when he comes he says That's it, now pay up. Which makes the guys angry and one of them says they won't pay a dime unless they can fuck them, and Billy says No way I'm going to take it up the ass from anybody. The guys don't try to insist on anything because they seem nervous about the whole thing, but when Billy tells them to pay up they say Go fuck yourself and start walking toward the street.

Billy throws himself down on a park bench and says We got to find some way to be making money, and they smoke another joint sitting there in the dark and now it seems funny what happened. Leigh tells Billy, At least we got our rocks off for free, but Billy says I thought we were supposed to get paid to get our rocks off, which makes them both laugh some more, and then Billy says in this quiet voice Do you ever think about taking it up the ass? I could do it to you if you wanted to.

Leigh doesn't say anything because he doesn't know whether that's something he wants or not.

Then it's maybe the next day or two days later—it's what he remembers more than anything else—they go out to Delta Lake, this time just him and Billy because Billy and Annette broke up back in the winter and this is the first time they've gone out to the lake since last summer. Billy's scored some poppers from some guy at the bar downtown, and when they get to the lake they park the truck in a picnic ground nobody uses much. They've brought a box with them and set it out on the hood full-blast, Mission of Burma, which Leigh doesn't like all that much but Billy's crazy about, and they start dancing to the music, flinging themselves around in the open summery air. Billy has a bottle of vodka, and they're trading swigs of it, plus they've smoked a little dope on the way out and while they're dancing to the music Billy'll reach up and give Leigh a whiff of popper, holding it there under Leigh's nose, and then he'll give himself one. It's a shiver sliding down like another shot of vodka only colder and sharper, sliding all the way down so Leigh shouts above the music to Billy, It goes right to your balls and Billy laughs, still moving to the beat, agreeing It goes right to your balls, and they keep on dancing and doing popper to keep them up there where they're floating in the warm blue day and everything's great, as great as things get, and then suddenly Billy starts coughing.

He starts breathing hard and it's a strange cough, nobody coughs like that, and then he sits down hard on the ground. He keeps coughing like he swallowed something the wrong way and one of his hands is digging at the ground, which is still wet from last night's rain shower. Leigh doesn't know what's happening, he just stands there and looks at Billy saying Billy, what's up? But Billy doesn't say anything, he keeps coughing that strange cough and Leigh can see how he's sweating and his face is red like it's going to explode. Leigh thinks maybe Billy's drunk too much. You going to throw up, man? he says, but Billy just leans over like he's going to try to touch the wet ground with the tip of his nose, and he does touch it but then he doesn't raise back up, he doesn't do anything. Leigh starts shouting for help—he doesn't know what else to do. There're some people a ways away at a picnic table who come loping over, some guys it turns out from the high school who put their hands on Billy but can't bring him around. They lay him out flat on the wet ground and one of the guys starts giving him mouth to mouth, straddling him and pumping away, but after a couple of minutes stands up and says It's no good, somebody call an ambulance quick.

When Leigh hears that, whatever holds him to the planet snaps and he starts howling, long gasping howls that pour up from somewhere he never knew he had inside him, long gasping throat-tearing howls. The ambulance is coming, somebody's just called it and it's on its way, but he knows it's not going to do Billy any good because you know when somebody's dead, you can tell it—it's like his mother, there's this thing that goes out of them and you can tell it's gone, and once it's gone it's really gone, it doesn't come back no matter how many ambulances you call.

And then this is the part that even now is not clear: Billy's lying on the ground, he's not breathing, and suddenly Leigh's on top of him, Leigh's kissing him and biting his lips and putting his tongue in his mouth. They've never kissed before, he's never even thought about kissing Billy but there he is kissing him and all these guys from his high school standing around, not doing anything to stop him because they're too amazed by it, too scared by the craziness of it.

Afterward it gets around, what Leigh's done—kissing Billy like that when Billy was dead.

The coroner says it was a heart attack, and later Billy's father says how Billy had a weak heart all his life and he knew about it, he went to the doctor a lot when he was younger. So he must've known what he was doing with the poppers and vodka and dope and everything, he must've wanted to go out like he did. It's what Leigh can never know, no matter how much he wakes at night to think about it, lying rigid with the hurt, motionless with it, he can never know whether Billy was doing it on purpose or not. He knows some people think yes, he was trying to kill himself and he thinks maybe it was true, Billy was just crazy enough to want to do something like that, but then other times he knows it can't be true, it's not the Billy he knew, and then still other times he remembers the time in the pickup truck with Annette and the way Billy looked at him, that strange serious look he can never forget on Billy's face.

III
NOVEMBER

Anatole can never get used to the early dark after the clock's changeover from daylight saving time. It feels tragic, a reminder of all sorts of other darknesses. But Mrs. Forman's house, as he pulls into the drive for the dinner party Craig has been importunate enough to arrange, is brightly lit, a haven of warmth and light. Everyone else is already there.

In the living room, he finds Craig and Leigh sprawled on the sofas watching MTV. They've obviously tried talking to each other, it just hasn't worked out, they have too little or too much in common. What Craig must be thinking: how it's a little embarrassing for his sister to be going out with a guy younger than her little brother. As for what Leigh thinks, well—he looks bored to death, he looks restless and insolent and uneasy. He's probably none of those things. Certainly he's dismissed Craig as too unlikely to lead to anything of use or interest to him.

"Here's the man," Leigh says in greeting—and it's warm, it's affectionate, Anatole thinks. As always. Their estrangement, whatever it is, is all on Anatole's side. Fucking Lydia doesn't seem to change anything with Anatole at all, as far as Leigh's concerned.

Tonight there's something about Leigh that's exactly on the mark. Ever since that day they spent in the City, there's been something different about Leigh. Anatole hasn't been able to isolate it, but suddenly it strikes him: little things, the way Leigh cuffs his jeans, subtle adjustments he's made to his hair—all those nuances that conspired to make him seem just a little behind the pace of the City's cutting edge: he's taken those in, he's incorporated them. There's something in that, so private and resolute, that takes Anatole's breath away. That's why I keep him, Chris, he says to himself. Because he wears Reeboks with a sort of genius.

Lydia and her mother are in the kitchen.

Mrs. Forman greets him. "Can you believe it, Anatole? She's actually helping her mother."

"Trying to learn how to cook?" he asks. The tone conveys, Thinking of getting married? Mrs. Forman's always tormenting her daughter with the assertion that Anatole's a fabulous cook, why can't she learn something from him? There's a spinach-and-sausage bread he often brings by that she adores. She seems, in fact, a little disappointed he hasn't brought any this evening.

"You go on," Mrs. Forman tells Lydia. "Trust the kitchen to me and Anatole."

"I'm afraid you might talk about me behind my back."

"Your own mother? Go on, now."

When Lydia's left the room, Mrs. Forman busies herself with the green salad. "I hate to do this," she says, "and behind her back, after all—but look, Anatole, can I ask a question?"

She doesn't turn around to face him. She slices a carrot into the salad bowl, deft strokes of the knife. "Friend to friend, Anatole, what's going on? I mean, she's twenty-nine years old. What's my daughter up to?"

It takes Anatole aback; he sits down at the kitchen table and plays with the salt shaker. He doesn't know what to answer. He and Lydia haven't rehearsed this particular scenario. He's on his own.

"What do you mean?" he says.

"Tell me about Leigh," Mrs. Forman commands.

"Well . . ." Anatole fumbles for words. "There's not that much to tell."

"Anatole, I have eyes in my head. This is the boy who was staying with you for a while, right?"

"He's still staying there."

"So what do you know about him?"

"Very little. Honestly." For the moment, he's embarrassed he knows Leigh at all. He feels responsible for having introduced him into this little world of theirs where everything has been stable, in place. He wonders if Mrs. Forman blames him for Leigh. He can't tell what's going on in her head.

"I worry about Lydia. I mean, what's she thinking? He's so young, he seems so, well, immature, that boy. And his haircut."

"I'm afraid I'm behind that one."

"Anatole!" She shakes her head. "It looks so unnatural. What tint did you use?"

"Just L'Oreal. His hair takes it in a wonderful way. Normally it's sort of dishwater blond, but very fine. He's got almost perfect hair when you get to know it."

"Anatole." Mrs. Forman's voice is all at once gentle and concerned. "Nothing's happened to hurt you, has it? My daughter hasn't done anything to stab you in the back or anything, has she?"

Anatole has to smile. He sprinkles some salt out on the table-cloth, watches how it piles up. He pushes it around with his finger. It feels strange having a conversation with Mrs. Forman's back. But she won't turn around—turning around would make it seem too much like a conversation that's actually taking place.

"I'm old-fashioned," Mrs. Forman goes on. "I don't approve of friends who do that to one another. If you can't trust your friends, who can you trust?"

"Maybe friends are the people you can trust least of all. Maybe that's why you make them your friends." He arranges the salt into long lines, like the spokes of a star. Then he scoops it back into a single pile again.

"Does that mean yes, Lydia's hurt you?"

"Everybody hurts everybody, Mrs. Forman. They get over it." He brushes the salt off the table, into the palm of his hand, then stands up to empty it into the wastebasket. "What're we having for dinner?" He puts his hands on Mrs. Forman's shoulders, massages gently. "It smells fantastic."

"Oh, you know me." She lifts the lid from the pressure cooker: steamy, fragrant pot roast she's seasoned with bay leaves and sage; potatoes, carrots, green beans. And in the oven, dinner rolls.

In the living room, Lydia sits next to Leigh on a sofa and feels completely alienated from every single person in the house. Okay, so Anatole's in an impossible position, she'd give anything to have gotten him out of this evening's torture—but her mother, Craig. She gets this sense Leigh's failed some kind of test already—that her mother and Craig have sized him up and, already, deeply disapprove. She's liked the idea of showing him off, she's liked the idea of going out with a boy ten years younger than she is, who has three earrings in his ear and spiky hair. But now it feels like nothing so much as an awkward adolescent kind of rebellion, this flaunting of Leigh—and she's more ashamed than anything else. They think Leigh's a nothing, they think she's being silly and they're embarrassed for her. They don't say it, but she can tell.

You get older, but nothing changes. You sit in your mother's house and you're still a child, no matter how old you grow. There's no point when the dynamics between mother and daughter suddenly become adult—it just doesn't happen. And she's furious, sitting there beside Leigh, wishing him gone, wishing herself invulnerable; she's furious with her mother for being her mother.

I should live in a city a thousand miles from here. I should change my name. I should have my own life and never look back at these people again.

"Everything okay?" Leigh asks her. He raises an ironical eyebrow, as if to say, So this is it? This is who you are? Maybe she doesn't even like him very much. Odd how this thought comes and goes with some regularity, this doubt: Why am I doing this? Sitting here in her mother's living room—how to account for the flatness she suddenly detects in Leigh, the abrupt suspicion that they've concocted him, she and Anatole, and there's not really anything there?

"Are *you* getting along okay?" She nestles against him. "It's not too weird, is it?" She likes how Craig ignores them both. This whole dinner party thing was his idea, after all.

"I've sat in lots of living rooms," Leigh tells her. "I'm an old pro." Nonetheless he seems shy, even upset. He has a way of pouting, a look that comes over him from time to time that seems to spell a complete, irreversible unhappiness. But then it always passes.

"I guess we're ready," Mrs. Forman announces, as if the whole problem has only been one of waiting. She and Anatole bring platters of food and bottles of wine to the dining room table: and then they all stand around awkwardly, not knowing where to sit, what the order among them is supposed to be. Mrs. Forman's a complete chaos of directives—but in a minute they finally sort themselves, Anatole and Mrs. Forman on one side facing Leigh and Lydia on the other, with Craig at the head of the table. "A toast," he says. "Does anybody have a toast?" But no one does—they only look round at one another with wineglasses held at attention. "Oh well." He shrugs. "To us."

"To us," they all say. It leads nowhere—silence comes down between them, they eat like nuns in a convent. Anatole's never been so aware of how disgusting the sound of five people eating can be. Nor how little five people can really know about one another.

He's not sure who's worst off—Craig, who knows nothing; Mrs. Forman, who knows just enough to be anxious; he and Lydia, who know just enough to know they don't know enough; or Leigh, who in the noisy silence of their eating is the only one who doesn't eat, who as usual just pushes the food around on his plate. In any event, Leigh's the one who finally breaks the silence. Afterward it will seem faintly sacramental, his tendency to talk into space just to see what will happen. An act not really any different, Anatole notices, from throwing beer bottles at the wall. When in doubt, do anything.

"I love pot roast," he says. Though he hasn't eaten it, he's just cut it up into little pieces and hidden it under the potatoes. "We used to have pot roast every Sunday after church."

He says it elegiacally, as if reporting a detail from a world that disappeared in some sudden unforeseeable cataclysm. "We ate in the middle of the afternoon, and then we all took naps. We did that every Sunday. It's funny, I haven't thought of that in a while. It's like it disappeared. And then it comes back, it's like it was there all along. My mom cooked potatoes and carrots like this along with the meat, all in the same pot. I guess everybody does things alike."

Somehow—miracle at the dinner table—what he says precipitates other talk, soon they're all talking, duets, trios of conversation that form and re-form around the table, and it's all natural, it's all the way it's supposed to be. Anatole heaves a sigh of relief—as if Leigh's proved himself; he's come to the surface from some deeps where he was hiding out. And poignantly. He's never heard Leigh say anything about the past. It means, when everything is over, Leigh might remember him one day. Anatole finds that thought strangely consoling.

It takes courage, after all, Lydia thinks, watching Leigh engage her mother and Anatole in a joust—somehow they've drifted into politics, they're talking about the Palestinian Liberation Organization and Abu Nidal, Mrs. Forman's going on about last month's hijacking of the *Achille Lauro*, the man in the wheelchair who got pushed overboard by the terrorists. Anatole seems to have heard nothing about it. But then he always lives in a vacuum. And would Lydia herself have heard of it if her mother didn't harp constantly on her Israel Bonds? "You just look and see, daughter. You think we're safe here? You think this is home? Nobody's safe. We thought we were safe in Europe. Our only home is where we have guns to defend ourselves."

Lydia feels friendly toward Leigh again, the way he started to talk, silly meaningless talk—and yet it was up to him, wasn't it? Because they'd all the rest of them proved themselves incapable. She knows her mother has seen through him in that moment, that perfunctory praise of her pot roast; compliments like that mean nothing to her, she's suspicious of them. She'll have found him lacking. Lydia can already hear how her mother will say it. And yet that's the interest, isn't it? How there's nothing there, and all of a sudden that nothingness will sprout a voice, it'll start talking, it'll be potent. It looses the logjam that's stymied more substantial souls.

"Have you heard any of the jokes?" Leigh asks.

"What jokes?"

"Klinghoffer jokes."

"Now, who's he again?" Anatole asks.

"The one in the wheelchair. The one who got pushed overboard." Leigh's surprisingly informed.

"Jokes?"

"Like—What does PLO stand for?"

It's become a conversation just between Leigh and Anatole. Mrs. Forman watches suspiciously, and Lydia's suddenly nervous.

"PLO," Anatole says. "I have no idea."

"Push Leon Over. PLO."

Lydia watches her mother. Suddenly they're all aware of the tension—all except Leigh, who goes on blithely. Or does he know and he's only testing things?

"Or this one," he says. "I hear all these at Denmarc. I think they make them up in the kitchen. What did Klinghoffer say when his wife asked him did he want to take a bath?"

"Leigh, these are dreadful," Anatole cries. "What kind of *people* do you work with?"

"He said, 'No thanks, I'll wash up on shore.' "

Mrs. Forman sighs wearily, a long-drawn-out theatrical sigh. "So what's funny"—she fixes Leigh with her sad-eyed stare—"about an innocent person getting killed by terrorists?" She shakes her head and grimaces. "This kind of humor," she says sadly, "I can't understand."

"Oh. Innocent people," Leigh tells her lightly. It's as if he's going to be dismissive—but then he says, "What if there's no such thing as innocent people?"

You're going to go far, Anatole thinks. Because Anatole's never been so sure as he is exactly now—the moment Leigh says this, smiling coolly, not unfriendly at Mrs. Forman, more impishness than anything else—what Leigh's future looks like. How the richest, the sleekest, the most unscrupulous will take him up. How for two or three years his star will be meteoric. He'll go to all the best places, he'll see amazing things. Anatole imagines how he himself will never see all this, it'll be some chic party on the Upper East Side. It makes Anatole sad because it leads so irrevocably away from him, so far beyond him— it leads to where he can't even see Leigh anymore, his figure disappears into the shimmer of his future.

"Innocent people are people just trying to live their lives," Mrs. Forman is saying. "All this other noise I just don't believe."

Evidently Leigh decides not to test it. He reverts to safer shores. He crumples his napkin beside his plate and says soothingly, "A wonderful dinner."

"Wonderful, and you only took two bites?"

"I have to watch my figure. I never eat. But I took delicious bites. Really I did."

And that's it, dinner's over (Lydia reproaches herself: I ate like a pig, I shoveled it in like a hog). They retreat to the sofas of the living room, where they lapse into scattered, impossible small talk (how's Reflexion, how was the trip to New York?—oh, fine; it was fine, nothing much to report). Craig's the first to grow sleepy, retreating upstairs with the excuse that he has to drive back to Boston tomorrow. His yawns seem to infect Leigh. "I'm exhausted," he confides to Anatole, nestling close on the sofa—they sip scotch, brandy, Irish Cream Mrs. Forman's brought out on a pewter tray. "Want to go home soon?"

"Soon," Anatole says. The word fills him with an odd kind of peace.

Lydia watches the exchange. She sits on the other sofa with her mother—and it's as if some strange trade-off's been effected. She doesn't know where anything stands—she walked into this evening with Leigh, now Anatole's walking out of the evening with him. The least Leigh could do is be faithful for a couple of hours, especially with Mrs. Forman taking it all in, coming to God knows what kind of conclusions. Lydia's annoyed that what she worries most is—How does the evening look to my mother, what is *she* going to think about it?

It's not easy being in love, she thinks, and then thinks, But I'm not in love. And in that moment she knows what it is, she knows what this whole thing is: she's not in love with Leigh, she's in love with Anatole being in love with Leigh. That's the real source of her attraction to Leigh, nothing more than that. It's because she's attracted to Anatole's attraction to him.

Lydia, you're sick. You're definitely ill beyond words. It's a realization that arrives inside her with a thud. I should really just leave, she thinks. I'm a monster. I'm screwing everything up for Anatole, who supposedly is the one person I like in the world. And why? Why can't I leave it alone? But she knows she can't—or she won't. Because of course there's also Leigh to take into account—he may be a wild card, but he presumably has needs too. She shivers, an electrical shiver deep inside her, replaying the memories as a voyeur shuffles through old photographs—the things they've done, the love they've made. She can think of each time separately, each one is distinct, special. And the odd thing is, he's not really that great in bed. He's awkward, he's a kid. It touches her, he's so clumsy with the moves. Which is what makes him just great. They're real. They're, well, sincere. It makes her think of Demian, the boy with the greasy-sweet hair. When everything's said and done, he was the only other real one, wasn't he?

All at once she doesn't like any of the reasons Leigh's important to her. A sudden spasm of self-hate—The only way you can prove to yourself or anybody else that you're still in the game is to steal from Anatole. And you haven't really even stolen anything. You wonder and wonder what goes on between Anatole and Leigh, and you know you'll never find out, and it drives you crazy.

When they're alone, she and her mother—Leigh and Anatole loosed to whatever common discoveries may occur—Mrs. Forman asks her, a quiet voice, "Set my mind at rest, Lydia. Will you do that?" They clear the dishes from the table, Lydia stations herself by the sink, ready to dry as her mother hands her the dishes she pulls from the soapy water and rinses under the faucet.

"What's bothering you?"

"If you could see the list. I know I'm just your mother, I know it's not really my business, all these things that happen. But remember your friends, daughter. This Leigh, he's nice, I suppose, but I worry. He's superficial, he's got a silly haircut. He's not for you."

"Should I call him and tell him that? Tell him you decided for me?"

"Me, I don't pretend to know anything. He comes with you, he leaves with Anatole. So what do I care? I don't want him to hurt people, this boy. I don't want him to hurt you, I don't want him to hurt your friend Anatole. He's not old enough to know."

"We're grown-ups, Mother, we can take care of ourselves."

"Nobody's ever old enough to take care of themselves. They always need other people to help them. As long as they're alive they need other people."

"Don't you wish. Really, Anatole and I can handle whatever it is we need to handle."

"Then there *is* trouble?"

"Why do you want there to be trouble? Mother, you're always complaining I don't know what love is. Maybe I do know, and you're just afraid to admit it. Maybe you have to pretend to yourself I don't know because it threatens you in some way. Maybe I'm in love with Leigh."

"And who is this Leigh in love with?"

She has to admit to herself she doesn't know, she has no idea. It frightens her, suddenly—because she realizes she can't imagine Leigh being in love. It's not something that enters the vocabulary she allows him in her imagination. What *does* he feel? About anything?

"Mother, surely you know enough about human beings to know not to ask questions like that. People have their private lives. There're all sorts of things they need. Not everybody needs love."

"I'm sixty years old, daughter, I've lived with my children, my husband who died. Everybody needs love. Don't tell me they don't."

Lydia feels they're moving toward realms that, even now, they can't afford to talk about. Fifteen years: her father's been dead that long. Fifteen years. Maybe someday they can talk about it, mother and daughter, but not yet.

So she retreats to her old stance, the long desperate years of growing up. "I can't believe," she says, half laughing, half in absolute exasperation, "I can't believe I'm twenty-nine years old and I still have to answer to my mother. I should really move to another town. Leigh and I should move to New York. Where does this platter go?"

"Did you live here twenty years, or what? The top shelf, under the butter dish. And save the bone—I'll make a nice soup tomorrow, you could come for lunch and have some."

Wrapping it carefully in aluminum foil, setting it in the refrigerator, Lydia complains, "On the subject of bones, I have still another one to pick. As long as we're in that mode with each other."

"Go on. I'm here all night."

"About Anatole. What I don't understand is, why you go on setting Anatole up against me. The way you take his side. The way you immediately assume I'm up to something bad, and that he's the innocent one in everything. There's a lot about him you don't know. That you don't see. Don't judge me just because you know me too well. It makes me feel very alone in the world."

"Oh." Mrs. Forman embraces Lydia, holds her close. "Oh, honey." They cling to each other for a moment, then, almost embarrassed, separate to wipe the kitchen counter, recork the half-empty bottle of wine.

"You see what I mean, though?"

"He can't take care of himself," Mrs. Forman explains simply. "Of all the people I've met in this world, he can take care of himself less than anybody. And another thing."

"Yes?"

"He's nobody's son."

Immaculate Blue: slow Tuesday with Chris idle behind the counter. Beneath fluorescent lights the store's gloomy. It brings back afternoons of childhood, storm clouds gathering beyond the bright schoolroom windows, sullen thunderclouds piling ominously above the low-slung houses of the Denver suburb where he lived. Once, in a violent downpour, he paced up and down the classroom, worried, wringing his hands, afraid of something, and even the teacher couldn't calm him. He was in the first grade. He thought everything would be washed away, his house, his mother and father, their new dark-green Pontiac.

When the door opens, he looks up and for a moment it doesn't register—kids like this frequent his store all the time, they buy bongs or roach clips, they browse the bins for the underground labels his is the only store in Poughkeepsie to carry. He knows a dozen of them by name, high school kids, unemployed punks. They hang out here for hours, it's a sort of haven from the dissonance of the streets.

"Hey," Leigh says. An insinuation of icy wind follows him in the door. "You didn't think I'd take you up, did you?"

"I haven't been holding my breath," Chris tells him. But his heart's jumped nonetheless. Wearing a faded denim jacket, Leigh looks almost, except for his hair, conventional.

"I've been busy."

Chris continues to write stock numbers in his notebook. "So I hear."

It seems to startle Leigh. "*What* do you hear?"

"Well, you can't be friends with Lydia and Anatole without hearing things." Chris glances up at him, a glance to test the waters.

"Oh, them." Leigh seems disappointed Chris knows them—as if he's forgotten that little fact of life.

"You don't sound enthusiastic."

Leigh shrugs. "You know how it is."

"Do I?"

"Maybe I'll tell you about it sometime."

"I'm not sure I'm interested." Chris says it cooly, then he smiles—it's a challenge. He's determined not to let this boy get the best of him.

"Are we defensive, or what?" Leigh asks.

"We're wary," Chris explains. "We hear things."

"Oh." It makes Leigh pause, he's thoughtful, even concerned. "Don't believe everything you hear."

"Well, I do. It makes things more interesting that way. It lets people get away with less."

"Like me? I mean, I just came in here to look for some records."

"Sure, and I'm giving you a hard time. It's the way I get my kicks."

"I get enough hard times."

"Do you really, Leigh?" Chris doesn't stop smiling, grimly, his smile to keep threats at bay.

Leigh looks at him, head cocked, eyes narrowing—there's almost the stance of a street fighter in him. "You know, I think I like you, Chris," he says at last.

"I wouldn't worry about that too much. You'll outgrow it."

They've established their territory, their terms. It is, Chris realizes, the first time they've ever talked without an audience. He's thought so much and so skeptically about Leigh that it's strange to have him standing here in the flesh. It's almost—well, disappointing.

"Anyway," Chris says. "You came here to buy records." After these advances, it's a retreat.

"Yeah, records."

Leigh looks around the store—the same proprietary once-over Chris saw him give Anatole's apartment that first night. "You know, like, I've heard of this place," he says. He walks around touching things—to put his imprint on them, or to make sure they're real? Chris lights a cigarette and watches him. "The house I was living in before," Leigh says, "the people who lived there used to come here. I told Anatole, I said, 'give me a hundred bucks and I'll buy ten albums.' His collection needs a shot in the arm. I mean, it needs a major fix. Ten albums is enough to make a dent in anybody's taste, right?"

The store's deserted: Leigh stands at the hard-core bin and flips through the records, every now and then extracting an album to set aside: The Replacements, Mission of Burma, Spiral Jetty. Chris watches his intentness, the way he bites his lower lip in thought as he pauses over Black Flag, then discards it in favor of the Pogues.

"Fantastic," he calls over his shoulder. "*Rum, Sodomy and the Lash*, my absolute favorite. Can we hear it? Can we play it here?" Without waiting for an answer he rips the cellophane off, and in an instant the Pogues' frenetic stomping rhythms fill the store.

"I love it," Leigh exclaims, turning the volume way up. "It's hot." Closing his eyes, he dances a couple of steps, then hoists himself up to sit on the counter. "When do you close up?" he wonders.

"I'm closed right now," Chris says, flipping the sign on the door.

"So what happens?"

"Now?"

"Sure. I'm not just going to take my records and run."

"Well, I have to clear the cash register."

"You need my money?"

"Keep it, it's on me. Anything for Anatole's record collection."

"Hey, thanks. I'll buy you a drink."

"You're making a nice profit on this deal, I see."

"Hustlers gotta live somehow."

The word startles Chris. "Is that what you are, a hustler?" It interests him, it suggests all sorts of things he hasn't granted about Leigh's capacity for self-knowledge.

"Aren't we all?" Leigh looks sly. He gives his head a shake—as if to make sure everything about him falls into place. "I'll even buy you dinner," he says, "if that makes you feel better."

"Better? About spending Anatole's money?"

"About whatever."

"You're incorrigible. Give me a minute to finish up here. There's a bottle of scotch behind the counter. Have you ever been to the Milanese?"

Out on the street the wind is strong and cold. Storm clouds, snow clouds. "And, like, just yesterday it was still summer," Leigh remarks.

Yeah, Chris thinks. It goes fast. It goes at the speed of light. That evening at Bertie's, summer, late summer, when Anatole first told him about seeing the boy sitting on the mall.

In the Milanese, Leigh's not hungry. "I'll just have the mussels appetizer," he tells the waitress. "Bring it with the main course."

"I'm only going to drink," he informs Chris. "I've got to watch my figure. You know, we should've ordered two carafes."

It's the sort of thing Chris might have said ten years ago. It makes him momentarily rueful. He feels old, he feels somehow gross and large, having ordered a full dinner to Leigh's spare appetizer. It's subtle, Leigh probably isn't even aware he's scored a coup—but for Chris it counts. He's been outdone.

"I hope the things you've heard about me haven't poisoned you too much against me," Leigh says a little abruptly. He's gulped his first glass of wine, he pours himself a second, apologizing—another line Chris might once have used—"I'm only fun when I'm drunk."

"I take everything with a grain of salt," Chris reassures him. "You're afraid there's poison about you?"

"Well, you never know."

"But you seem on rather stellar terms with both Anatole and Lydia these days."

"Am I? Is that what it looks like? I was at this dinner at Lydia's mother's house the other night—you should've been there, Chris. I felt like some kind of rag doll that's getting tugged at from both sides. I mean, like one's got one arm of me and the other has the other arm and they're tugging, they're tugging. It hurts."

"I can't rescue you," Chris tells him.

"I don't want that. I just want to have a friend. I mean, I can see it's not Anatole's fault and it's not Lydia's fault. It's just something that happens, but once it happens, what can you do? I want them both to have me, but they can't, because the only way either one of them wants me is for the other one not to have me anymore. I mean, anybody else could have part of me, they don't even want all of me— it's just that they don't want the other one to have even a little piece of me."

"They go back a long way, Anatole and Lydia," Chris says. "There's a whole history there. You can't unravel it. Even they can't. It's gone on way too long, since way before I knew either of them." He sips his wine reflectively, leans back in his chair. "In fact," he says, "you might say I had exactly the same experience with them." That thought, not having occurred to him before, disturbs him. He tries to see if it's really true, what he's just said. To protect himself from the implications he lights a cigarette. We're only jealous of the young, he thinks: we revenge ourselves by falling in love with them.

"Then you can see what I'm saying," Leigh tells him, an edge of misery in his voice as the waitress sets his mussels before him, black shells in a dish of bright diavolo sauce. "Do you think"—he picks with his fork—"do you think they'd be better off if I just left?"

"Where would you go? What would you do? I don't know anything about you"—Chris studies his mound of calamari rings as if suddenly uninterested in eating all that food—"I can't give you any advice."

"It wouldn't be the first time. Just pulling out and leaving."

"You haven't been living in Poughkeepsie very long, have you?" Leigh shakes his head. "I came in April. I was living in this house with these lesbians. I don't even want to talk about it."

"And before then?"

"Before then. Well. It's a long story."

"It's always a long story," Chris tells him. "I have a whole meal to eat; I have plenty of time to listen."

"You know, it's amazing," Leigh says. "I mean, the three of you." He smiles, almost fondly—"Talking and talking and where does it get you?"

"It gets us older. You come to a point, Leigh, where you realize everything you do it just gets you older. You're not there yet. It's why we like you."

"You too?"

"Well, don't get too many ideas. I'm staying as far out of all this as I can."

"But you're interested in me?"

"I'd like one or two facts, is all."

"So you can add me up?"

"So I can have something to go on. I look at you, Leigh, but I don't see you. I don't think anybody sees you. Maybe that's your secret."

Leigh grimaces. "You're being silly like everybody else."

"People are always being silly about one another. That doesn't keep them from trying."

"Trying?"

"From coming back to the same two or three things."

"Like?"

"Like basic things. Like where you came from. Like who you were before we knew you. Before you made yourself up to fit whoever you thought we wanted you to be."

"I don't get it. I mean, I don't get what you're asking me for, Chris. I really don't."

"Oh, simple things. Like where you were born. Like where you lived when you were a kid. Like how you grew up to be the way you are."

"Which way am I?"

But Chris doesn't answer, and Leigh only smiles. Of course he likes concealing things: it's the only power he has, and he knows better than anyone that once he gives it away it's gone, it's no use to anybody. It's only good so long as he keeps it, and even then it's not good for anybody but him, and if it's only good for him then it's not worth anything anyway. So in this instant Chris feels sorry for Leigh. At the same time, he's hooked, he's engaged by all this dodging about, these smiles that say no.

"I mean," Leigh is saying, "you could ask me any question you want."

"And you'll answer it?"

"Sure. There're always answers, if you want them."

"That doesn't give me much to go on, does it? What if I want answers I can trust? What if I want to be sure?"

"Try me." Leigh shrugs. "See what happens."

Chris shakes his head. "Maybe we should just eat, then, and not talk anymore."

Leigh pauses with his fork half lifted to his mouth "That's not what you want to do, though, is it?"

He chews slowly; his eyes don't leave Chris. "Okay," he says at last. "You want to know where I was born?"

"Yeah." Chris eyes Leigh slyly, even humorously. "I want to know where you were born."

"Well, okay then. Ramstein." He lets the word hang in the air. "That doesn't mean anything to you, does it?"

Chris laughs. "Ramstein," he says. He savors it. "An air force brat. I should've known. That's you, isn't it? There's something about you that should've told me."

Leigh watches Chris.

"See," Chris explains. "My dad was a colonel before he retired to get rich. I grew up on air bases. I can tell an air base kid like that. It does something to you. You can't disguise it."

Leigh grins; it's as if he's been caught at something. But he also seems relieved. "Yeah," he says. "I don't really remember Germany. *Ich möchte Brot mit Senf.* I want mustard on my bread. That's the only German sentence I know. I remember that one. We lived there till I was five, then we moved over here, Griffiss Air Base."

"I know Griffiss," Chris says. "It's up the river, right? Near Rome. I mean, I've never been there or anything. But I know it. So really you're just an upstate kid."

"An upstate air force brat. If you want to call me that. So there you have it. But see"—Leigh sounds fierce, even dismissive—"all this stuff, Chris: it doesn't have anything to do with who I am right now. You could find out a million things like that, and it wouldn't have anything to do with anything. There's just nothing back there. It's not good or bad. It's just nothing."

Suddenly Chris feels very sad, very empty—something in Leigh's tone empties everything right out of him. Because Leigh's right. There's nothing. It wells in him, a physical sensation—but then it passes. And he wanted Leigh to be different from those boys in the hotel rooms of Lexington Avenue. He'd wanted him to be more real.

Where Leigh's hand rests on the tablecloth, delicate, the bones spreading from his wrist like a fan out into his fingers with blue veins mapping the clear skin—Chris wants to reach out and cover that hand with his own. Because it seems so utterly vulnerable in this instant, both of them seem vulnerable, he and Leigh both, sitting on top of pasts that mean nothing and that can't help.

"I know," Chris says, gently as he can. "I know all about that."

He looks up to find Leigh staring at him. It's a grave stare. For an instant—trick of candlelight, the wine, whatever—Chris sees it, he sees what must have thrilled Anatole that first day in September. Our Boy of the Mall—he hasn't heard that phrase in a long time, but for once, despite all the ridiculous and degrading things that've happened, it seems exactly appropriate.

"I thought you would," Leigh is telling him. They don't stop looking at each other—not studying one another so much as just contemplating the intimacy that's suddenly fallen over them, covering them wholly with its shadow.

It's a high-water mark, from which the flood gradually recedes. Chris plunges into his calamari with a vengeance, Leigh seems content to order another carafe.

Later, as they stand by the car in the parking lot, Chris is at a loss. "I should take you back to Anatole's, right?" He doesn't know what he wants—he wants to end this evening as quickly as he can, he wants to shut it out. Also he wants to prolong the bright moment just a little longer. The wind's damp and cold. Part of him's thrilled to have established this unholy connection with Leigh—he feels they *understand* each other, that they've communicated something; but at the same time he feels guilty; it's involvement, even betrayal. "I'll pay," Leigh insisted in the restaurant, but Chris stopped him, he wouldn't allow it. Anatole's hundred dollars—it would be too awful. As it is, there's something uncomfortable in these transactions behind his friend's back, an advantage taken. I will not be, I refuse to be another Lydia, Chris tells himself. He wants Leigh safely deposited at Anatole's, he wants his hands clean.

"Anatole's," Leigh says. "Yeah, I guess I should get on back. I should inflict his new record collection on him. But let's do this again sometime. I mean, like go to dinner, or have a drink. It was really fun. It was good for me, Chris."

"It was good for me too," Chris has to admit. "But I feel pretty strange. I have to tell you that." He hasn't been completely honest in years. It feels odd.

"I don't understand."

"Look, you're shivering. Let's don't just stand here. Get in the car. It's fucking freezing out here."

In the car, Chris starts the engine, the heater, but they don't go anywhere. They sit and Chris says, "Look, this is a little hard to talk about. I mean, I don't know everything, but I *do* know a lot about you and Anatole, and you and Lydia. They're both my friends, and"— he sort of laughs—"I don't quite know what to do. I mean, you *know* how complicated all this is. I don't blame you for getting involved with Lydia, because Anatole, even though he can be wonderful, he doesn't really have the right to want you to be something you're not. I mean, I don't *know* exactly who you are—what you're up to, what you really want—I don't think any of us know that, and I think you probably use that to keep all of us interested in you, one way or another. That's not the point. The point is that I owe it to both of my friends not to make things worse than they already are. I'm afraid even getting to know you better is going to do that. There's no way for it not to. Can you see how I might feel that way?"

Chris can't really see Leigh in the darkness of the car's interior, but he feels him shrink into himself. "It makes *me* feel like a piece of shit," Leigh says, his voice young, hurt, aloof.

"No, no, it's not supposed to," Chris pleads. "Leigh, I think what we've found out this evening is, when you add us both up, we come out to about the same number. Does that make sense?"

"Chris, I just want to be friends with you."

Chris wonders what he's being talked into. He thinks of the Puerto Rican boys in the hotel on Lexington Avenue, how there the script's uncomplicated, in some sense pure and incorrupt, a model of hygienic relations with the world of strangers. He opens his mouth again with the definite sense that later he'll look back and think, This is the point where things went wrong, this is the moment I regret.

"Look, I'll be honest with you, Leigh. Completely honest. If things were different, I mean, if everything else hadn't happened, and this were a different town or whatever, if all the things that are going to fuck this up weren't around, I don't know . . . But things *aren't* different, nothing's going to make them different. Still, take it for what it is. Okay?"

He looks over at Leigh—who sits with his arms folded tightly across his chest, his legs pressed tightly together.

"You're still shivering," Chris says.

"I know." Leigh laughs quietly—it's a laughter of knowledge, Chris recognizes it because he's laughed that way himself. "I'm not shivering because I'm cold," Leigh says.

"I know that." Even to say it is to acknowledge something, to step across some boundary.

"I'm confused. I feel scared, Chris. It's exciting. Like starting out on a trip where you don't know where it'll lead. Like getting in a car and just driving."

"I think we'd better get you to Anatole's."

"Please don't get me wrong." Leigh reaches out and touches Chris's arm. Nobody touches Chris. The touch thrills him. "I'm not a bad person."

"I don't think you're a bad person."

"I'm a better person than you think I am. I want to let you see that, somehow. I mean, not on Anatole's terms or Lydia's. On my terms and your terms. Just us."

"But it isn't just us," Chris tells him. "I wish it was, Leigh, I really do. But it isn't."

"But you don't even give it a chance. You talk yourself out of everything before you even try it. That just makes me so sad, Chris."

It strikes Chris to the heart—as if Leigh's found him out in a way he's begged Anatole and Lydia to, for two years, and they've either refused, or been unable to.

"It's safer that way," Chris jokes. "You don't get AIDS."

"AIDS," Leigh says. "We're all going to die anyway. It doesn't make that much difference. I mean, when they start shooting off the missiles."

"I'm afraid I'm just a coward, then. I want to hold out to the very end. It's something I'm committed to. It's my personal version of suicide."

"Then I'm sorry all we can do is talk"—Leigh's voice tense, disappointed—"when it's not going to get us anywhere. When it's just going to depress the hell out of both of us." With a gesture of anger, or frustration, Leigh flings the car door open and steps out.

"What're you doing?" Chris asks through the open door.

Leigh shakes his head, lips pursed grimly. "It doesn't matter. I want to walk around some. I don't want to go back to Anatole's yet. I don't want this to end just like this." And he slams the door.

Chris is out of the car too; in an instant they face each other over its mist-beaded roof.

"You're being silly, Leigh. Come on, I'll take you to Anatole's. We'll call it a truce."

"Walk with me," Leigh says. It's so peremptory, it catches Chris off guard.

"Where?"

"Anywhere. Who cares?"

A little park at the base of Main Street, fronting the Hudson—they walk the quarter mile, it's cold, misting—Chris is all ajumble, and yet he's happy. They don't talk, they just walk, they get wet. The little park's deserted, the Hudson scours the shore with quiet persistence. They sit on a bench, Chris and Leigh, the floodlit suspension bridge looks fanciful, nostalgic; a mile upriver, the old train bridge is unlit except for a red light and a green light to warn low-flying planes of its complicating presence. Otherwise it's just a pattern of darker darknesses against the night's own dark.

"I've fucked this whole thing up, haven't I?" Leigh asks resignedly. "I've been like the bull in the china shop."

"Well, not exactly a bull. A gazelle in the china shop. But you've probably broken things, yes. I'm just being frank when I say that."

They sit close to each other, Leigh puts his arm around Chris, draws him close to him. And Chris acquiesces. He breathes deep, the cold night air, Leigh's warmth, the young comforting animal scent of a boy's body. Meditatively, he strokes Leigh's hair: the moment unattached to anything that will happen on one side of its moment or on the other, a narrow territory of honesty, of tenderness bounded, even guaranteed by those two looming bridges, one alive, one dead—from both of which, with some regularity, people a lot like Chris and Leigh jump to their deaths.

They lie in bed, the near memories of their lovemaking linger powerfully. This flesh, this miracle. He'll grow up, he'll be like us. It's Lydia's only consolation in the face of his devastating youth. Whatever we are now—she's speaking for all of them, for her friends: because it's not just a simple matter of *her* anymore, is it?—whatever we are now, you'll eventually have to be that in one way or another. I wish you luck. It's hard, it's probably not even worth it—but we're cowards, we go through with it every single day: day after day, we go through with it.

"It's funny," she says. Odd, to break the silence after lovemaking—though this doesn't so much break it as simply extend it. "I've been thinking."

There's something in this stillness that seems to promise her she can say anything. They've cleared some space, their bodies have solved something between them, and now in this emptiness—"My father," she says. "Everybody thinks he died of a heart attack. But he didn't."

She watches where Leigh lies, arms folded behind his head. He stares at the ceiling, his eyelashes are, well, heartbreaking.

"He killed himself," she says. "He shot himself with his old army pistol. There was never any reason anybody knew." She watches him to see if she should go on. But he's imperturbable, his eyes blink now and again but that's no sign of anything. That's just nothing. So she goes on. "It was in the summer," she says, "we'd had dinner on the picnic table on the patio. I remember everything about it: we had pork-and-beans and London broil and macaroni salad. Dad cooked on the grill. He had a beer. Rolling Rock, that's the kind of beer he always drank. I was always asking for a sip. We'd just finished eating, and he went in the house, he said he'd be back in a minute. Then we heard a gunshot. He was lying in the bedroom, between the bed and the wall, and the wall was all splattered with blood. It was bright red, it almost looked like paint. For an instant we thought it was a joke or something, then my mother started screaming. My brother was away at summer camp. He doesn't know. Nobody knows. My mother and I've never talked about it. It's like it never happened. She tells people he had a heart attack."

Leigh doesn't move. Under each arm, there's a fluff of blondish hair. "How old were you?" he asks at last.

"I guess I was fifteen. I don't know why I wanted to tell you that."

She watches him watch the ceiling. His eyelashes blink up and down. It's perfect. It makes her feel absolutely alone.

"You know," Leigh says, "it's all right to kill yourself. There's nothing wrong with it."

"I've always wondered how it affected me," Lydia says. "I mean, if I'd have been different if that hadn't happened. I think I blame my mother, I think he wouldn't have done it if she somehow hadn't been the way she is."

"How is she?"

"I don't know. It's just, every once in a while I look at her and think, She drove him to kill himself. I can't say why, but I don't forgive my mother. When I was in high school, in college, it was really bad. It's better now, but I still don't forgive her. You know what the first thing she said was? She said, 'Oh my God, the wall's ruined.' See, they'd just had the bedroom repainted that summer."

Leigh raises himself on one arm to look at her. "Anatole likes your mother a lot, doesn't he? He says nice things about her."

"Anatole doesn't get a lot of things about people. He doesn't see things. And they're a lot alike, if you look at them in a certain way."

Leigh doesn't say anything. He reaches over to the nightstand to look at the clock. "I've got to be getting back in a little," he tells her. His chest has definition, his bare shoulders are thin but perfect.

"Leigh," she asks, "you don't have to answer this, but tell me: Why do you have to sleep over there every night? I mean, what is it about Anatole's?"

"He's got a comfortable bed," Leigh says, and kisses her lightly on her eyelid.

"No, really. Tell me." Where he's leaned across to look at the clock, she lies under him.

"What if I said I was in love with him?"

"Are you?"

He looks at her and grins. "Who knows?" But he sounds sad, dejected.

She holds his arms, she's afraid he'll move, and she likes him lying on top of her like this.

"Do you want to have sex with him?"

"I might."

"But you never did, did you?"

He looks away into space, the ceiling. "No," he says, "I never did. You don't have to worry."

"Oh, I'm not worried. I was pretty sure you weren't like that.

But, you know—tell me if you ever do. I don't want to be the first woman in Poughkeepsie to get AIDS."

"Maybe I've already given it to you."

"I doubt it."

"Who can know?"

"You haven't given me AIDS, Leigh. I know. Now stop that. You're trying to evade the issue."

"Oh. The issue."

"It makes me feel a little abandoned, you know. To be feeling so close to you like this, and then for you just to up and say, 'Okay, I have to go sleep in somebody else's bed now.' " She caresses his chest, his brown nipples annealed to his skin like pennies. "It's not cool to mention it, is it?"

"No, go on, mention whatever you want."

"It's just, sometimes I don't know where I am with this whole thing, Leigh."

"You don't always have to be consulting a compass, you know."

"It's a habit. You get older, you need to know where you are. You don't like being lost anymore."

"Older. That's all I hear these days. Even Chris. He was harping about it the other night. Growing older. You're not *that* old, you're—what?—twenty-nine, thirty?"

"Not *quite* thirty, please. I still have two months. And anyway, I didn't know you knew Chris. Were you with Anatole?"

"Do I need a chaperone? Chris and I understand each other."

"Oh? Well, that's nice. What do you mean, 'understand'?"

"Well, we sort of confessed it to each other. We went out on a limb together. We went to the Milanese, we had dinner."

"Was Chris giving you the treatment or what?" As she says it she massages his temples, he looks into her eyes.

"What does that mean?" he asks seriously, looking at her, into her, his eyes dark brown. Can you really see directly into somebody through their eyes? And if you could, what would *that* mean?

"I'm just being cynical," Lydia teases. She touches the tip of his nose with her fingertip, trails down across his lips, slightly swollen with all their kisses, his chin. "I'm trying to see it the way Chris would." Actually, she's amused, she's even thrilled she's caught Chris in this flirtation, or whatever it is.

"He's special," Leigh tells her.

You're so naïve, sweetheart, she thinks—but says, "He is. You're right. If you can get through his shell."

"But there isn't any shell. That's what's so, I don't know, so wonderful. It's all right there. He's completely honest."

"Are we talking about the same person?"

"We're not. You and Anatole, you talk and talk, but you don't get anybody right with all your talking. They're always different from who you think they are."

"Well, let's not talk anymore, then, okay?" She moves her hands down to his hips, cups his tight, adolescent buttocks in her palms. She can feel him get hard against her.

"Pretend I'm Chris," she whispers to him as he begins to move against her, "if that makes you feel better. Is it sexy to think of me as Chris?"

An immense distance at once falls between them; he draws back and looks at her—that sullen, estranged look he gets from time to time. Instantly she's sorry she said it: a stupid thing to say.

Before Leigh, the last person she fucked was Chris. A terrible thought, too strange even to glance at.

"What a dumb thing to say," she apologizes. But he's lost his hard-on. He pulls off her and sits on the side of the bed, not touching her; he looks totally defeated by something inside himself. She reaches up, rubs his back—there's a pea-shaped birthmark halfway down his spine. He doesn't respond to her touch, but he doesn't shrug her aside either. Earlier this afternoon she put new film in her camera she never uses, and over Leigh's protests—"You don't want a picture of me; I take terrible pictures"—she snapped a roll of twenty-four. Leigh sitting on the sofa, bare-chested, barefoot, his faded jeans unbuttoned one button. Leigh stepping out of the shower, hair slicked back, a pink towel around his waist.

"You're like a hornet buzzing around with that thing," he said. "Now, cut it out."

"You're cute when you're annoyed. I only have two shots left. Now, smile."

"I hope you loaded the film wrong, I really hope that."

An act of desperation, a way of proving to herself, come some future, that all this was true, that it really happened once. Snapping those last pictures, she felt—This act of salvaging him on film guarantees I'll lose him in the flesh. For half a moment she was ready to expose the roll to light, obliterate all those traces of her sudden loss of confidence in everything. But then she didn't: she's always been greedy, she's always hoarded against the empty futures that become, more and more, self-fulfilling prophecies.

"I'm sorry, okay?" she says, caressing his bare back. He doesn't look at her. She doesn't have a clue to whatever he might be thinking. "I just got carried away."

"I think we're on totally different wavelengths here," he says finally. His voice is careful, as if he's spent the last couple of minutes rehearsing this. He's holding everything in abeyance, he's letting go as little as possible. "Maybe we should just be straight with each other for once."

"We're always straight with each other. We're the only straight people we know."

He won't acknowlege it, and once again she's in the position of regretting immediately what she's said. He insists on deflecting her attempts to defuse whatever it is she's triggered. He bears right down on it. "You know I hate to talk," he tells her, "but we've got to. Otherwise I'm just going to walk out of here or something. You're starting to freak me out, you and Anatole. All this using me for this or that. I'm just not sure how much of it I can take. I can always get out, you know. I'm good at just walking away. I've done it before."

"I don't understand what you're saying," Lydia tells him. But she does, she does understand. She's known this would happen.

"Maybe we need to cool off a bit, Lydia." He's reached down to the floor, picked up his shirt, and now he starts to put it on, button it slowly. "I mean, like stand back and take a look at things in perspective."

Part of her is relieved—at last it's come, now she doesn't have to wait and wonder what form it'll take. But Chris. She can hardly believe it.

"So Chris seduced you?" she asks, her voice hard-edged and narrow. "Or did you seduce him?"

"It's not that, Lydia. You're not hearing what I'm saying. It's like you don't want to understand. See—that's what I'm talking about. He lets me be whoever I am. He's not always trying to make me something else."

"Oh, and that's what I do?"

"You and Anatole both. I can feel it. It makes me uncomfortable. Look, I'm confused about all sorts of things. I just feel that, well, with you and me, it's not helping things much, our going on together like this."

"What the hell do you mean, 'things'? Leigh, you can't just walk into people's lives and turn them upside down and then say sorry, it was a mistake, wrong number. You have to take some kind of responsibility for what you make happen."

"I just feel like you've taken advantage of me." Leigh flings the accusation bitterly.

"That's just not true, Leigh. I swear—" But she stops midsentence. Denying it only makes it *seem* true. And Leigh's suddenly burst into tears. There's something absolutely terrifying about it. He throws himself on the bed, his face turned to the wall, and sobs, deep heart-rending sobs of an intensity and despair she's never heard before from anybody. She doesn't know what to do. She reaches out to comfort him, to pat him on the shoulder. "I hate you," he cries. "I hate you. Leave me alone. Please, just leave me alone. Keep your hands off me."

It pierces her. She sits stone-still, her heart's carved out of ice. She watches his back heave with sobs. Then she gets up and puts on her bathrobe.

"I'll be in the next room," she tells him. "If you need me."

He doesn't say anything; he does nothing to indicate he's even heard. In the living room she sits on the sofa in a stupor of confusion and hurt. What sense does any of this make? It's all flung at her out of nowhere, it's like a nightmare where absurd unanswerable accusations pursue you and you can't answer them, even by trying to deny them you confirm them. Was she right at the very beginning—that first night at Anatole's, when Leigh was so drunk, out of control? Is he really just an unstable, even dangerous kid it's crazy to be involved with at all? Can it be that her mother, of all people, has been right? In the next room she can hear his sobs—they go on and on, it's frightening, unearthly, more like the sounds of a wounded animal than anything human. She's horribly touched—it seems possible she's really in love with him, willing to sacrifice anything, even herself, for his happiness—at the same time she doesn't want this boy in her apartment anymore, he's too much for her to bear, she just wants to be rid of him.

I *haven't* been using him, she assures herself fiercely—while at the same time the realization surfaces: the reason she told him about her father, it was to impress him, it was somehow to try to hold on to him. Like everything, it was doomed to fail. Perhaps—who knows?—it even, in its way, provoked all this. And yet—this must have been coming for some time; whatever discharged it was only accidental.

At last his sobs subside, there are long minutes of silence. Then he appears in the doorway, fully clothed, looking worse than she's ever seen him. "I don't have anything to say," he says.

It's as if they've never known each other. "You don't have to," she tells him, the way she'd tell a stranger. She doesn't get up. He doesn't make any move to come to her. "Just promise we'll talk about this sometime," she says briskly, more to reassure herself than anything else. More to keep the pain at bay.

"I don't know if I *can* talk to you anymore," he says, his voice sullen, withdrawn, absolute. "I'm going now."

"I'm not going to stop you. Respect me for that, okay?"

He doesn't say anything. He's not even looking at her. Some storm door's crashed heavily shut inside him, he's protected from whatever it is he can't afford to face.

He's crazy, she thinks, listening to him descend the stairs, slam the front door. He's more lost than any of us. So he has youth, he has beauty—those are only accidents, in a few years they'll disappear and then where'll he be? Because except for those accidents, those jokes of circumstance, terrifyingly (she's seen it tonight) there's nothing there at all.

And she thinks: Chris and Leigh, Chris and Leigh. What impresses and devastates her—pouring herself a tall glass of ice-cold gin, rummaging the refrigerator for something to eat (she's ravenous, she doesn't care how fat she gets)—is the simple *logic* of it. The logic that discards her and Anatole alike, that reaffirms their status as—didn't she put it to herself once this way?—allies in futility? She walks around her apartment, she stands facing the wall and leans her forehead against its cool smooth surface, and all she can say to herself is, The logic, the logic.

It makes Chris uneasy: how he's taken Leigh to the Milanese, how they've sat at the same table where he and Anatole usually sit, how he's ordered the calamari he always orders. What could he have been thinking of? All that seems worse than having sat with Leigh in the park, and touched him, and let himself be touched, and said things he probably shouldn't have said—though when he reconstructs their conversation, no single sentence seems to cross any borders, there's no one moment he can point to as in itself a mistake. Still—these things always get back, one way or another: Anatole'll find out, he won't understand, he'll be hurt. Because Anatole has that great talent for letting himself get hurt. It makes Chris wince to think about it— a talent that almost but not quite approaches genius. And Chris is angry with himself for *tempting* Anatole's talents to aspire to genius. That whole evening with Leigh—what can it look like but a wanton betrayal, a calculated desecration of the little ritual of biweekly dinners he and Anatole settled on long ago as a replacement for all those other difficult and thwarted things?

He hasn't wanted to see Leigh again. He's wanted to wash his hands in cold clear water and have done with it. But there are smudges, they show up on everything you touch. And it can't be forestalled— it's exactly a week later that Leigh's waiting for him when he closes up Immaculate Blue. Leigh leans against a wall, collar turned up, one foot propped back on the wall, hands in the pockets of his jean jacket—

and he really is good-looking, he really is something extraordinary. Smoking a cigarette, he holds it between thumb and forefinger, it's burned down to the quick. He survives the cliché gracefully, he flourishes within it. And Chris cringes. Did I look like that? Was that all it consisted of?—the ability to act out, unconsiously or not, a few clichés with a lit cigarette and a nice profile? When was it he stopped being the cliché and started believing in it?

He can't help it. He's glad to see Leigh.

"Hi, Leigh," Chris says a little grimly. "Waiting for a bus?"

"You could call it that." Leigh smiles, falls in step with him, still sucking on the stub of his cigarette. Chris likes the way boys walk and smoke at the same time, there's something so intent and purposeful about it.

"Where're you going?" Leigh asks.

"What if I have things to do?"

"You don't, though, do you?"

"No, I don't. All I need is to find somewhere to get a drink."

"Bertie's," Leigh suggests brightly.

"Preferably not Bertie's."

"There're people there you don't want to run into." Leigh's blithe, as always, with his basic assumptions.

"I'm ashamed of being seen with you, is all."

Leigh laughs his laugh that Chris will still remember years later, when all this is long over. "Hey," he says, flinging away his cigarette ironically, "you can afford to slum it for an afternoon." With his elbow he nudges Chris, their shoulders bump, they collide for an instant, friendly as kids; then they walk on.

And Chris thought he managed to be firm the other night, he thought he made it clear there was no hope. He admires that Leigh still refuses to take no for an answer. It makes him think maybe Leigh's better than any of them. He'll go farther, he'll learn more.

Just past the Main Street mall, where Main Street proper resumes its seedy progress, is a bar called the Congress. It looks closed, but then it always looks closed. Chris and his friends never come here, there's something vaguely unhygienic about it. All of them agree—anybody you'd meet here's not somebody you'd want to take home with you. It's the kind of place Daniel will frequent as a breather between more dangerous spots like the Nite Cap and the Silver Spoon Lounge, bars he dares with some regularity when he's on angel dust and in drag. That's okay: Chris isn't afraid of running into Daniel. They've had a long-standing truce of mutual indifference.

Inside the Congress is fetid and gloomy. It's dark enough so that you can't really see anybody. Antlered heads gape from the walls; the decor, if you can call it that, is Bavarian brauhaus. At lunchtime a hangout for businessmen, after six it turns into a sort of gay bar. Not a real gay bar, as Anatole will tell you—not like Prime Time across the river: but a Sort Of gay bar. The few times Chris has been to the place, late at night, there's been desultory dancing to a jukebox in the corner; and lined up at the bar, ten or fifteen men, all either too fat or too thin to be healthy; cheerlessly they nurse mixed drinks and glance at the door to see whoever's coming in; while two or three close-cropped dyke couples in bowling team T-shirts sit and shout at each other in the other room.

But right now, six-thirty on a Tuesday, there's nobody here at all except the bearded bartender. He's dancing behind the bar to Sting, who sings moodily about the Russians and nuclear war. He's stoned, or drunk. His eyes glisten, he plays rhythm on the smooth bar top. "Two double scotches," Chris tells him. "Johnnie Red." When he turns to hand Leigh his, he notices there's someone sitting at the far end. He must have come out of the bathroom. A middle-aged man, he wears a brown leather jacket, ordinary business pants. His hair is graying. He smokes carefully, the way Europeans smoke.

"We can sit in the other room," Chris suggests. It's a dark side room where there are tables. The bartender follows them, tunes the TV mounted in the corner to MTV, but leaves the sound off. Leigh stands to divest himself of his jean jacket and the loose-knit sweater he's wearing. Chris can hardly see him, but his white T-shirt seems luminous in the light from the TV. The antics on the screen are depressing, without the sound they're ridiculous. But Chris can't really take his eyes off them. They seem an accompaniment to something heartbreaking but inexplicable.

"Well, here we are," he says.

Leigh gulps his scotch in one gulp. "Here we are. So what have you been thinking? Since last time."

"You jump right in, don't you?"

"I'm young, I'm impatient. You've gotta act fast with me."

"So I see." Chris takes out a cigarette to light—it's something to hide behind. Leigh reaches for the pack and takes one too. "Since when've you started smoking?"

"Since I decided it was cool. Since I started watching you."

"Corrupting minors isn't my thing, really."

"I'm eighteen, remember. Anyway, I'm already corrupt."

"Eighteen, sure," is all Chris says. "And I'm fifty."

"Well, you're well preserved. I like older men."

Chris laughs but he's not amused. He's bored and aroused. He hates it, but Leigh's presence is intense, and he remembers with a sort of swooning disbelief that cold night last week in the park, in the rain. Get out of here, he warns himself, disengage, disengage. But under the table, Leigh's long legs fumble with his own, engage them. Leigh sort of laughs, more a murmur than a laugh.

"Cut it out," Chris warns, but it sounds more playful than anything else. As if by magic, now that they've finished their drinks, the bartender returns, carrying two tumblers brimming with scotch.

"Telepathic bartender," Chris admires.

"Not really," is the reply. "These are compliments of Ed."

"Ed?"

With a flick of his head the bartender indicates the end of the bar, where the middle-aged man has been sitting. Turning around, Chris can see him in the other room, his back framed by the open doorway. He's not looking at them. He smokes imperturbably, methodically, the way someone might masturbate. The smoke blossoms above him, hangs there in a cloud.

Something in Chris says, Don't accept these, you don't know what these will get you into. But Leigh's already taken his in hand. And Chris remembers: Leigh's accustomed to accepting drinks from strangers, it's his whole life.

"To Ed." Leigh raises his glass a little ironically. "Whoever he may be."

They clink glasses. The sound's hollow, a bell gone dead. "He must have heard you saying you like older men," Chris teases. "I'd be careful if I were you."

"Don't be silly." Leigh sips the fatal drink with gusto. "It's you he's after. He's going to steal you away from me. I'll be bereft. I'll start hanging out in bars like this from sadness."

"You know, Leigh"—Chris watches him as he drinks—"you're very silly."

Leigh grins—there's something cold in the grin. "Otherwise I'd be dangerous, right?"

"Who knows, kid? I mean, just who can tell?"

But he doesn't touch his scotch. He doesn't know why: he just doesn't touch it. Call it superstition.

"So can we talk more about us?" Leigh asks.

"You don't understand. There's nothing to talk about. See, I've finally reached this point, I feel like for the first time I know where I am, I know who I am. I don't want to mess with that."

"And I'd be messing with it?"

"Anything would mess with it." Is he really saying this? But he goes on. "What I know about myself is that I have to be very careful." He looks at his scotch but doesn't touch it.

"That's all?" Leigh looks restless, annoyed; he shifts about in his seat. "I don't even know what that means, 'careful.' "

"Well—you get to this point, you've hurt too many people—" He really wants the scotch, he needs it. But he won't have anything to do with it, with that man sitting in the other room at the bar, whom he's conscious of even though he can't see him. "I hurt them because I made them think I was one thing but I wasn't. I mean, I didn't even know who I was. I just sent out contradictory signals all the time and let them think whatever they wanted to. I let them fall for whoever they thought I was."

"And you decided that was bad?"

"I decided that was bad, yes. And I decided I have to live all that down. Do you understand what I'm talking about?"

"No. Not really. Look, are you going to drink that scotch? Like, I want to get drunk. I don't want to just sit here drinking politely."

"One day you *will* be dangerous," Chris says. "Maybe not yet, but one day." Leigh lifts the tumbler and swallows.

"We should get double scotches this time," he tells Chris. "And keep talking." He hops up, disappears round the corner into the other room—then sticks his head back in. "Because I want to know everything."

Everything. Chris watches the TV screen while he waits. Waiting in a dark room for a boy he feels himself circling toward, the way water goes down a drain. It's a video from last spring: Cyndi Lauper's living in a house trailer with her boyfriend. He's long-faced, bony. Her hair is spectacular. In the video it's autumn; they're white trash barely making ends meet, but they're somehow happy in an autumn sort of way. He thinks he remembers how the song went. A sad song— it was very popular last spring, he used to like it at the time. But he's forgotten the tune, he can't remember it at all, even though it feels as if he's seen this video a thousand times.

"What took you so long?"

Leigh settles before him. "That Ed guy wanted to buy these for us."

"What'd you say?"

"I said sure. What do you think?"

Chris groans silently. But this is the way Leigh is, he tells himself. It makes him queasy—he wants to leave.

"I think he might come in here and sit with us," Leigh says.

"You talked to him?"

"Just to say thank you. He seems okay."

"Yeah, sure. I'm sure he's okay."

"You're too suspicious of everybody, Chris."

"I've had bad experiences."

"So tell me. I'm interested. I've told you about *me*. It's only fair."

"I don't think so," Chris says coolly.

"I do," Leigh tells him. "I think you owe it to me."

Chris studies the boy. Maybe I do, he thinks, Maybe I do. It's difficult territory—terrain he can't, even now, see clearly. It's things he's never talked to anybody about—not Anatole, not Lydia. He sighs and lights another cigarette. At least if he's going to do this, he can do it right. "It was a long time ago, Leigh. It wasn't here, it was in another town. These two people I knew, a guy who was my roommate at Cornell and his sister."

"And?"

He isn't sure he wants to go on. He shakes his head slowly, bemused that Leigh's the one finally to draw this out of him. "We were living together," he says, "it was during the summer, and the three of us were living in the same house."

"So far so good," Leigh coaxes. "They were both in love with you? It's always the same. Which one were you in love with?"

But Chris can't go on.

"It's very complicated," he tells Leigh. "I thought I wanted to talk about it, but now I don't think I do."

Leigh's look is gentle, sympathetic. Chris shakes his head and grimaces. "It's not fair of me to do this to you," he apologizes. "It's just too . . ." But he's paralyzed, he can't even find the words.

"It's okay," Leigh tells him. He reaches across the table to touch Chris's hand. And Chris lets him. The contact feels, for the moment, important.

"Terrible things happened, Leigh. This woman Michelle, I ran out on her when she needed me. I just disappeared, I left town. She still doesn't know where I went. Nobody does. I can't explain it, Leigh. It's just something I did."

"You did it for no reason?"

"See, her brother was in love with me. I didn't understand how in love with me he was. I mean, I thought I knew him pretty well. We'd been roommates for a year. We'd been, well, close. But I was wrong, I didn't understand a single thing about him. I guess I encouraged him. I mean, I didn't know what to do."

"So did you like him?" Leigh asks.

"Did I like him? It doesn't really even matter—I mean, when you look at it now. He was very unhappy with who he was. He must've been very angry and lonely, all sorts of things must've been going wrong for him. It just fed into everything else. Everything got so fucked up so fast that nobody could go back and undo anything once it started."

"You said you ran away. That doesn't sound like running away, if it was all over."

Chris inhales deeply from his cigarette. He lets his lungs fill, then gradually lets the smoke out. He's taken this into his body and released it and it hasn't changed it in any way—it just disperses the way any smoke would disperse.

"I should've been there to help. I should've been able to say, 'Part of this is because of me.' But I couldn't. Somewhere out there in the world right now there's somebody who thinks I'm a completely terrible person. A moral coward. And she's right. In terms of her life, and her brother's life, I *am* a completely terrible person."

"Could you get back in touch with her?" Leigh trying to be helpful, but only sounding very young. "Could you work things out?"

"No." Chris is firm. "There's no way to go back and change the things that happened, no way. All you can do is get as far away from it as possible, and hope she's managed to do the same thing."

"Look," Leigh says. "I really think this is getting us somewhere. You and me. But I have to go piss. Come looking for me if I don't come back."

And I'm lying even to Leigh. Or if not lying, then talking around the truth in ways that aren't courageous. Do I want to impress him? Even now, do I want to shield him in order to encourage him? Chris thinks it with a sort of wonder. He can't believe it. It seems to him right now—a terrifying insight—that he doesn't even have a clue to what it is he's about. There are so many Chrises, so many sanitized versions shut up in so many different rooms in his brain. Doors open and shut, he moves from room to room, he has no idea where he is, no idea.

He remembers it exactly. He was sitting on the sofa rereading *Franny and Zooey*, a book that had been very important to him in high school. Michelle's one-eyed kitten was asleep on his lap. The morning was warm, sunny; there was a fan on in the window. Then Michelle was in the doorway.

She didn't say anything. She walked over and sat down on the sofa beside him. The kitten looked up, then nestled back down to sleep. Chris laid *Franny and Zooey* aside and looked at her.

"What's up?"

She didn't look at him. She stared at the doorway she'd just walked through.

"Michelle?"

"John's dead." She said it in the flattest voice he'd ever heard. He didn't understand.

"What do you mean?" he asked her.

Turning to look him in the eye, her voice still completely without expression.

"He's dead. My parents called. His car ran into a tree."

Chris knows instantly—he killed himself, he drove his car into a tree on purpose and nobody knows except Chris. To everyone else in the world it's just one of those inexplicable things, what everybody always fears. But he knows, he alone knows why John drove his car into a tree.

Nothing to do with me. It's got nothing to do with me. His mind clanging shut against that inadmissible fact. But around the edges there's a searing light—I didn't know, Chris thinks, the wind knocked out of him: I just didn't know, I *couldn't* have known.

Surely there were other things. There had to be other things.

There was the letter that came two days later. He stood there holding it, terrified—then crumpled it into his pocket so no one would know. As if anyone *could* know. Then he took a long walk, the same walk he'd taken that day six months before, in a blizzard, the morning after he'd first slept with John. Out beyond the Plantations now drowsing in summer. Out to where the apple orchards began.

People don't kill themselves for love.

Just last September he'd been in the Student Union and seen a sign—Read This and Weep, the sign had said, and he stopped and read. A girl from Israel, a new graduate student, had jumped off the Cascadilla Gorge bridge. She was homesick, she was lonely, this new country made no sense to her and she was afraid she wouldn't be good enough for graduate school at Cornell. So she'd killed herself. He hadn't wept when he read that; he'd felt a kind of contempt.

His walk had carried him in a long arc back to the stone bridge over Cascadilla Gorge. He stood there in the sunlight; out over Cayuga

Lake thunderheads were building, there'd be a storm by afternoon. On the other side of the valley the hills were green and still as sleep; the creek a monotonous seethe of white water. What had John thought as he drove toward that tree? How long had he known he was going to do it? Had he been afraid, or had he felt in that moment what love really was? Try as he might, Chris could move no farther into the dead boy's brain than he could into that Israeli girl's. There was only a kind of wonder—John's gone, and all this is still here, it's all the same except for the tiny hole he fell through.

Taking the letter from his pocket, he tore it carefully into little squares. Whatever it said, he didn't want to know. It wouldn't be able to damn him any more than he was already damned. So he let it go, he let John go: watched it fall, a fluttering fall of snow on a summer afternoon. It falls among the fir trees, the boulders of the creek where he and John and Michelle spent whole afternoons sunbathing, it falls into the tumbling waters and is gone.

Leigh's talking to Ed in the bar; when Chris turns around to look, he can see him framed in the light of the door—he looks particularly vulnerable in his T-shirt, his thin arms. He looks as if he's on the verge of moving away from Ed, coming back into the dark room where Chris sits—but something keeps holding him there. Is it something Ed's saying? Chris can't hear, of course. But Leigh keeps making a move as if to go and then staying a minute longer. Ed has wheeled himself around on his barstool, he faces Leigh nonchalantly, legs crossed—there's something cool and appraising about the look on his face. Now let's see who he's really interested in, Chris chides Leigh silently. Leigh smiles, laughs his laugh that's light as driftwood; Ed reaches out and pats him on the upper arm, smiles. The gesture's fond and corrupt—it makes Chris shudder. He turns away: and in an instant Leigh is back at the table. "I got accosted," he says. "But I escaped." Touching his chest with the palm of his hand. "Anyway." He composes himself. It's as if that little encounter didn't happen, as if Chris didn't witness anything. "I still don't see why whatever happened between you and your girlfriend and her little brother has anything to do with you and me," Leigh complains.

"It has to do with trust, I think," says Chris.

"Oh. Trust. You use all these big words, Chris. But look, we're going to have a visitor." Chris cranes around in his seat to see Ed lumbering into the room where they're sitting. The guy moves much less gracefully than he sits. He looks, Chris thinks, like someone who's been drinking whiskey for hours, maybe years.

In his heart he feels cold; everything warns him they should have left at the first sign of trouble.

He can't resist being hostile. But Leigh's friendly.

"Thought I'd see if I could get a party going here," Ed says affably. "What is it about queer bars, they never get going before midnight? Afraid the makeup will show?"

Chris is never sure in retrospect how these things happen. One minute Ed's standing at their table, a complete stranger, the next minute he's sitting there with them, tossing back his scotch and laughing and it's as if they've known him forever. Is it part of Leigh's special charm, part of the mystery that surrounds him, his uncanny ability to move not against people but with them, taking them into his space, altering himself to fit whatever motions their presence enjoins? If that's it, then the bare fact just has to remain: it's a kind of genius.

Ed's talking about himself.

"That's fantastic," Leigh interrupts. "You *own* an airplane?"

"I own *two* airplanes. I've got this little Piper cub, that I've had from way back; and then last year I bought a Cessna, it's a dynamite bird"—he clicks his tongue to convey the precision, the style of the aircraft.

"Where do you fly it?"

"Oh, around. I take it out over the river, fuck around a little bit. Loops and barrel rolls, that sort of thing. Cheap dogfight tricks. What I really want to do is be a stunt pilot. But I took it up too late. See, I was respectable for way too many years. You wouldn't believe it. I woke up one day and saw where *that* was getting me. Ta ta to the old family—I was a new man. That's when I started flying. I mean literally and figuratively." As he says it, he reaches out and touches Leigh on the arm—insinuating; but also to reassure him?

Chris wants to alert Leigh somehow—this guy's a phony, he's

repulsive. But he can't because Leigh's listening. He's getting into it. And Ed continues to talk—about how a couple of months ago he was flying down over the City, he was completely lost, and it turned out, boom!, he was right over LaGuardia, the guys in the tower were going crazy, trying to get him to acknowledge them. "Hell, I wasn't about to acknowledge," he says. "They'd slap a fine on me stiffer than a teenager's dick, if you'll pardon my French. I ditched my radio comm and just got out of there quiet as I could. Anyway, you should come up with me someday. If that didn't scare you off."

"I've never flown in a little plane. I mean, of course in jetliners, but that's probably different."

"It's not even in the same ball game. A Cessna—it's just you and the sky and the Good Lord. You know, only angels and sea gulls get a chance to feel that way. You got the whole world floating out there below you, and you're up there and the wind's rushing by—it's really loud up in one of those little planes, it's not like you'd think—and you feel like, this is it—I can go anywhere, I can do anything. You're just up there above the whole world."

"I'd like to fly," Leigh says. "I'd like to learn how."

"You're looking at a great teacher," Ed tells him, pointing with his forefinger at his own chest. "I'll have you flying in no time."

And this isn't what we're really talking about, Chris thinks. We're being led along, we're not our own anymore. We're his.

And they are, it seems, his.

"Why don't we go back to my place?" he suggests. "I've got a locker full of venison, I shot it up around Woodstock last weekend—we'll drink a little red wine, I've got this Mendocino cabernet that's just dynamite with a little venison . . . I've been yakking about myself—I want to hear all about you boys. I'll bet you've got some flights that'd put my little Cessna to shame."

"Well," Chris says. He doesn't want to go to Ed's house, he can't stand the man. But he also doesn't want to let Leigh go alone. It's irrational, but he feels he needs to be on hand to protect Leigh. Which is crazy, of course—Leigh's fully capable of handling himself. Perhaps it's nothing more than Chris's disbelief that Leigh would have any interest in going to this man's house in the first place—because Chris feels almost jealous, he feels he's in danger of being dropped for someone more interesting, more novel.

But then they're following Ed's bright red Porsche along the arterial, and Chris has to say, "We don't have to do this, you know. I mean, we don't have to go back to his house just because he invited us. We could cut out right here."

Which wouldn't, Chris thinks regretfully, be the first time he's ditched somebody on the way home from a bar. How do they remember him, those people he let pick him up, but then he managed to disappear from, opening the door at a stop sign to vanish into the night?

Leigh's busy fiddling with the radio. He keeps punching buttons but none of the stations he finds interests him. He rummages through Chris's tapes. Finally he puts on Bronski Beat, *The Age of Consent*.

"I don't know. What do you think? I'd *like* to learn how to fly. That'd be fun. I think he'd be a fun guy to know. You know, somebody you could have a couple of scotches with and really talk to."

"Do you think that?"

"I don't know. We can leave whenever we want to, right?"

"Turnaway runaway" is the refrain from Bronski Beat. It haunts the way any song will that you've danced and danced to.

Ed's house is very large. Brooding, mossy-roofed Tudor beneath pines. An outcrop of rock the driveway circles round, planted with rhododendron, their leaves curled tight with the day's cold. It could be a Japanese print, it's so stately and evocative. Ed ushers them inside with a liquor-flushed grin. "Somebody light a little fire," he says, "and I'll make drinks. You boys like martinis? I make legendary martinis."

He's so confident, so in control—he must have done this a thousand times before, hustled unwary strangers back here from bars. The living room looks like the kind of place where things have happened. The walls are oxblood-red lacquer. Darkened, mythological paintings hang in frames of darkened gold. It's a room with the ability to absorb all sorts of things having happened and then retain its composure perfectly—which, like Ed, is florid, rich, cluttered. A succession of Persian carpets spread across the dark floors, two potted palms frame the entryway into the dining room. Floral chintz, suitably time-darkened, covers the sofas and armchairs, in the corners of which blood-red tasseled pillows have been tossed.

Leigh has the calm and alert eyes of a thief. He goes over everything as Ed disappears into the kitchen to rattle bottles and break ice cubes. The coffee table stacked high with art books. The bronzes on the end tables—Siegfried, a supplicant nymph, a hefty bull mounted on a block of blood-dark marble Leigh picks up to examine, then sets back carefully. Everything looks old, authentic, substantial—and Chris, watching Leigh's catlike movements, all the boy's alertness called suddenly into play, Chris is convinced he can know exactly what Leigh must be thinking. It makes him wince—because what he sees, what he suddenly understands is this. Everything *they've* offered him, each of their various offerings, his and Anatole's and Lydia's—they've each been paltry compared with this. What's a boy from Rome, New York, on the make, to think? Compared with anything they can offer, someone like Ed must look irresistible. Chris has the picture clearly in his mind: how Ed will swoop down and grab Leigh up into flight with him, and there'll be no looking back. How could there be?

They were way stations, they were all three points of rest on the pilgrimage. So it began in a bar and it ended in a bar. There's a melancholy pleasure in the shape of all that.

"Look," Chris says on impulse. Any minute now, Ed will be back in the room. "I'm going to leave. I'm walking out of here. You don't have to come with me if you don't want to."

"Leave? Why?"

"I don't want to be here. I think maybe you do."

There's a longing in Leigh's eyes, but what he says is, "I don't get it."

"I guess I'm asking you to make a choice."

"What kind of choice?" Leigh looks puzzled—he knows he's being tested.

"About what you want. What's best for you. If you go with me nothing's going to happen. There's no future with me. I'm trying to prove that to you."

"And if I stay here?" Leigh looks around at the room, drinking it all in like some rare liqueur.

"Who knows? Anything might happen."

Leigh considers it. "I'll go with you only if we can fuck."

Leigh puts it so bluntly, so unangelically, that Chris feels his penis swell with excitement. He tries to look as aloof as possible, but he's back in that school bus, he's squeezing the door shut as tight as he can.

"No," he tells Leigh. "Like I said, nothing's going to happen. Nothing."

Leigh looks at him—he seems almost ready to cry, and it breaks Chris's heart. But he can't let it break, he has to be ruthless with himself. This is what you want. To be out of it like this. To wash your hands of it. Anything else is too terrible to afford.

"You don't want me?" It's a forlorn cry.

"I don't want you, Leigh."

Leigh throws himself down on the sofa. He doesn't look at Chris. He twists the tassel on a blood-red pillow. "I'm staying, then," he says at last.

"I thought you would." Chris pauses to look at this boy one last time. Because he won't be coming back, this is it: he won't see him again. He resists the urge to take him in his arms like a little child, to hug him tightly. Instead he says, "Be careful, okay? It's terrible out there."

Leigh doesn't say anything.

Balancing three martini glasses on a tray, Ed has stopped discreetly in the doorway. He seems to realize what it is he's won. He stands confidently. They stare at each other for a moment, Ed and Chris, then Chris turns his back on him and walks out the door.

It's long after midnight, Anatole expects Leigh back—either from Denmarc, if he's working there tonight, or from wherever: because no matter who he's out with, he always comes back. It's the rent he pays.

Two, two-thirty—Anatole stays up drinking, watching David Letterman, the late movie, the ranting stomach-turning preachers of the religious station; finally, embarrassed at being so parental, he goes to bed. But he doesn't sleep. He gets up, takes two Valiums, a last long swig of scotch—it doesn't help. He lies awake, his body rigid, listening to every sound the night makes. How silent, how alive with noise. His whole body is a listening ear, everything in the city takes place on the surface of his skin, the occasional noise of traffic, sirens in the distance, the random and varied creaks as his apartment decays around him. The sound of the blood in his own veins, a sort of unsettled roaring, the current of a complex branching river. There's never silence, the body's always generating its own noise, a machine working away steadily, relentlessly, no matter how you'd like to quell it.

He listens for any signs that might betray Leigh's approach. The sound of a car, footsteps on the stairs. The click of a key in the lock. But there's nothing.

It had to happen, he thinks. There was never any guarantee, any agreement between them that Leigh would come back here every night. It was unspoken, a tender, rueful gift on Leigh's part to a relationship he couldn't engage or sustain. Anatole hasn't realized how used he's become to sleeping next to Leigh—without him the bed feels huge, a desert in the darkness. They never touch, he and Leigh—only late at night, when they're both asleep but have floated to the surface simultaneously, as if responding to shared dreams, they sometimes roll against each other, they embrace in their sleep, furtive heartbreaking intimacies that in the morning are far closer to dreams than to anything that's actually happened. So that Anatole never knows whether he dreamed that embrace, that silent groggy grappling and touching—or whether it really happened. And if it happened, well . . .

But tonight, there's just this emptiness, this shallow concave absence in the sheets next to him.

Leigh's at Lydia's, he must be.

Lydia. He conjures, for the thousandth time in these last three weeks, the image of Leigh and Lydia making love: it's too unbearable, it's sweet and provoking and intolerable all at the same time. It makes his soul writhe with loneliness and envy. He knows it just makes everything worse, not to be able to control his imagination: it's an indulgence like picking a scab: but as soon as he relaxes his mind even a little—those Valiums didn't do anything—that's the image that comes crowding back in.

It makes him want to cry. Everything he's depended on, he's depended on without any objective evidence to support his belief in it.

Around five o'clock, exhausted, he falls asleep. He dreams. A vague, upsetting dream: He and Leigh are in a town—it's sort of like Poughkeepsie but not quite, familiar and mysterious at the same time. Something terrible's happened, they're trying to get home. He can hear air-raid sirens. They come to a little square—cobblestones, a few straggling trees, their leaves sad and brown. Leigh sits down on the ground and confesses, in a strange, garbled voice, "I can't go with you. I have to go the other way"—indicating with his hand the direction they've just come from, a direction where there's something terrible, whatever it is they've been running from. And Leigh pulls something from his pocket, it looks like a piece of bone, only it's translucent, it's glowing, and Anatole realizes that medallion means Leigh really *does* belong to the other side, that he *can't* go on home with him . . . only Anatole now realizes he doesn't know where home is, that wherever he thought home was involved Leigh going with him, and that without Leigh the place he thought was home isn't home anymore. Some other place is home, though he doesn't know where that other place is (but it has to be in this city, this is where he grew up . . .).

Around seven he wakes, it's sunrise, a strange sun hovering in a November fog: blood red, more like a sunset than a sunrise. He feels hung over, though he hasn't drunk any more than usual, a half liter of scotch. Everything seems different, displaced. He walks around the apartment in his underwear—it's chilly, damp with the fog. Everything in the world's disoriented. Human beings have no place. Life is horrible beyond description.

All day at work he waits for Leigh to call, to explain or apologize (he has fantasies) or at least to reassure him, but nothing happens. He can't concentrate, his hands are unsteady, he feels hollow the way he does after nights of too much cocaine. When one of his regulars complains, looking in the mirror, "Oh, Anatole, it looks horrible, what did you *do?*" he's at a complete loss for words. It's Daniel who steps in to say, "Not to worry, honey, it's the shredded wheat look."

All day there's a sense of unreality, as if last night's dream is reality, and *this* is the dream, the unreal life, this vacant aftermath of some terrible, equivocal parting. He wonders should he call Lydia just to check? He'd feel stupid doing it, he feels so alienated from her that he can't bring himself even to pick up the receiver. It would be just too humiliating. He'll wait it out, Leigh's bound to come back.

"If you want to talk about anything," Daniel tries to console him, "I have ears, you know."

"When it's all over," Anatole tells him. "I'll tell you everything. I'll make your ears *burn.*"

Because suddenly Anatole has this queasy sense that, indeed, it *is* all over. Or soon to be.

After work he goes straight home, breathless with the anticipation of finding Leigh there—but at home there's no note, no sign Leigh's been home all day. He walks from room to room, drinking scotch from the bottle and listening to the records Leigh brought back from Immaculate Blue last week. But he doesn't like them, he hates them, they sound raucous, violent, they're just ugly. He doesn't understand. It's music that leaves him behind. Maybe if Leigh were here he could *get* to like it.

He drinks late into the night, but there's no consolation, the world's empty, boring. There's nothing worse than waiting. Because that's what hell will be—waiting and waiting for that person you expect to call, to show up, and he never, never does. And still you wait; your hope becomes your humiliation, you go on hoping, endlessly, knowing all the time it's no good, it's rotten.

Drunk and scared, Anatole rummages through the little gym bag Leigh brought over one day from the lesbians' house where he had been staying before he met Anatole. Leigh hasn't taken it with him, wherever he's gone, and Anatole interprets that as some sign of hope. He goes through everything, layer after layer of neatly folded clothes. But there's nothing; nothing he finds is anything that might identify Leigh as someone who has lived. There's some bikini underwear in different colors. A little worn, a little urine-stained. Two pairs of jeans, one considerably more faded than the other, a white cotton broadcloth shirt, long-sleeve, some T-shirts—the one that says RELAX, the one with Life Sucks, Then You Die in small letters across the front. A pair of flip-flops Anatole has never seen Leigh wear. A beat-up pair of black loafers. A black sweater, thin at the elbows. That T-shirt with the crayon drawings on it—which he never wore again, as if embarrassed by it. But kept packed away. Otherwise, nothing personal; because all the clothes Anatole has seen before. Without Leigh, they're just lifeless, clueless. Leigh owns no personal things. There's something disturbing in that. Anatole hasn't expected a diary, but maybe a letter Leigh got from somebody once, maybe a photograph of somebody or somewhere to remind him of where he's been, who he's known. But there's nothing. It's just blank.

It makes Anatole remember: a day soon after Leigh moved in, and Anatole was dying of all the mysteries that haloed the boy. Leigh taking a shower, and, shameless, nervous, Anatole went through his wallet—a social security card, a driver's license, New York State, showing place of residence as Rome, New York. Height 5'10", weight 130, hair brown, eyes brown. No other identification. Twenty-three dollars. Tucked in a fold of the wallet there was a slip of paper with a phone number on it. Anatole wrote it down, but never called it. He put it somewhere. He tries to think. In the top drawer of his bureau, back in back where he keeps important papers, his car insurance, his birth certificate.

Number in hand, he sits down on the bed and dials. It's an act of complete desperation, something flung out into the emptiness that threatens to overwhelm him. A recorded voice greets him, telling him he has to dial a 1 before the number. He hangs up and dials the number with a 1 before it, and an operator comes on the line. What area code is he trying to call? It's not a local call, he needs an area code to complete it. But Anatole doesn't know any area code, the paper only has seven digits and no area code and it could be anywhere.

Anatole sits on the bed and looks down at the gym bag, which contains everything tangible that he can be said to possess of Leigh.

He feels completely alone, he feels completely at the end of things.

Next day, he overcomes his reticence, his humiliation. He calls Lydia.

"I haven't seen Leigh in over a week," she tells him when he asks. Her tone's offhanded, cool. It startles him.

"We had a fight," she explains.

"A fight?"

"I really don't want to talk about it, Anatole. If you can understand that."

"Sure," he says. "Of course." Over a week ago. Anatole tries to figure it out. Leigh's been gone only two days. It couldn't have been because he fought with Lydia, could it? He didn't mention anything like that, but then Anatole can't imagine that he would have, their relationship's so circumscribed these days. He feels achingly isolated from Leigh, he wishes he knew what was going on, he wishes he was in a position where he could afford to know and not be destroyed by it.

"You might try Chris," Lydia suggests.

"What do you mean, 'Chris'?"

"Chris. You know, our good friend Chris. You don't know the latest?" Her tone is arch. It sounds like more than he wants to talk about over the phone.

"Listen, Lydia," he says, "do you want to have a drink after work? I feel like I need to talk to you."

There's a pause, he doesn't think she's going to say anything, but then she says, her voice quiet, conciliatory, "I could use a drink."

They meet at Bertie's, Anatole's tense as if he is going on a date. He can't imagine Lydia'll really want to talk to him about her fight with Leigh—he's surprised, knowing her, she even confessed to it over the phone. But he also feels as if there's something life-or-death about this conversation. She's already there when he arrives. Strange emotions—for an instant he can almost imagine they're back in the summer, any ordinary day after work, before all this happened.

"So what's this about Chris?" he plunges right in.

"You really don't know, do you? My guess is, if Leigh's not at your place, he's probably moved in with Chris."

"That doesn't make any sense. They don't know each other."

"That's what I thought. Apparently they *do* know each other. They're madly in love."

"It's not possible," Anatole says. "It really can't be possible."

"I'm just reporting what Leigh told me. Before he dumped me."

"He dumped you? Just like that? Leigh doesn't dump anybody. Look at me. He's a master of prolonging the agony."

"I guess he just used me up a little bit faster," she theorizes bitterly. "My apartment's not as nice as yours."

"It just doesn't sound like him. Something's wrong."

"Does anything sound like him? Come on, Anatole, the kid's a floating disaster area, anything's possible with him. They should put signs around him—Danger, Stay Clear."

"But *Chris?*"

"Darling"—the word's icy, the way she uses it—"have we *ever* known what Chris was about? I mean, really? I think he's finally showed his true colors."

Anatole can't believe it, it goes against too much he's established, painstakingly, as true. He's made his peace with Chris, after all, by coming to realize that there wasn't anything personal in Chris's not wanting to sleep with him. It was just that Chris wasn't interested in men. If that was true, that was okay, it was just one of those deplorable facts of biology. But now—if he really *does* sleep with men, if he's slept with *Leigh*, if Leigh's slept with *him*, then it must be something in Anatole he doesn't like, something that doesn't attract him. Him. Them. Either of them.

He tries to muster some sort of last defense against this, but there isn't any defense.

"Even if Chris *is* gay," he says passionately, "which I think *very* unlikely, I simply refuse to believe he'd do something so crude as this. It's not in good faith, it's not like Chris. I *know* Chris: he wouldn't do something he knew would hurt somebody. If anything, he goes too far in the other direction. He's"—he searches for the word—"fastidious."

Lydia looks stricken. She picks at her fingernail and won't look at Anatole. "Maybe he didn't mean for us to find out. Did you think of that? Maybe Leigh spilled the beans when he wasn't supposed to. You know how it's hard not to brag."

"No, no, no." Anatole is adamant, even hysterical—"I *refuse* to believe that, I'll die before I believe it. Even if he knew it'd never get out, he wouldn't do something like that. If Chris has got anything, he's got a kind of, I don't know, scrupulousness. It sets him apart from the rest of us."

"You're sure about that?"

"It's the only thing in the world I'm sure about." He knows Lydia's always been a little skeptical of Chris, has made fun of his cigarettes, his too-good looks. Still, he's willing to put himself completely on the line for Chris.

"Well, I wouldn't be sure," Lydia tells him flatly.

"What do you mean?"

"I just wouldn't be sure. Oh Anatole"—her voice sinks, like a little boat that crests a sea swell, pauses an instant, then falls into the deep trough between waves. "It happened so long ago, it doesn't matter now. But you shouldn't go around fooling yourself. I know Chris has been your friend. I know he's been important to you. Integrity may be what Chris likes you to think, but it isn't his strong point. It just isn't. I *know*."

"I still don't understand."

"You don't want to."

"I do. I'm sure it's a mistake, some kind of misunderstanding. Whatever you're trying to say, you have to spell it out if I'm going to believe it."

Lydia sits for a long time. Anatole's hyperaware of everything: the desultory hum of conversation at other tables, the television running New York news above the bar—the nightly repertory of murders, scandals, drug raids, AIDS. "I really don't want to say what I'm going to say," Lydia tells him. She doesn't look at him. She looks at a spot on the wall above his head, as if studying the slow progress of some spreading stain there. "I never wanted you to know this, but we've come to the point where it has to get said. You have to try to see all this clearly."

"Go on," he urges as she stops.

"Remember back when you were all gaga about Chris, you were calling me up all the time with the latest tiny step you'd taken in the direction of each other?"

"Sure."

"That was in the summer, remember"—she speaks very precisely, a lawyer rehearsing a witness—"and then in the fall you introduced him to me. But the two of you were still fencing around with each other, it was driving you crazy."

"How can I forget?"

"Well, while all that was going on, he seduced me."

She looks right at him, then she looks away again. "You're making that up," he tells her. She has to be making that up. There's some reason she needs to lie about it.

"Listen to what I'm saying. He fucked me, Anatole; all the time you were thinking he was interested in you and being so sensitive with you, he fucked *me*. I mean, I feel terrible about it, I wish it never happened and that's why I never said a word. I didn't want you to know. But it *did* happen, and you've got to know that about Chris. Like I say, it was a long time ago, I hope you can realize that it was a long time ago. But I've known this about Chris for a long time— I've watched you fool yourself about him completely, and I haven't said anything because I knew you were in love with him, and I guess I always think that's a good thing, to be in love with somebody. But you have to come to terms with the truth—no matter how much you think you can trust Chris, you can't *really* trust him. Whatever he may say about not hurting people, it's a smoke screen. When it comes down to scratch, he's as slimy as anybody else, he's just as desperate and cornered as the worst of us, the only difference is we admit it and he tries to pretend he isn't. And I think that makes him a lot worse than both of us."

Anatole's trembling, he feels he's going to vomit. All he can think is, Either I hate Chris or I hate Lydia. And the worst is, he doesn't know which one, he doesn't think there's any way to know.

"I don't know what to say," he says. It's fallen apart, and he can't put it back together. It just lies there shattered. He gets up from the table, he can't stand being here in this bar, in her presence. "I have to think about all this," he says.

But out on the street's no better. The buildings of the Main Street mall, old bricks painted long ago with advertisements, now peeling, fading; abandoned upper stories, glass broken out, gaping wounds: the whole street's an aftermath of something terrible. He walks furiously. Around the corner, Immaculate Blue's closed for the evening, locked tight. Its window-front array of bongs and pipes, its feeble potted geraniums—he's never noticed how tawdry it all looks. So this is how the life goes out of things. He doesn't know what to do. If he's going to go over to Chris's apartment, he should've drunk more: he'll lose whatever edge might allow him to say the things he needs to say, he'll fumble, he'll look pathetic. He's so angry with Chris, with Lydia, both of them, neither of them—his brain stumbles in circles like a drunkard even as his body feels completely lucid, rigid with its awful clarity.

He's never been able to think things through clearly, he's always been at the mercy of his feelings. Back on Main Street—he just went around the block, he just walked in a circle—this is where it started, that bench, a boy touched by a trick of September sunlight, an accident of grace spilled thoughtlessly into the profaning world. And now he's gone, disappeared, who knows if he'll ever see him again? He flings himself down on the bench. The wind's cold, unforgiving. No illusions. He'd give anything to turn back the days, hold that first perfect moment again, that hazy golden afternoon.

Where was it he lost track of that first fervor, that trembling annunciation of angels, Our Boy of the Mall? Gone, it takes with it everything. He jumps up in a terror of loneliness, he runs to the parking lot where his car is. Suddenly he has to get to Chris—if he wastes even an instant, this too will fade, he'll not be able to hold on even to Chris.

He need Chris's assurances, he needs to know.

When he gets to Chris's apartment, Chris's car—that sleek Mitsubishi that says everything and nothing about him—is parked in front. Anatole slides in behind it, then waits before getting out. It's possible Leigh's in there right now, isn't it? It's possible this may really be the end of everything. He'll walk in the front door, he'll surprise them. In an instant everything will be clear. And he thinks—I don't have to do this; I could drive away this instant and be done with it. Then before he knows it he's out of the car, before he knows it he's knocking on the door.

Chris is in his bathrobe, scotch in hand. "I was just going to take a shower," he says. "Come in. You look like you just murdered somebody."

"Can I have a drink? I need a drink."

He sits—collapses, rather—at the kitchen table. Chris sets the scotch bottle and a tumbler in front of him, and then sits down across the table and lights a cigarette. Anatole peers at the bottle, picking it up, hefting it as if it's a curiosity. Then he pours himself a half glass.

"So I guess I can relax," he says. "He's not here, is he?"

"Don't be so cryptic. Really, Anatole, you look awful."

"Leigh. He's gone. We don't know where he is."

"He's gone?" Chris frowns. "When?"

"A couple of days. I thought maybe he was staying with Lydia, but he's not. She hasn't seen him. They had some kind of fight or something—but that was over a week ago. She hasn't seen him at all. I didn't even know they'd broken up. He didn't tell me anything about it. He acted like everything was the same as it was."

"When exactly was this? I mean, when was the last time you saw him?"

"He didn't come home two nights ago, and he wasn't home last night."

"Did he take his stuff with him?"

"He didn't have any stuff, really—just some clothes. Everything's still there. It's not like he cleared out or anything. He just vanished."

"Are you worried? I mean, should we call the police? Do you think something's happened to him?"

Chris seems at once so caring and sensible—it calms Anatole, it almost makes him forget his rage. Surely everything'll be okay; Chris'll take care of everything.

"I don't know what to do," Anatole says. "I came over here, I thought he might be over here." He finishes his scotch in a long, harsh swallow. "I thought he might have moved in with you," he admits.

Something accusatory in Anatole's tone puts Chris on guard. "Why would he do *that*?" he asks cautiously.

Anatole's grim. "You *know* why, Chris, you *know* why."

Chris can only smile helplessly, hold out his hands palms-up to show he knows nothing.

It makes Anatole shake his head, a gesture of weariness, disgust. "Leigh talked to Lydia," Anatole says evenly. "He told her everything."

"And she told you?"

"Yes."

"But I don't understand. Told you what?"

They look at each other, Chris genuinely baffled, and Anatole says, "Everything." He says it clearly, bleakly, and all at once Chris knows. His heart goes white. It bathes him like a fall of clear light; he's known for a long time it would come, he's wondered how it would happen, what form it would take.

Anything he says, he realizes, will sound like feigning innocence. He can't say a single word. He only watches as Anatole pours out a torrent of accusations, this black river that's broken its dam, tears up everything in its raging path. "Chris, I look back at everything, our friendship, everything, and it just makes me sick, it's like this thing that I can't even think about, I can't even comprehend it." Tears run down his cheeks, some pressure of betrayal forces them from him, the way statues in churches sweat blood. "All the time," he says, his voice breaking—"all the time I thought one thing was going on, and it was something else. I had everything figured out exactly wrong, and every-body knew I had it wrong but nobody told me, you just played along because I don't even know why, because it was easier for you that way, you and Lydia and Leigh. Every one of you. I mean, I don't care, I really don't care who's fucking who anymore. It's just that if every-body has to lie to everybody else then there's just not anything, is there? And that's what it is, Chris, that just"—he shakes his head, he can't even say how it makes him feel, this discovery that everything, everything's been rotten all along, and he didn't know it—"What it is, it's you lying to me about not fucking Lydia and lying to me about not fucking Leigh. That's what it is, that's what just makes me feel like such a complete fool, Chris, like such a complete piece of dirt. Like with Lydia, it just doesn't make any sense to me, why you wouldn't tell me, so I'd go on making a clown out of myself, trailing you around and being in love with you—and all the time what were you doing? Were you enjoying it? Did it make you feel powerful, or important? Was it funny for you to watch me going through a nervous breakdown because I was in love with you and you wouldn't let me get close to you, and all the time you and Lydia were laughing about Poor Silly Anatole behind my back? I've tried to think about it—I'm trying to be logical about all this—but I just can't, I can't think through to the bottom of it."

"Anatole, Anatole." Chris puts both his hands on top of Anatole's hands, he strokes them urgently as he tries to see through the storm of Anatole's words, to glimpse their still source. "I just want to know this one thing. Okay? Everything else, it doesn't matter. But just this one thing. What did Lydia tell you Leigh told her? I just need to know that one thing."

"What did she tell me? She told me Leigh admitted you and he were sleeping together. I mean, it makes sense. He broke up with her, he's going with you. Just like that. I didn't want to believe it, I didn't think you'd do it. I mean, I thought you were a friend. You're no more of a friend than Lydia. At least she didn't lie. At least she didn't pretend she was one thing and then do something else."

"So she told you Leigh told her he and I were sleeping together." Chris repeats the information mildly. It's a source of wonder. In other circumstances it might even be luminous, this confusion of tongues. He's seen pictures of wolves caught in traps, their plangent eyes, how they wait for the hunters to arrive.

"I wanted to believe she was making it up," Anatole goes on—though he lets Chris continue to stroke his hands, he doesn't want to relinquish this last bit of contact—"I wanted to think she was lying. But then, how can I trust you, Chris? I've always trusted you, and now I find out you've been lying to me for years, you've betrayed me before and I didn't know it."

"I've betrayed you before. I'm sorry, Anatole. You don't know how sorry I am. But I haven't betrayed you now. I haven't fucked with Leigh, I really haven't. I've stayed clear of it as much as I possibly could. You can't believe that, I know you can't. I know *why* you can't, and you're right not to."

"How *could* I believe you, Chris?" Anatole cries. He leaps from his chair, makes for the door as if unable to stand Chris's presence for even another instant. "Anything you say to me now"—he flings the accusation at Chris—"how could I believe you?"

"You couldn't." With it, Chris hears the price for his whole past, how it gathers weight and guilt, how it gets paid in a single instant. "Whatever I say"—Chris follows Anatole to the door—"it couldn't make any difference now."

For a moment they're both motionless, they confront each other in the doorway like fighters. Then Chris lunges forward as if to attack, and Anatole staggers back against the door. They grapple; Chris wraps his arms tightly around Anatole and holds him there, against him, holds him tight as if to claim him against everything that threatens. And Anatole doesn't dare move. He holds himself rigid against Chris's embrace, not returning it, not making any move at all. Only suffering it.

Tears streaming down his cheeks, Chris kisses him on the lips.

"No," Anatole cries. "No." He refuses to believe anything. He can't afford to. Without looking back he's out the door, he's running for his life from the one thing he's spent the last two years living for.

Lydia doesn't move. After Anatole's gone from Bertie's she sits and stares at the tabletop, the little bit of spilled beer, how the corner of a paper napkin greedily laps it up. Did I just do what I just did? she wonders, tracing with her finger the edge of the beer, feeling a sense of calm, a resolve. It's the way people must commit suicide—spur of the moment, a sudden amazed disbelief that it's already too late, that it happened just like that. Falling from a bridge, everything about you screaming No, I didn't mean to—but also a peace too terrible even to contemplate, the peace that says I've done it, I can't undo it, it's out of my hands.

She's relieved she can't hurt Anatole any more. She knows she won't call him, because she doesn't want to apologize. She wants to have done exactly what she's just done. We all have to wake up sometime, she thinks. Even Anatole has to wake up sometime.

She surprises herself. She's lost Leigh, she's lost Anatole. What does she feel but numbness? It crosses her mind that if she fails consistently to be a good person, it's not because she's bad but because she lacks something that would free her from the perverse necessity of ruining things once it's in her power to ruin them. If she were stronger, more capable. But how? Her mother accuses her of not being able to love—as Lydia sees it, that's all she ever does, love and love and love, a lighthouse throwing its light in handfuls out into the unwelcoming dark.

She moves in a dream. Driving these streets, this city where she grew up, this city she's tried to flee but always come back to, as if to her fate: these avenues, these bare maples that line the avenues, these old forlorn houses the bare maples fail to conceal. Midway up Hooker Avenue there's a 7-Eleven convenience store. Around a public phone in its parking lot five or six teenagers have gathered. It's the sort of group Leigh might have been a part of had he never met the three of them. For a moment she fantasizes that he really *is* there among them, among friends his own age, untouched, incorrupt—but he's not. And anyway, these kids are not quite his type. They're all high punk: Mohawks, bald heads, fluorescent pink hair teased into breathtaking spikes. Long barbaric earrings dangling from their ears. It's cold out, but they seem impervious to it. They're dressed in black, they wear boots with metal studs. One of them has a skateboard with the flag of Great Britain painted on it. The back of his jacket says Fuck Dancing, Let's Fuck.

She slows the car to a crawl. Punks in Poughkeepsie. She sees them around, hanging out on street corners, appearing at Bertie's on Wednesday Punk Nights (she remembers how Leigh materialized among them that night on the dance floor). Where do they come from, how do they live? She witnesses them with a kind of wonder, she feels a palpable kinship for these kids who, with their haircuts and clothes, want the impossible. To transcend their time and place, to be beautiful.

What if she stopped the car, went over to them? She has cocaine in her purse; she'll share with them, she'll get to know them, these dangerous boys painted like warriors, these girls who are dark and deadly and intimidating.

On an impulse she wheels her Chevy into the 7-Eleven parking lot. Her heart is beating faster, it strains against her rib cage. She breaks out in a sweat. I dare you, she tells herself. But dare what? She dares herself to prove she hasn't died.

Getting out of the car, she walks over to the phone they cluster around but do not use. Except for the boy with the flag of Great Britain skateboard, their backs are to her; he stands before them, rocking back and forth on his skateboard. "Yah," he's saying. "She don't fucking know anything. Hey, Dana, she don't fucking know anything, does she?"

The girl called Dana's got jet-black hair. She ignores the boy with the skateboard. The back of her jacket says Butthole Surfers. She looks off in the distance and smokes a cigarette. "You're such a fuckhead," one of the boys tells the skateboarder.

"Oh yeah, tell me." He spits. No one seems interested in the exchange, and they don't continue it.

"Hey look at that," one of the other punks says. A small private plane is buzzing the city. It seems to circle the 7-Eleven, droning steadily in the blank sky. The boy with the skateboard waves.

"Don't wave, stupid," the girl called Dana tells him. "You're such an asshole," she pouts. She lights another cigarette.

"What's wrong with waving? It can't even see us."

"Maybe it'll crash," says someone.

They haven't seen Lydia approach. She's so close she could speak to them in a normal voice and they'd hear. Five steps and she could tap Dana on the shoulder. For a moment she thinks she'll shoulder her way through, stand in their midst at the phone booth and make a phone call. But she doesn't know who, in the whole city, she'd call.

She could call herself, she could dial her own number. It would ring—ten, twenty times. There'd be no one home.

At the last moment she veers aside and enters the fluorescent squalor of the 7-Eleven. You can't do it, she thinks: can't connect with anything anymore. She's fragile, she almost staggers under the impossibilty of everything she faces. No more Anatole, no more Leigh. She's on her own for the long haul.

Moving among the aisles of doughnuts, candy bars, comic books, she thinks she can understand why so many people secretly long for the nuclear war to come and annihilate the world. Maybe we can't wait to be dead, she thinks, maybe we do everything we can to be dead. It makes her defiant. She doesn't care, she doesn't care. Thank God for gin, for butter brickle ice cream.

Resolutely she goes up to the freezer locker (death to everything, death to the whole world) to pick from the Popsicles and ice cream sandwiches a quart of Ben and Jerry's, imagining how she'll settle down in front of the TV, watch some Ida Lupino late movie, console herself by slugging gin and eating her way methodically but relentlessly through the quart. But instead she reaches into the next locker and takes out a Lean Cuisine lasagna. Why? She stands there looking at it, not sure it's an accident.

So is this hope? Is it the least she can do?

She wonders—hefting the cardboard container, this promise of less than three hundred calories—where is he? It'd be completely like him, wouldn't it, just to disappear without a word, vanish as magically as he arrived . . . And yet she worries—something bad will happen to him, he's doomed, it's written all over him the way they wrote on his T-shirt that first night when they led him home from Bertie's.

There'll be other hands than theirs, less gentle hands.

As she pays for the lasagna and a bottle of seltzer, she notices through the window that the punks have abandoned the phone booth—disappeared as if they were never there. It saddens her, it's a sign of something.

She wonders what she'll say to Anatole when they run into one another next. Will they be like old lovers who now have nothing much in common? They can't go back: that much she knows. None of them can go back. And who knows where forward will be? Three hundred calories. Maybe she'll really do it this time, maybe she'll change her life. She might even move to the City and get a job in publishing.

If it comes to pass, then maybe Leigh's the one she'll have to thank for it. Because Leigh was nice, she thinks. For a moment he gave her some hope. He never said she was fat.

But then he never said anything about her body one way or the other.

When it comes, the end, it comes all at once; it comes with the speed of light.

Chris is leaving Poughkeepsie. He doesn't know where he's going—he'll find that out, he tells himself, when he gets there. His plan is to drive west, maybe back to Denver, the haunted neighborhoods of his adolescence—as if all those miles might undo something, might discover what forces mysterious as weather led to this, Poughkeepsie, the age of twenty-six when everything shudders, falters, refuses to go on.

Yesterday he went down to New York. The hotel on Lexington Avenue, this last time, it's a skinny blond white kid from New Jersey with an oversized cock, and a graceful self-assured Puerto Rican teenager. He likes it when they don't know each other in advance, he likes the cautious exploratory moves they have to make with each other. He makes the blond kid fuck the Puerto Rican. The Puerto Rican boy's agonized groans as the blond kid enters him give Chris that feeling he gets only rarely, but that is the real object of his quest among these derelict boys—he feels farther away from himself than he's ever felt, he feels he's lost his way back to himself, that when this awful exhilarating estranging moment is over—the boy's face contorts, becomes ugly with pain, pain is a greediness that takes him over—he won't be able to find his way back to himself, he'll be freed, liberated into some great cool vacant space, the space his personality used to fill. It's all he wants, that great moment of nothing. He feels as he felt as a child, in that school bus, when he tried to cut his little cousin in two. Cries of pain coming from a great distance, as if something both monstrous and poignant is being born—like any birth, in fact; like death.

Afterward, after the boys have washed and dressed and left, the Puerto Rican wincing bravely, the New Jersey kid chattery and nonplussed, Chris stares at the filthy towel thrown down to protect the bedspread. He circles the bed, it fascinates him, the bloodstained, shit-stained towel, this only trace that what has happened has happened (otherwise he might have hallucinated it)—but he won't touch it to throw it away. Let the maid find it, the old Spanish woman who trundles her cart up and down the hall all hours of the day and night— she's doubtless seen worse. This evidence of the world: it's almost a holy thing, Chris thinks, a sacrament.

Midafternoon: he's locked Immaculate Blue, turned out the lights. He does it briskly, he registers nothing except the bare fact— I won't see this again. It's not the first time he's locked a door behind him. Now, moving about the rooms of his apartment, excluding himself object by object from their embrace, he packs methodically. Of all the apartments he's had in all those different cities, this has been his favorite, these bare white walls, these maple floors the color of honey. The sun in the afternoon through west-facing windows.

Disappear, disappear. That night he let Leigh go, relinquished him the way mystics lose the world—he lay among ineradicable dust balls on the bare floor and listened to David Bowie, the *David Live* album they should have called *David Dead*, it's so weary, so heartbroken; he drank scotch and listened to the music and tried to believe he wasn't really going to give it all up again. It baffles him, what to do to stop the brain from boring insistently deeper and deeper into itself, its desolate catalog of dreams, Michelle's cries of love those nights in that house in Ithaca, John lying awake upstairs wanting to die, to die; desolate catalog of boys observed, defiled, expelled from dingy hotel rooms off Lexington Avenue; Leigh's voice, unforgettable in its airy nothingness: "I'm not shivering because I'm cold," he said. These acts could all be remorseless. You could die from them.

There comes a point when you just get too tired of it all. You might consider suicide, but you're not courageous enough for that.

You're just coward enough to change cities, step into yet another disguise, pretending you can fool yourself just because you fool others now and then, for some short golden breath of time.

The afternoon light through west-facing windows. He really is going to run away one more time. Never again he told himself when he moved here, those first quiet wonderful days in Poughkeepsie when he knew no one, when he went about the business of taking over Immaculate Blue with a chaste sense of purpose, an aloneness that wasn't lonely but rather serene, careful, expiatory. And then one day in June, on the train back from New York, he met Anatole.

It's funny. He blames Anatole. He blames him for being vulnerable, for falling in love, for being blind and manipulated. He blames Anatole because he's been in love with Anatole for two years and hasn't understood till now, now when it's too late to make any difference.

He moves through the empty blameless rooms, floating in light like a ghost. The telephone sits stranded on the bare floor, forlorn the way last objects in rooms always are. Before he even knows what he's doing, Chris has picked up the receiver, he's dialed, he listens to it ring. Maybe for once, he thinks, on the verge of hanging up and yet unable to resist the possibility that suddenly occurs to him as a challenge, a defiance—maybe for once.

Anatole, he says, Anatole. The phone rings and rings, and there's no answer. It's a mild sound after a while, its insistence more soothing than urgent. Twenty, fifty, a hundred rings. But he doesn't hang up. He lets the phone keep ringing, carefully almost reverently he sets the receiver on the floor, and taking one last glance around he leaves the apartment, he locks the door behind him.

At some point during the night Anatole wakes to a sharp wind jarring the windowpanes, tossing and snapping the branches of the big scotch pine behind his apartment. The whole house shakes, an enormous invisible body is hurling itself against the walls.

When he flicks on the bedside lamp, nothing happens. He's had dreams like this—the lights won't come on, only a sinister brown filament glow; and for a moment he panics, his heart hurts in his chest. But then it's clear: electricity's out. He moves about his apartment blindly, it's a ship rolling against battering waves. Everything feels at once precarious and exhilarating, a precipice the wind continually offers and revokes. He can't help it—in the pitch dark he trembles violently, happy with something he can't name. This is the way springs must come in Russia, when the ice fractures all at once and a violence of flowers overtakes the landscape; it's like being on the verge of falling in love, that brink where anything's possible, the whole world trembles with unbelievable promise.

Then he remembers: I've lost Leigh.

In the kitchen he gropes for the scotch bottle, finds it, drinks a long stomach-warming swallow. I've lost Leigh, I've lost him for good. It comes over him like a flood. He sinks down on the cold floor, cradling the scotch bottle as if it could hold any comfort, and he cries. He cries long wrenching heart-sobs. He sobs because it comes to him with such numbing clarity, the truth about his life: how he fails to be a human being. How again and again people take him up, they befriend him. And then it happens—there's this point they reach, some of them sooner, some taking years to find their way to it—but it always happens. They reach the bottom of him, a moment so final that they know that whatever happens, there's no more of him there. They've found him out, sounded to the full those lies that are the only substantial thing about him. And so they leave him, they move past him and he can hold nothing back.

He sobs because he knew this all the time, from the very instant he saw Leigh—not that first time on the mall, sitting there like any ordinary miracle among the hazy debris of a September afternoon, not then, because that could be excused as an accident, but that second time at Bertie's, when he came back after Anatole knew he'd never see him again, and that time it was fate, it was something he had to walk up to boldly and encounter, whatever the outcome might be, because if he didn't face that moment he'd never face anything. And he did face it—as he watched Leigh dance, the only important body among a hundred unimportant ones out there on the dance floor, he put out of his head that knowledge, that suspicion he'd always nursed about himself, and instead moved bravely on saying to this perfect stranger, "I was watching you. I admire good dancing," forgetting that this girlish boy filmed with sweat, wiping his face on his T-shirt, this beautiful boy couldn't possibly be interested in him, they couldn't possibly have anything in common except the vital accident of their both being there.

You can't forget that, Anatole tells himself. You can't ever forget that. You can fool yourself again and again, but it's going to end up the same. How many more times will you huddle on the kitchen floor and sob in the middle of the night because once more you've been left behind to be just yourself?—that thing that's all you have, and that's not enough.

He empties the scotch bottle in a long last swig, then heaves it against the wall. Do this in memory, he thinks. The bottle hits the wall but doesn't shatter. It rolls across the kitchen floor hollowly and comes to rest against the refrigerator. He picks it up and hurls it against the floor. But it's unbreakable. Again and again he throws it, hard as he can, against the walls, against the stove, the refrigerator—it recoils with a racket but it stays intact, it survives.

"Hey," the woman downstairs calls up, her voice muffled by the floor that separates them. She bangs the ceiling with the handle of a broom, loud thumps that surround in a ragged percussive circle the spot where Anatole stands barefoot. "Hey, I'm trying to sleep, I have an important meeting tomorrow," she yells. "I need a good night's sleep. Don't you have any respect?"

Is it possible Anatole feels at this instant only love, wild and impossible as the storm that uproots everything? Earlier this evening the phone was ringing insistently, ten, twelve, a hundred rings—but he wouldn't answer it. It wouldn't be Leigh, he knew: it will never be Leigh again—and he was afraid it was Chris or Lydia calling. He didn't want to talk to either one, he didn't think he could. What could he say? I'm sorry? I'm sorry for all this mess?

But then he did pick up the receiver anyway. Because if that's what it took, then he was going to say it, whoever it might be. That he was sorry. That now here he was, reduced once again to himself, and himself only, in a nakedness and quiet of soul that might, just might be able to make broken things right again. But on the other end, only silence. "Hello," he said, "hello, who is this?" He listened and listened, but there was nothing. He put the phone down, and picked it up again, but the dial tone didn't come back. And he couldn't sever the connection. He didn't know where it led, maybe it was only a prank. But all of a sudden he *depended* on the connection. It was just there, there wasn't anything he could do about it, but now it was necessary, it was absolutely essential.

And it's still there, the receiver lying on the kitchen counter—if he picks it up he can hear his way into that empty space, whoever's on the other end hasn't hung up. He doesn't know who it is—but there it is, the connection, and for some reason it's unbreakable.

It's funny, it's impossible. He's laughing through his tears. The clown of God—that phrase from a film about the Russian dancer Nijinsky. It's been in his head for months, he hasn't been able to place it. Now he has this image of Nijinsky gone mad, collapsed on the floor like a spent puppet (he and Daniel saw the film in Rhinebeck; Daniel cried, his face was shiny in the light from the screen). The clown of God. Maybe there's courage there, he thinks, maybe it can see you through. Still sobbing but also laughing, he can't tell where one stops and the other starts. Salty tears run down his face, he tastes them with a kind of amazement that they really are salty, they're salty as the ocean, the great drowning sea they all came from, he and Leigh and Chris and Lydia, the five billion people in the world who don't matter much.

"Do you hear me up there?" the woman downstairs is yelling. Again she bangs on her ceiling with the broomstick. "Have you gone crazy? Do you hear what I'm saying? I'm trying to sleep down here."

And Anatole shouts back, stomping on the floor, jumping up and down, laughing and crying like a maniac, "I'm just trying to stay *alive* up here," he cries. "Don't you understand? I'm just trying to stay alive."

ACKNOWLEDGMENTS

My thanks to Meg Blackstone, my editor, and Harvey Klinger, my agent; James Day and Bob Richard, astute early readers of the manuscript; Jerome Badanes and Marianne Burke, for those many summer nights on the back porch; and especially Christopher Canatsey, whose ineffable contributions have been not so much to this book as to my life.